ISBN 13: 978-1-60489-093-8 library binding
ISBN 13: 978-1-60489-094-5 trade paper
Library of Congress Control Number 2012930432
Printed on acid-free paper.
Printed in the United States of America by
United Graphics

Hardcover binding by: HF Group
Typesetting and page layout: Joe Taylor
Proofreading: Joe Taylor, Jane Elias

Cover painting: Jason Covert
www.jasoncovert.com
Cover design and layout: Jeffrey Bucari
www.jeffreybucari.com
with special thanks to Steven Sergiovanni at Mixed Greens Gallery
Author photo: Jeffrey Bucari

Story acknowledgements on page 226

first edition
6 5 4 3 3 2 1

CONTENTS

MARGINS OF TOLERANCE

FLOATING

Inside the hallowed gates of the Monasterio de Santa Catalina, suspended between the fortressed walls made of dyed volcanic *sillar,* carved in infallible black lettering above the primary archway, is one word:

Silencio.

Silence is sacred. Silence is respect. This I have been taught. This is expected of me.

Spitting distance to the *catedral,* the humble *hostería* where I work. Right off the Plaza de Armas on Calle Jerusalén, fourteen tasteful rooms, with ceiling fans and minibars and 24-hour hot water. Satellite television—my favorite amenity, my steadfast companion at the front desk. I sit and gulp down American TV shows. Maury Povich, *Blind Date,* Jessica Simpson and her cross-eyed husband. Later, at night, the magnificent *Sex and the City*: Carrie and her spicy friends conquer New York and order men from a menu. Here we have room service from 6 a.m. to 10 p.m., where we offer local specialties along with continental fare. So: *Rocolo relleno. Ocopa Arequipeña.* But also: Goat cheese salad. Mississippi mud pie.

9:17 a.m., I am rearranging the tourist brochures when the phone calls begin.

"Francisco, *mi polluelo*."

Mama named me after her favorite saint, Francis of Assisi, patron saint of animals and against solitary death. She hopes to find salvation through me, clear up the devastation left behind by my vagabond father, who blew through her life like a hurricane. Thirteen times a day the phone will ring.

"How's work?" she asks me. I have been here seventeen minutes.

"Carmelita is singing like a sparrow," she tells me. "Jorge has come down from Trujillo with the twins."

Carmelita, our next-door neighbor. Jorge, her son. The twins, Carmelita's grandchildren.

"Two years old already!" Her voice is sticky with joy. "I will receive them this afternoon. Fatten their cheeks with sweets. It will take my mind off things." She sighs. What she does not say: *Mi hijo*, when will you get married and start a family? I too want to wake up to the faces of my grandchildren, sew them mittens and booties, stuff their cheeks with *dulces*.

She does not speak them, but the words strain the muscles of my soul.

A gringo named Columbus arrives at ten o'clock. The sun has caramelized his hair and bloated his skin. He sports camouflage shorts, a petulant smile, the weekend stubble of someone ten years younger.

"I don't like my hotel," he broadcasts to the world. "Do you have a room for a few nights?"

His eyes flutter about our plain lobby, sending pinpricks of unrest through my bones. But what can I do? Business is snailing along as

Eric Sasson

it does in October, and the *patrón* always finds excuses to blame me. *We must update our website, Francisco. Network with travel agents, send moist girls to the bus stations to lure the backpackers.* Never mind that backpackers won't pay our rates.

The gringo stares up at the board to my left and then at me, provoking me to do better.

"It's sixty-five *soles* a night," I say, hoping I have struck the right deal. Less than half of the listed rate.

"Internet access?" he asks.

"The cabins are down the hall."

"Can I see the room I'll be getting?"

"Of course, *señor*."

I ring the bell for Inez, our head chambermaid. The ancient elf dribbles down, the heavy clop of her shoes echoing against each stair. She looks at me, startled, before glancing suspiciously at our guest.

"Show the gentleman number four," I tell her.

They return not two minutes later. "Let me see something better," the gringo says, flashing his teeth. I hand Inez the key to room no. 2, the most superior in the hotel. When Columbus returns, he seems pleased.

"And how much would that be?" He flattens his palms against the counter. His hands are thick and the hair sheathing his arms runs all the way down to his fingers.

"It's fine," I say. "Sixty-five *soles*."

"I'll be back in twenty minutes," he says.

Mama calls at 10:52 a.m.

"How's your knee?" I ask. Mama's left knee keeps her home most of the time. It requires an operation, which will cost us a small fortune. The government should pay, but they won't. They will tell us they will pay, and then schedule the operation after she is already dead. There are no honest politicians in Peru.

"The saints must be deaf," she says. "My life has not fifteen cents of happiness. I won't be able to move soon."

"Don't say that," I tell her. Normally a few sentences between us lulls the tempest of her anxiety. But my words are of small comfort lately.

"I feel so alone," she says, and then pauses. She wants the words to sink deep, to plant seeds within me. "Good you have no children. His name doesn't deserve to be carried over."

If only she meant this. But I know she is finding excuses, so I offer only a sigh.

"Ghosts visit me at night. Poking accusations at me. They want answers, *hijo*. I don't know what to tell them."

"I have a guest to deal with," I say.

She hangs up the phone.

Here are my answers, Mama: I am forty-three years old. I have managed a hotel for almost as many years as I have not. I have access to all of America on the make-do television by the front desk. I dream of floating.

Sometimes at the end of a late shift, before I come home to the cold meal you have left out for me, I go to the gay bar. For an hour. Sometimes I am lucky and I find compassion in the back, and compassion puts his lips around my cock until I am unburdened.

Sometimes I hear you when I get back. You talk in your sleep, did you know that? I try to be still and eat my potatoes. I listen and you shout, "Oh, Sebastian!" and it sounds like floodgates releasing. It sounds like the end of the world.

I do not have the answers, Mama. I only have questions.

At 11:15 the house phone interrupts my favorite soap opera, *Days of Our Lives*.

"I'm unable to obtain an outside line," Columbus says, in a distastefully formal Spanish.

"Give me the number and I will dial it for you, *señor*," I say, in English.

"I want to make a call from my room," he says, switching to English. He thinks I have not understood him.

"We must dial the number for you," I say.

I hear his teeth chatter. "Why?" he asks. A one word accusation.

"Our phone system is set up this way. I apologize for the inconvenience."

"This is ridiculous!" he barks. "Where's the privacy?"

He seems very loud to be so concerned with privacy, but I do not tell him that. Instead I apologize again. "We will never compromise your privacy, *señor*," I assure him.

He grumbles, then gives me the number without further words. Twenty years I have been a hotel manager, and I have trained my voice to the proper pitch. I'm told that animal trainers do the same. The animals expect a certain tone. They are not docile otherwise.

Most requests are ordinary: extra towels, wake-up calls, directions to the monastery or the crafts market. Some are more specific: sheets laundered in fragrance-free detergents, requests for a Bible to be removed from the nightstand drawer. Some men ask me for the phone numbers of escort services; I refer them to the yellow pages. Once a man called to tell me that his girlfriend had somehow managed to get her foot stuck inside the toilet. I grabbed a plunger and a toolbox and scurried upstairs.

The woman had one pant leg twisted around her thigh when I

arrived. A towel covered her hair and face, as if she were a Saudi cleric's wife. All that was required was extra leverage. One good yank and we managed to release her. Other than "thank you" and "you're welcome" the couple and I exchanged no words and I asked no questions.

I left the room and disappeared down the stairs, like nothing had happened.

At 11:34 a.m. Inez is sitting beside me, running through an inventory list. When a commercial comes on I study her, the way she drums her pen against the notebook. She bites her lip and her eyes dilate and I know conclusions are being reached, which she then jots down on her paper. Silently we sit, the noise of the television speaking for us. We have worked together for almost a decade.

"Shower caps," she whispers.

Six months ago I entered the service closet looking for lightbulbs and found Inez rooted down like a tree stump on the floor. Her face was frozen, her eyes scattered like those of a fish freshly caught from the ocean. "Rodolfo is leaving me," she whispered, into the air. It must have killed her, to allow herself to reveal this to me. We have been so formal with each other. I didn't know what to say so I pressed a tissue against her face and smoothed down her hair. "Go home," I said. "You shouldn't be here." I was trying to be compassionate, but it came out wrong. She thought I was concerned she would embarrass the guests.

Since then she has found solace in God. Jesus saw an opening and wasted no time moving in. She and Christ have always been chummy, but now they are best friends.

"Air freshener," she says.

I look up. Columbus comes down from his room, shouts "Hey

there!" at us and heads off to check his e-mail.

At 11:54 a. m. a young tree enters the lobby. He is taller than the sky. Other than that he looks like everyone's second cousin. His eyes are so eager to please that I worry he might be looking for a job. He is about to ask me a question when Columbus barrels down the stairs.

"Mauricio!" Columbus shouts, extending his arms wide.

Mauricio accepts the embrace inelegantly. His lower lip tremors and his skin grows goose pimples. I doubt these two have ever met before.

"Come on up!" Columbus says, so casually. Inez curves her prosecutor's eye to me.

"Sure," the tree replies, with a voice too small for his bark. He bounces his head at Inez and me: *Buenos días, buenos días.* Don't think we don't smile back. Of course we do. But unless they are blood, men do not invite other men up to their room. This is not done, and Mauricio knows this.

When they are gone, Inez turns to me. "I'll never understand it," she says.

"Señor Columbus is having a late breakfast," I say. I use humor as a shield.

"*Por favor,* Francisco!" Inez whispers, shaking her head to stop the wickedness from nesting in her hair.

I like to take my lunch in the plaza. Pigeon shit is everywhere. The plaza belongs to them, and we are just guests. Papito in his wheelchair selling batteries. The children running and laughing, their lips blue with candy. The policemen blowing their whistles. All of us, guests.

I find my bench: southwest of the fountain, where the light lingers late into the day. I close my eyes and wait. There's not much else I can do, except feed the pigeons. I listen to the sounds. Sometimes the sun is sympathetic. Sometimes if I keep my eyes closed long enough, the world vanishes and there is silence, only silence. I find safety in this moment, when nothing changes, nothing asks to be updated. Time stops and I can breathe in my dreams.

Luisito approaches me at half past twelve with his stool and footrest. I have just unwrapped the sandwich that Mama has prepared for me.

"Uncle," he says. His eyes are milky and hard.

He knows I will not refuse him. He reaches for my right foot. I watch him spit into his palms, drag his fingers through the paste to prepare the pigment. He is slow, scrupulous, and thorough.

"How is business, Uncle?" he asks.

"Tomorrow is another day," I say.

"Do all the rooms have cable TV?" He undoes the laces of my shoes, gently.

"Yes," I say.

"I want to learn English," he says. His left hand holds down my ankle. I swallow hard, because I am aroused. Not thirteen years old, and I am aroused, because his hand lingers, because I am so much more naive than he is.

"I will study in an American university. And own my own company. And build my own plane so I can fly all over the world."

I close my eyes and imagine the world he aims to inherit. Colonies in space unburdened by gravity. White robes. A universe without clocks. The saints are absent because we have become our own saints.

"Can I spend the night in one of your rooms, Uncle?"

I look down at my feet. My shoes have become new.

"The subtitles can teach me," he says. "You can stay with me and we can watch together."

"Excellent job," I say. I pat him on top of his head, place one *sol* into his open palm and smile as best as I can. But I know: my mouth is trembling.

"See you soon," Luisito says, winking at me, the coin already deep in his pocket.

My father was not a religious man. He even used to watch television on Sunday mornings. Mama and I would come home from church and he would be sitting on the couch in his bathrobe with a plate of leftover *anticuchos* by his side.

"Sebastian, turn it down!" Mama would scold him. "The neighbors will hear."

"They are watching themselves," he would reply. "With the volume off."

He would grab me by the hips underneath my stiff suit and balance me on his knee. "In America, *hijo,* the television sets are as big as small cows." I'd watch his eyes kindle when he spoke. "They have boxes that let you switch the channels without getting up."

Mama sneered. "You should teach him history, instead of filling his head with nonsense."

"We make history every day," he responded. "Tomorrow this moment will be history."

At 2 p.m., I turn to Bravo, for *Queer Eye for the Straight Guy*. On American TV, the *maricónes* are shrill and conspicuous. They are unafraid to call attention to themselves, to flirt with other men, to speak their minds.

Inez comes and stands beside me. She helps herself to the roasted *cancha* we put out for the guests, and she reads the subtitles, and when she finally understands what she sees her pupils dilate and her nose climbs up her face and she says, "Sodomites!" the way a scientist yells "Eureka!", like she has found the 118th element.

"God have mercy on the damned," she proclaims. Her eyes swim upward, toward room no. 2, and I nod, and I laugh, because laughing is acceptable in this instance. Because we will keep watching the show anyway. We will watch and hang on every word, no matter how damned the world is.

Mama calls again at 3:11 p.m. "The mailman can only carry bills."

My mind is preoccupied so I agree with everything she says. I have to call the credit card company to verify one of yesterday's receipts.

"Are you listening," she asks.

"Of course," I say. The TV is on, and Inez is mopping the lobby. She is humming an old tune, a paean to God.

"We used to sing of our ancestors," Mama admonishes me. "When I was a girl, in Moquegua. I can still sing any one of those songs."

"*Sí,* Mama."

"The world has amnesia now."

She is upset, my mother. Because she has fast-forwarded to her deathbed and she cannot hear her name sprouting on the lips of her relatives like wild mushrooms in dense forests. She cannot see the tears collecting in pools like shrines to commemorate her. Who will sing in the chorus of her posterity, bake her memory into ancient recipes?

When Mama looks at me I remind her that we are nothing.

"Why don't you listen to me?" she asks.

Silence. I am not listening. I am not following directions.

Five o'clock: The zesty Judge Judy occupies the TV set and Columbus poodles past me out the front door. Not five minutes later he returns with a local boy: about four seconds older than eighteen, his skin as downy as a goose's ass. The gravity of shame pulls his gaze to the floor; meanwhile Columbus bares thirty-two teeth and says, "Nice evening, isn't it?" I manage to return the smile but keep my focus squarely on the young shoat, whose eyes cannot admit to being there. I smell the anticipation rising like hog sweat to the surface of his skin. Twenty-five years separate us, but I know what he is thinking: *Please let us have no acquaintances in common. Please let this man forget my face.*

I know, because I have had these thoughts myself. I have nurtured them well.

Fifteen minutes later, I turn down the volume. Room no. 2 is directly above me. I hear: the wobbly whimpers of a thirsty newborn, the deep-seated grunts of a dog protecting his bone. I close my eyes and imagine the gringo violating the child without a condom. The boy keeps silent as Columbus plants his seed inside him, like a flag on top of the moon.

He just never came home. There was no quarrel in the morning, no embarrassing looks or lingering hugs. He left for work whistling, carefree and joyful as always.

Mama knew early. At 2 p.m., I came home from school sooner than usual to find her prostrate on the floor. It was like she was on a different planet, where the gravity was stronger, so tightly was her body pressed against the ground.

Quickly she sprang to her feet and greeted me. There was no mention of what I saw, no discussion over dinner as we entertained his empty seat. Even later on, she never directly said to me, "Your father has left us." It was something inexpressible, like faith. It was supposed to be my shelter.

If only she knew how much I wish we could thrash it out together. We could imagine him in Lima or New York or Abu Dhabi. We could give him another family, with three greasy children and a cocker spaniel. We could have him pack this family into a station wagon and drive them off a cliff. Even the damned dog.

Anything is possible, if only we allow it. But we don't.

Mama calls at 6:52 p.m.

"After church on Sunday, we will go to Sachaca," she says, with a sadness that sounds like authority. "I will treat you to a special lunch. Marisol can come along. You like her, don't you? She has such a soft smile."

I do not respond.

"Time is a rapist, Francisco. Please do this for me. My dreams are becoming brittle. They are so fragile."

I say nothing. I want to tell her that my dreams are also fragile, fragile and murky, like pearls shucked too early from an oyster. I want to tell her of the dream that will not disappear, a dream of that special day in my life. 1968. I am six years old and Mama, Papa and I are on the coast. The sky smells densely of January and I am making sand castles. Papa beckons me into the ocean, where the currents are crushing and seductive. Mama yells, "Come back!" but Papa and I are daredevils, we are titanium.

The waves approach like cannibals. I can hear them beckon for my life. Papa holds me underneath my arms. He asks if I am afraid and I tell him no, even though I am shivering. He asks me again, this time much louder, and I scream "No!" again. A wave is about to eat us alive. Papa lifts me up into the clouds. He says, *If you are not afraid, then scream, Francisco, scream,* and I look out to the mouth of my executioner, and I scream, scream like the dead scream for the living, scream like emancipation.

Papa throws me into the ocean. My body sinks under the water and I tumble and I lurch, and I hear a silence so vast that I am terrified, but right before I die I rise to the surface, like all things that float. I am lifted up, into Papa's embrace, and he is laughing and kissing my neck, my lips—he opens my mouth with his kisses. My mother screams bloody murder because it is sick and terrible what has happened but I know nothing of sick and terrible so I kiss my father back everywhere on his forehead on his neck deep deep kisses.

For a single moment in my life, I am three hundred feet tall.

When a third man approaches the desk at 7.45, I am lost in *Entertainment Tonight.* He asks for Columbus and I don't hear him at first, because it is illogical. I turn to look at him and it is worse: I recognize his face.

"Disculpe?"

"Estoy buscando Señor Columbus."

He forwards his gaze upon me. How strange to see his eyes up close, looking blankly into mine. I was once a hand on his knee in a movie theatre. Six or seven years ago, I can no longer keep track. We were watching *The Shining,* and when Jack Nicholson started to chop down the bathroom door with an ax, we allowed ourselves to scream. For several seconds I squeezed, and then I relaxed my hand. He did not move it.

We went out to a café and Mama saw me. She was still walking then. She saw two men sitting in a café, and one of them was her son, who was supposed to be managing a hotel. How smoothly she kept her cool. Her eyes caught mine, and the truth passed between us faster than sound, and then she turned her head and kept walking.

I froze for a second, before I threw ten *soles* on the table and said good-bye to a man I could have created memories with. As I ran over to her I thought: finally I have dislodged the stone stuck in my mother's throat. Instead I encountered a mirage. Her smile was as pure as murder when she said, "Francisco, what a surprise!" and I knew, with that cruel smile, that she knew all along. She had known for eternity.

Still I said nothing. Because the lines my ancestors have written on the backs of my mother's hands are also written on mine, I said nothing.

Like I say nothing now.

I call Columbus to inform him he has a guest.

"Send him up," Columbus says.

"Of course," I say, without hesitation.

Is it possible the American is still hungry? I close my eyes. I hear Angelina Jolie's name on the television. I feel a gnawing in my stomach, a cancer rising in my throat, burning my tongue. My hands tremble. I have to ground myself. I will my fingers to pat down my vest. I straighten my tie, smooth out the lines on my face, and foist a welcoming smile upon my lips. But my anger refuses to concede.

I grab the receiver and dial Columbus.

"Señor Columbus?"

"Yes?"

"Will the gentleman be spending the night?"

"Excuse me?!"

"The gentleman that just came to your room. Will he be spending the night? We will have to charge you the double rate if so."

"Ex*cuse* me?!"

"I asked if—"

"I heard you the first time. How dare you. I'm hanging up now.

I will speak with your supervisor in the morning. Do not bother me again."

"But *señor.*"

He slams the receiver down.

At 8:30 p. m. the phone rings. Four times. Seven times. When there is a pause, after the eleventh, I pick up the receiver and disconnect it from the cradle.

8:52 p. m., eight minutes before my shift ends, Columbus and his final conquest descend the stairs together. He dangles the room key in front of my face and wishes me a pleasant evening. I nod and say, "*Sí, señor. Lo siento, señor.*"

I clutch the key to room 2 in my hand. My fingers shake. My heart is disengaging and rising. My body knows: I will soon do something wrong.

My feet send me up to Columbus's room. Inside, the crisp scent of semen lingers in the air like a hangover. I don't know why I am here but I know I must be. I swagger onto the unmade bed. The sheets are damp, rich with sweat. My head spins. I grab a pair of used underwear that is hidden between the pillows, and I bury my nose inside it. I sniff and picture Mama's face on the Sunday after Papa left, her small look of victory as she pulled a loaf of freshly baked bread from the oven.

This cannot be taken away from me, I tell myself, as I bounce on the bed. I turn my head. Everywhere I look, a flood of products: styling gel, ultraviolet protection, six-megapixel digital camera, iPod. And then, piled neatly on the floor, in a dark corner: alpaca scarves. Hand-sewn legacies on blankets and brightly patterned tablecloths, *Cerveza Arequipeña* t-shirts. Cloth finger puppets, with which, I imagine, the gringo tickles his suitors' anuses.

Travel Journals. Journals! He swallows our culture and spits it out in individually wrapped souvenirs. My throat is dry like from a dentist's vacuum. I begin to pick up Columbus's possessions, tossing them against the wall: flip-flops, travel guide, sleeping bag, sunglasses, mosquito spray. Tourist *paella. Ceviche mixto.* It feels right, this cleansing. I am creating new memories.

I don't know how long I've been here when Inez walks into the room, but I am dancing.

"Santa Lucia," she says, before putting her hand over her mouth. She closes the door behind her and draws the curtains tight. "What have you done, Francisco?"

I see no reason to answer, so I continue to dance.

"You must stop. I understand you are angry. So much . . . filth." She looks up to the sky, where her eyes find answers. "But we cannot do the Lord's work. Let eternal hell be his punishment."

I look over to her face. Tears are ready to sprinkle down. Tears like holy water. I laugh. What else can I do? I laugh and laugh. God bless Inez. So sacred are the ignorant.

"Go downstairs, Francisco. You must calm your mind. When I am done here the gringo will never know what happened. It will be our secret."

I'm laughing so hard I can no longer feel my tongue. *Our secret.* But for her sake, I pretend to calm down. When I approach her she startles back, so I prayer my hands underneath my lips and close my eyelids. "Forgive me, sister," I whisper. I reach out for a hug and fearful as she is she still accepts my embrace. I kiss her on each cheek and whisper *"Dios me salve!"* into her ear, and she says, *"Sí!"* so I repeat it again, *"Dios me salve!"*, this time with more conviction and she says *"Sí!"* even louder and then one last time, *"Dios me salve!"* and then I am spent.

I open the door and leave Inez to her duty. Down the stairs, I drift. I cannot feel my feet. Am I floating? In science-fiction movies they promise us hovercrafts. In the future we will all float.

Right as I reach the last step I hear the phone ring. Inez must have replaced it. The clock on the wall reads 9:17. I am due home. I grab the handle and shout "Mama!" into the receiver.

"But how did you know it was me?" she asks.

"Telekinesis," I reply.

"Why are you still there? The chicken is withering."

I don't say anything.

"Francisco? Francisco!"

The television set is still on. It is always on. I can stay and watch *Friends* or *Dawson's Creek* or the Anna Nicole Smith show. I can stay, because Inez is upstairs arranging our secret and Columbus will return and know nothing.

"Answer me, *hijo!*" Mama whines.

"You saw me," I whisper.

"What?"

"You saw me," I repeat, louder. "You know."

"*Dios lo cuide!* Come home, *hijo*. You are scaring me."

"You know. You know. You know."

I can hear the tears coming. But I will not stay to listen. Let them slick down her face and seal up her mouth. Let them dive off her chin, burn holes through the floor as they drill down to the earth's core.

When I walk outside a local band is setting up. They wear traditional costumes and in their hands they hold flutes, mandolins made of armadillo shells, llama-bone panpipes, and timpani. The lead singer says, in English: "My friends, authentic music of the Andes people, special price only 20 soles a CD." The tourists clap appreciatively. They look forward.

Up ahead the plaza looks murky. Few people linger. The pigeons that remain are groggy, drunk with bread. I should sit down and reflect, but I can't. So I walk. Past the *catedral,* so luminous and inspiring. I make a right onto Avenida Santa Catalina. In the distance, I see her: the walls of the great city within the city.

I approach the gates. The monastery is glowing inside. It is too late for a visit. Besides, I am sure I will not find inspiration here tonight. For four hundred years, 450 nuns took refuge inside this shell, abandoning their families, their loved ones, all but their God. They congregated in the wombs of chapels and cloisters, sacrificed their lives for souls less fortunate than theirs.

The world was dead to them. History tells us they expected nothing. But I have to imagine some of them were curious. I have to believe that these women fantasized, fingered themselves, opened their lips for sounds that weren't soft prayers. But I understand: sometimes walls are more liberating than doors. There is so much freedom in the silence. For years I sank into it, allowed it to lull me into a glorious coma.

I pick up a small stone and toss it hard against the wall. It makes the tiniest spark. No one can hear it. But I can.

Satisfied, I make a left onto Calle San Francisco. Teenagers cluster outside of cafés and bars. Everybody is drinking, chatting, having a good time. Their laughter rises, like helium. I look into their eyes and I see thunder. They are jumbo jets and cruise liners and, soon, hovercrafts. They are the future. If only they were time-travel machines. But they are not.

I keep walking. Despite visions of jumbo jets and electromagnetic trains, the promise of rocket ships spitting on the speed of sound, I have to keep walking. Mama, can you hear me? The world spins on its dizzying axis, and here we are, still walking. Not even—crawling.

No more.

My feet keep moving. I walk, and though I don't know to where, I know I am ready. Even if I am only walking home, I am ready. Ready to break the surface.

Somewhere, the voice of my father is calling out to me. He tells me, *Scream, Francisco*.

So I scream.

DEAR GUY IN 24B

Dear Guy in 24B,

I don't like Zach Galifianakis. I do not crave Jack Black. I don't get off on bearded trolls, pleasingly plump fellows with self-deprecating wit, with class-clownish *joie de vivre*. I have a boyfriend. Theo is smooth and thin and will remain that way until his coffin. I adore his cool skin, I like to feel it quake when I tickle it with my tongue. I'm exceedingly satisfied with our sex life together and impressed by our ability to keep things fresh.

So when you entered my row on the plane, you didn't really do it for me. Just one look and I knew you sweat a lot, that your sweat was sour and milky and that it coated your skin like a varnish.

And yet.

You sat beside me and offered the gentle nod of the forcibly acquainted. Up close your paunch was smaller than I'd assumed, your arms gaunter, your unsexiness more sexy. You reached above to turn the air-conditioning knob and fuck, that stain on your undershirt was somehow mysterious now, the tufts of strawberry hair sprouting from under your arm egging me to look further.

But no, that wasn't it. I had just seen a hottie in the terminal. The jock at the urinal next to mine had a big schlong, and I know you're supposed to keep your eyes to yourself but, well, not likely. And so I'm on the plane and I see said hottie board, this lacrosse player type—you know, the kind of guy staring was invented for, the kind so far out of my league lookswise and bodywise and agewise that it's painful to know he's alive. We're talking I-need-to-drop-trou-and-masturbate-right-now hot, and if it weren't for societal norms I'd do that quite often.

Not making my case well, am I? Okay, so I don't masturbate in public. But I do fantasize about it, and likely I was doing so when your koala-bearness came and sat next to me. And then maybe it transferred to you, I don't know. But trust me, not until you thrust your leg against mine. Seriously. *Thrust*. Not rested. Not brushed up against. And so you might say, "Well, Todd, you were taking up my personal space and I was giving you notice." No, darling. You *invaded* my space. I remember it *very* well. You were a good inch and a half into my side, and your knee was all up on my tray table too. And let's not forget your arm, *pushing fully up against mine* on the armrest, we're talking skin-on-skin action, I'm feeling your red pelt rubbing up against my darker hairs, I'm hearing your hairs whispering to my hairs, *What's up babies how you doing tonight?*

Yeah, hairs don't whisper, but yours practically did. Still think you were claiming your territory? Granted, some people are like that. Some people have a vague sense of boundaries. But do these same people *leave* their arms and legs resting against others for two, four, seven minutes? And when I started moving my leg not away from but rather *further against* yours, did you need to keep your leg flush against mine? How was I supposed to interpret that?

How about a fucking sign, dude. *Dude*. How about *some*thing to let me know—not infer, or guess, something obvious to *let me know,* unequivocally, that my frottage was a major no-no, that what was

Eric Sasson

going on between us was unambiguously one-sided. Because when you start rubbing back, I'm going to get the wrong kind of hint. The kind of hint that could've easily been avoided had you, say, moved your leg after five or fifteen or even *thirty* seconds. Or maybe you could have sighed. You know, one of those deep, frustrated-with-the-asshole-beside-you sighs, one of those not-so-subtle moves we give to people who insist on flirting with us when we have no desire or patience to be flirted with. After all, we wouldn't want to give the wrong impression. We don't want the older gentleman sitting beside us thinking we're gay, or hell, maybe we don't care if he thinks we're gay because it's not like there's anything *wrong* with being gay, it's like a minute past 2011 for goodness' sake and we're enlightened people, we're flying from Miami to New York, not from Tuscaloosa to Colorado Springs; hell, we can even *be* gay, right, and still not be interested, it's not a necessary thing to enjoy some guy rubbing up against you on a plane just because you happen to be same-sexually inclined.

You, meanwhile, decided to do nothing. In fact, it's not really fair to say you did nothing, because you did do *something:* You kept yourself pressed against me. Your leg and my leg were Siamese twins for almost two hours. And why did you allow this? I imagine you've come up with reasons. Allow me to cut through your bullshit excuses one by one:

Excuse # 1. I had my headphones on.

I see, you were listening to *music,* and somehow this means what, that I didn't exist? That all you have to do is concentrate hard on Dylan's or Springsteen's lyrics and then you can shut out the demands of the real world? (Fuck yes I'm stereotyping here. Although, to be fair, you looked more like a Dirty Projectors guy. Or a Fleet Foxes guy. In other circumstances, I imagine we could've taken in a show at McCarren Pool and smoked some of my neighbor's seriously sweet weed together. But no, you had to Be Like That.) If that's the case, I wouldn't want to be around you when, let's say, a building was on fire or someone needed medical attention. You're not my go-to guy on 9/11. Just sayin'.

Excuse # 2. I didn't really notice what you were doing

After all, you were watching *How to Train Your Dragon* on your laptop. Which, by the way: a*dor*able—one of those mini-notebooks that couldn't weigh more than a toy Yorkie and had all those fun geometric patterns on the outer shell. Where did you get it? I'm still a little jealous. And, hate to stereotype again, but a wee bit *stylish* for a straight man, don't you think? I mean, are you really surprised I thought you were gay when you're watching a Disney movie on a petite laptop?

You know what else didn't help you? *The Omnivore's Dilemma.* Okay, the beard and the book screamed "hipster" to me. But hell, a lot of those boys are gay, and the hairy cub thing is all the rage now. Does this happen a lot with you? Do people assume you're gay all the time, and do you tell yourself you're fine with it, since in some ways it means they think you're put-together and modern and culturally relevant? Does it gain you traction with the ladies, who read you as soft and sensitive and lay down their guard and then bam—in you go for the kill?

I hope the book helps you assuage your guilt. I bet you've given up high fructose corn syrup. I bet you're a member of some co-op and you tell yourself it's perfectly fine to eat meat so long as it's grass-fed, locally sustained, and humanely treated. You're making every effort to avoid products coming out of the industrial-agribusiness machine, ergo you're a moral person. A bit easy, don't you think? I mean, can't we just tell the omnivore: Hey, no dilemma. Just don't eat *everything*. Talk about having your meat pie and wanting to eat it too. If it smells like hypocrisy, it probably is. Just sayin'.

But back to you not noticing, which, granted, might've been a reasonable excuse if it happened once. Or twice. But I'm pretty sure it happened seven times. That's right, I touched you *seven times,* the last six of which could not be construed as accidental. And out of those seven times, you adjusted and pulled away from me *once*. So really, let's just admit that you knew what I was doing and decided to do nothing about it.

Excuse # 3. I'm not a confrontational person and I thought if I ignored you, you'd stop.

There *was* something very Papa Smurf about you. You didn't strike me as the kind of guy who gets worked up about things in public. You're an internalizer. The shy geek holding up the wall at the junior high prom. The dutiful squirrel, collecting and storing his outrage acorns in the mulch of his psyche.

Is this why your girlfriend likes you, your quiet strength? Does she see steely resolve in your medium-length hair, your fashionable-but-not-fashion-forward cargo pants, your sensibly-striped crew-neck sweater? I bet you shop at J.Crew together. I bet you have a joint Costco account, and you appoint one Sunday every two months to stock up on laundry detergent and toilet paper and industrial-size oatmeal. I bet you counter those savings by buying artisanal mushrooms from the organic produce stand, I bet you splurge on aged balsamic vinaigrettes and mango-baby-daikon mustards, I bet every other dish you cook together has shallots in it. I bet you never have to tell each other that you love one another but that you do it anyway, all the time.

Theo doesn't like it when I cook. Mostly we eat out, usually Thai or Italian but never Mexican, because Theo says New York doesn't understand Mexican cuisine. He couldn't come down with me to Miami this time, which was truly a shame since my mother was really looking forward to meeting him; she had baked a Sacher torte for the occasion. It's not easy getting away from the office when you're a young upstart like Theo. He still has to prove himself to his superiors and he can't be running off on long weekends when he's *this close* to getting promoted to assistant vice-president of communications—which of course would mean more responsibility and fewer long weekends—but I get it, it's his career, and just because I don't really have one doesn't mean I can't understand how important it is to show you're reliable and willing to go that extra mile for the sake of the team. I can be a team player too. I just wish Theo understood that we could be our own team, a team of just us two.

Anyway, so here's what I don't get. If I hadn't said anything, we both would've gotten off that plane without either of us acknowledging what had happened. Don't tell me I beat you to it. The plane had already *landed* when I apologized for teasing you, and even after I said it, you said nothing—*nada*—for three, maybe four minutes. I had silenced you with my confession. In fact, allow me to suggest that what bothered you was not the fact that I had *touched* you, *repeatedly,* but that I had broken the spell of our tacit flirtation by daring to talk about it. Because once I talked about it, suddenly it was *real*. Suddenly you had to think about it whether or not you were complicit. Suddenly you needed to affirm your heterosexuality, suddenly we're back in sixth grade, where the worst thing to be called is "fag" and damn if that fear doesn't stick with you through life, right?

Which brings me to my next point:

Excuse # 4. I'm not homophobic and I felt uncomfortable judging you.

This is my favorite excuse of all. Because clearly there were only two options: saying something and instantly "exposing" yourself as a homophobe, or quietly allowing a stranger to touch you and remaining the open-minded liberal that you are. In fact, you played that one really well—not only didn't you say something the entire flight, you didn't even want to move out of the way of my hand. Gays have been persecuted for like, ever, and here you are, offering up your body as penance for all the bad shit straight people have done to us from pre-biblical times. Thank you, Father Fucking Teresa.

See the problem with that argument, sugar, is that you *did* judge me. Remember? Remember when I apologized for teasing you and then four minutes later you clucked your tongue and said the plane wasn't a nightclub? Remember when I said, *I'm sorry, you should've said something* and you said, *I don't have to say something. That shit just ain't done, man.* (BTW, loved the "man" at the end of that sentence. It's like all-too-flagrant code for "I'm straight." Needless to say, gay men never call each other "man" or "dude," unless we're making fun of you breeders.)

Now, if you really wanted to be the bigger man, you could have said, "That's all right. No harm done." Or, "Not interested, sorry," or even, "What are you talking about?" which of course would have let me know that you didn't want to embarrass me—that you were going to play stupid for both our sakes and move on. But however noble your silence seemed, the second you opened your mouth all of that fell by the wayside. Trust me, I'm really noble in my head too.

You remind me a lot of my father. He also likes to defer to my sense of morality; he too only judges when prodded. When I was eighteen and I told him I wanted to be an interior designer, he nodded and pulled his glasses down his nose and looked at me with his pseudo-forgiving eyes and said, *I see. Well, I hope that works out for you,* making sure to sound upbeat even while his words seemed vaguely cruel. And when that didn't last, and I went into commercial voice-over work, he also remained unspecific and neutral. And when I failed at that, more nothing. I would ask for advice while I kept hitting him up for loans—to pay off my other loans, to make my rent, to feed my three cats—and he would be delightfully resolute in insisting that I do *whatever makes me happy.* He never understood—still doesn't—that I just wanted to be accepted for who I was. I want him to appreciate me, not as a way for him to measure his capacity for tolerance, or as a genetic extension of his shrewdness or determination, but rather as a separate being, fully and uniquely my own, warts and all. Is this too much to ask?

Probably. Probably I can't ask for the kind of love my father isn't capable of giving, I can't ask for saplings of empathy to take root in the fallow soil of his soul. The man has worked hard enough. He deserves to be left alone with his newspaper and his ESPN commentators and his HD instant replays. He shouldn't have to constantly be pushing away my clingy, needy arms as they brush up against him, seeking approval or love or even just the opening of his bountiful wallet, a wallet that took many hard years of work to fill, first on a retail sales floor, then as a store manager, then as an owner of one, two, three affordable children's fashion stores in midtown Manhattan.

Sigh. Had things gone better between us, I could've had a story for Theo. We've been all about the role-play lately; Theo says the extra oomph these games have been lending our sex life is really healthy, and I fully agree. And Theo wouldn't have been jealous. Not at all. Let's say you and I had clicked and suddenly you had a blanket over your lap and I was giving you a hand job; I think Theo would have approved. He would've told me that opportunities such as these aren't meant to be passed up—that's what living in the moment is all about. Which explains why a few weeks ago he told me about the time he had sex in the bathroom at Bloomingdale's with that guy with the faux-hawk from the gym who just happened to be browsing the Kiehl's aisle at the same time he was. *What are the chances?* Theo said. And he's right, it's not like the gym is anywhere near Bloomingdale's. Apparently all the time he's sucking this horse-hung god in the stall he's imagining telling me about it, how hot it was, and fuck if he wasn't right and I got insanely hard, and sure there was the initial rush of resentment because we hadn't talked about sex outside the relationship, but then Theo got really graphic and so *into* it, into having the story *get me off,* I just couldn't resist his urgency. The story had this vicious momentum and it was either stand outside like a sad fucking bystander or just go with it and let it overtake me.

But now I won't have a story for him. I guess I could make stuff up but I wonder if I really can. Theo's going to want visuals; he's going to dissect my play by play and I might buckle under the pressure. I might not be able to describe what your penis felt like in my hand. I might not know exactly how you tried to stifle your moans as you came or whether you closed your eyes, and if my story doesn't ring true, then Theo might get upset that I haven't lived up to my side of the bargain. *I can't do all the work, Todd,* he's said to me. And he's right. Fuck. If you'd just smiled at me or said something flirty, I could have gone home and turned Theo on and then he could've believed in us more. Instead I'm sitting in front of a computer at half past three in the morning, typing you a letter that you'll never read or ever even know about, wondering about my life choices. Do you think I lack boundaries? That I'm socially retarded? Well, let me tell you something: I wasn't breastfed through my tweens. My parents didn't walk around the house naked. I wasn't molested by any of my uncles because I've never had any uncles. Plus I was *really* popular in grade school and popular enough in high school. I don't have that much pain to take out on the world. Sure, I have issues, but I'm not such a bad guy. If you think about it, isn't it very human, this yearning, this desire to connect with someone, even strangers? *Especially* strangers. We all want to feel alive, don't we? I was just tapping into the universal knob of lust that's out there. Can you imagine harnessing the energy of all the lust in the world? Imagine a machine that could turn lust into fuel, imagine where we could go. I'm not saying I'm due a medal of honor here. I'm not saying you should congratulate me on my willingness to think outside the box. I'm saying you were complicit. I mean, if I'm allowing that I was somewhat responsible, can't you be a bit flexible too? Can't you try to understand why I'm angry?

I don't even know what I want from you. An apology? For what—calling me out on my shit? An acknowledgment that you and I aren't that different? Who the fuck cares if we are different? What's wrong with being different? I'm not going to feel guilty for not being as uptight as you. You know what? I bet you've rubbed up against a lady or two in your day. No, even better: you've rubbed up against a *guy* or two or fifty. I wasn't the first person to respond to your not-so-subtle cues, and I won't be the last. I thought I was horned up by this scenario, but maybe it's you who was. Maybe nothing gets you hotter than turning guys on and then turning them down. Maybe, in those unspoken minutes when you and I communicated via our limbs, you were experiencing the kind of taboo pleasure that hours of fucking your girlfriend could never live up to. Maybe this is just what you do and you didn't want me calling you out on it. Sorry for exposing the truth, dude.

I should really go back to bed. Theo's going to wake up in a couple of hours and he likes it when I make his morning espresso and butter his English muffins. I don't have anything forcing me up at five in the morning but I do it anyway because I love Theo and I don't want him to resent my leisure, which to be perfectly fair isn't all that much, considering how much time I spend tweaking my résumé and applying to every job I might be halfway qualified for. I'm thinking of taking an antique appraisal class at the New School. I just know I'd be good at it, and both Theo and my dad have been super supportive, as it's one of those jobs that's loosely associated with the arts that also happens to pay well. We'll see. I wonder what it is you do. You're probably some sort of social worker. You're probably an executive assistant at a not-for-profit who plays in a band on the side. Clarinet. No, accordion. You play accordion in a klezmer Pixies revival band, with gigs in dive bars in Ridgewood, and you all wear fedoras and skinny ties and you're all über-talented musicians, and if your lead singer's voice and the crowds knowing hoots are all so preciously ironic, it's totally unintentional. I know. I *get* it.

Does it make you feel good to see how bitter I am? I bet it makes you feel sad. Appropriately sad about the human condition and all us fuck-ups who aren't as self-actualized as you are. But you know what? Pity is the most narcissistic impulse of all. Condescend to me and you'll just reinforce all my prejudices about you being a smug know-it-all. I'm not leaving you much room to be human, am I? I'm sorry. I'm bitter, remember? Can you see past all that? Can you bore your way through my cynical outer shell into the gooey vulnerability beneath? You have to admit: At least I'm trying to get in touch with my feelings. At least I'm trying to understand both of us here. We don't have to hate each other. I can be the lamb and you can be the lion and we can lie down together. We can beat our swords into ploughshares and not cast first stones and all that fantastic hooey, and yes I'm quoting scripture because even though I'm an atheist, I'd bet the Vatican's net worth that you're not, so I thought I'd reach out to you in a language you'd understand. I'm sorry for all the vitriol earlier. I was just ranting. Don't you ever feel the need to rant? Don't people piss you off sometimes so much that you want to write them letters, and don't you ever start writing those letters only to realize you're not half as pissed-off as you thought you were? I'm sure, under different circumstances, we could've been friends. I could have, for instance, mentioned that I had read *Fast Food Nation* and seen my fair share of documentaries on the evils of ethanol and dolphin poaching. Likely that would've given us the platform to jump off into all sorts of topics, like Chomsky and vinyasa and composting, and you would've mentioned your girlfriend's soy collective and I would've mentioned Theo's upcoming silent auction for God's Love We Deliver and you would've said, *Yo, that's cool,* and you wouldn't have even *blinked* when I said Theo was my boyfriend, your furry red eyebrows wouldn't have even arched a *nano*meter. By the end of the flight we would've bumped iPhones to trade contact information and I would've invited you out to Cobble Hill because you'd read up about the scene there and were *dying* to check it out, and you would've said, *Great meeting you, man,* and I wouldn't have minded that man, not one bit.

Why don't we imagine that happened instead? Maybe it did. Maybe I'm just imagining the endless wait for the airplane door to open, having to stand beside you as twenty-three rows of the slowest people on earth tried to wrest their bags from the overhead bins. I'm just pretending that I had to look away to avoid seeing you fidget and squirm, and it's not like when I got off the plane I went to a stall instead of a urinal, it's not like I told myself I couldn't be trusted at a urinal anymore. It's not like I called Theo on my way out of the airport and when he asked me how the flight was, it's not like I saw you waiting in baggage claim averting your eyes, it's not like I gritted my teeth and said, as calmly as I could: *uneventful.*

You must know I'm not as batshit as this letter makes me out to be. I'm bright and caring and a really good listener. Ask anyone. I'm not a pervert. I'm just a normal guy. Like you. I think we should move on. Can we? Move on? Please?

Yours truly,

Todd.

GETTING THERE

Johannesburg, apparently, has little patience for tourists. The airport bus has been suspended, and the visitors' bureau informs Roger there's no public transport. "Even if there was," the woman behind the counter says, "you wouldn't want to take it." He's advised to find himself a driver. "Take a card. You'll need it," the woman says.

Roger heads outside for a cab. The sky is overcast. His head is hot, his mind exhausted and exhilarated. He's been looking forward to his adventure for weeks, has chosen South Africa over India, Japan, and Thailand, not just because of the wild animals but also because of its sense of living history: any country that could move from apartheid to one of the most progressive constitutions in the world in under two decades has to be admired. And yet a sense of foreboding gnaws at him. Something could really go wrong here. So many potential pitfalls: rampant violent crime, a host of insect-borne illnesses, not all of which can be combated with the antibiotic regimen his doctor has put him on. And then the minor detail of South Africa having one of the highest HIV rates in the world.

He's reminded of this by numerous billboards on the ride to his hotel in posh Sandton, ads explicitly warning the populace to protect themselves. The air outside is pleasant and not too warm. When they hit Alexandra, a dilapidated shantytown that abuts Sandton, he sees boys getting haircuts in slapdash tents, women whose tattered blouses barely cover their breasts, all in plain sight of the plush green suburbs directly above.

The hotel isn't plush, but it's bright. The receptionists are gracious, although the answers they give to his sightseeing questions are shaky; no one's pretending this is a tourist friendly town. He needs to check his email but the hotel's Internet service—a small room behind reception with one terminal—is down, so he treks to the nearby mall. There are no sidewalks, and no one else is walking but him. Around him he sees car dealerships, tall, manicured bushes, high walls and gates—gates everywhere.

Sandton Mall is sparkly and oppressive. The men sport Italian suits and the women oversize sunglasses. The stores are overpriced, sterile. And yet the size of the crowds suggests it's clearly the place to be. He's offended by the inexorable whiteness of the shoppers, still being served by black salespeople. Is there no intermingling? And then he remembers: he *picked* this neighborhood.

At the Internet café, he logs on to Gaydar to retrieve his messages. He chatted up a dozen men before stepping foot in South Africa, secured phone numbers, wrote down pithy descriptions beside their names, like "nice lips" or "huge cock" or "likes it rough." But his prospects disappoint: mixed-race Andre has a sister coming into town and suggests meeting the following day. The other Andre in his mailbox is also otherwise engaged. None of the others have responded, which is upsetting. He considers entering the chat room to scare up some action, but instead he researches bars. The two that look promising are both in Melville, several miles south.

Later that night, after showering and little rest, he descends to the lobby and asks the front desk to call him a cab. The receptionist—a lanky black boy named Thapalone—smiles and says he'll be off duty in ten minutes and will drive Roger to Melville for a hundred rand, as it's on his way home.

In the car—a smudgy two-seater—Thapalone smokes and listens to talk radio, which Roger assumes is in English even though he can barely make out the words. Thapalone talks about Times Square and the Knicks and Roger nods, pretending to recognize the names of the players. Roger opens his window and feels a timid breeze. In the distance rise the lonesome skyscrapers of downtown Joburg, the only tall buildings for miles. The streets are too still; it irritates him. Other than the occasional stray dog, he sees nothing but cars, trees, streetlights, and walls, behind which must be the people. Very scared people.

They pull up on Melville's main drag and he's relieved to see signs of activity. As he's getting out Thapalone invites him out to a party the next night in Braamfontein, promising lots of free booze and tasty young girls. Roger thanks him and says, "Sure, see you tomorrow."

The first bar, Statement, is too small. The patrons remind Roger of frogs in a pond. He walks the long stretch downhill to OH! Bar—which is livelier, if thoroughly unoriginal. Gay bars the world over seem to doll up with the same narrow range of accessories—video jukeboxes, sassy drag queens, pumping house music, unisex bathrooms, and mirrors everywhere—yet it's precisely this familiarity that comforts him.

He orders a gin and tonic from the muscular goatee behind the bar and does his once-around, landing on a stool by the railing opposite two go-go boys in Doc Martens and skimpy yellow Speedos. He surveys the possibilities, puzzled once again at how white the crowd is. Where are the black boys? Do they have their own bars? Though New York isn't much different. He could usually count on one hand the black men at any given bar in Chelsea. When he asked his gay black friend about it, Marcus harrumphed.

"Lots of brothers on the down low," Marcus told him. "And the ones who aren't don't care for Chelsea."

"Because white boys are bitchy?"

"Not necessarily," Marcus said. "Or rather, not *just* that."

Roger didn't follow up. The gay box seemed grotesquely small already. He couldn't imagine compartmentalizing it any further, limiting himself only to gay Jews. Not that that would be a small box, in New York.

A short, brawny type with flirty eyes and a wide forehead glances restlessly at him. His tapered Oxford and dress pants peg him as a tourist in this sea of t-shirts and jeans. Roger glances back, blankly; he isn't interested, but he's eager to speak to somebody.

The man sidles up beside Roger. "So," he says. "Where are the good places around here?"

Roger laughs. "I have no idea," he says. "I got here this afternoon."

"Me too," the man says. "My bus from Mozambique broke down on the highway."

Roger recognizes the accent. "You're from Brazil," he says.

"Ricardo," the man says. "I live in Mozambique now."

"Roger." He shakes the man's hand. "So how'd you get here if your bus broke down?"

"This Mozambican recognized the bus and stopped." Ricardo's eyes canvass the room. "He drove me here and helped me find a hotel."

"Lucky," Roger says. "You speak English really well."

"My MBA is from Florida State." Ricardo shrugs. "We need to find the action," he says.

Eric Sasson

Roger laughs at how much better "action" sounds with a Brazilian accent.

While Ricardo fishes for information from some locals, Roger heads to the bathroom. On his way out he spots a pretty face checking him out in the mirror. Seashell-smooth skin and dark hair and eyes, and the first black customer he's seen all evening. Or at least half-black; Roger isn't sure. The boy's t-shirt reads "I'm the Life of the Party" in bold, shimmery sequins and his eyes say, *Follow me,* which Roger does, down the spiral staircase to the dingy dance floor.

The boy sashays onto the floor and turns around, beckoning Roger with oscillating fingers. Roger smiles and negotiates the crowd. The boy releases an enthusiastic squeal and pulls at him, squeezing his ass. Within seconds, his tongue is down Roger's throat. Roger is too caught up to resist, and is pretty sure he doesn't want to, anyway. They'd be putting on a show, if the others cared, but they don't. The boy grinds against him. He thrusts his hand up Roger's shirt and works his moist fingers around his chest, nuzzling his head against Roger's neck. Roger breathes in the sweet tartness of the boy's citrus shampoo.

"I love hairy men," the boy purrs.

Roger smiles, wondering if he's old enough to be the boy's father. "How convenient," he says. "I like smooth guys."

"I'm K—" the boy says, but the music is loud and Roger isn't sure if it's Kinlana or Kinlabi or something else.

"Roger," Roger says. The boy makes happy noises. He chews on Roger's upper lip, massages Roger's cock through his pants.

"American Roger," K says, exaggerating every *r*. He backs up against Roger's body, wraps one hand behind Roger's neck while running the other down his thigh. The theatricality seems excessive, but Roger gives in to the moment. He wonders if there's someone for whom this ritual is being performed.

The song dissolves into another. K fans himself and sighs. "Come," he says, taking hold of Roger's hand. Roger follows up the stairs, to a back room beyond the bathrooms, one that is terrifically dark and almost empty, with convenient nooks and velvet couches that huddle in corners. The boy takes him to a couch. They feel each other up.

"You're sexy," the boy says.

"So you live here?" Roger says, the first and only question of importance to him.

"Of course. I'm *real* hard for you. See?"

He guides Roger's hand to his cock, which is indeed hard, and large.

"Let's go to my hotel," Roger says.

"Are you a businessman?" K asks. "Imports and exports?"

"No. I'm on holiday," Roger says. "Are you in university?"

"My first year," K says. "I'm nineteen."

The number should appall him. But Roger isn't any less turned on.

"Why don't we go back to my hotel?" Roger suggests, again.

"I can't," K says. "My friends are waiting for me."

"So tell them you've met someone."

"They're waiting in my car."

Roger's eyes narrow. "Why?"

"They're sleeping. They're straight. Gay clubs bore them."

"So why don't they go to a straight club?"

"Because I have the car," K says, as he reaches for Roger's fly. Roger tenses, but doesn't resist. K wriggles down and Roger closes his eyes. He feels a warm moistness on his cock, hears a soft pop, smells the sharp musk of sweat that's not his own. *My first African experience,* he thinks. But then he shudders: it's all happening too quickly. The boy is so aggressive. What if he's on drugs, or has herpes? Roger remembers the billboards on the drive from the airport. He hears a humming in his ear, the drone of nearby conversation. His neck trembles, his lungs seize up. He pulls K's head from his crotch and tells him to stop. K glances up, confused.

"What's wrong?" he asks, twisting a few wisps of Roger's chest hairs between index finger and thumb.

Roger bites his lower lip, investigates the boy's gaze—his eyelashes are fluttering, but otherwise K's expression is hard to decipher. Roger wonders whether he's supposed to say something back. Something funny, or affirming, or sexy.

"Nothing." He forces a smile. "It was great." The words limp out of his mouth.

"I bet," K says. "I really should go. My friends are waiting."

The boy pops to his feet, brushes invisible dust off his shirt, runs his middle fingers across his eyebrows, back into his hairline.

"Wait. What?" Roger says. "I mean, I'm sorry. Tell me more about you. Are you really South African?"

K laughs. He bites a hangnail off his thumb, flicks it at Roger. "Does it matter?"

"I don't know," Roger says. The boy's indifference, the brusque nature of their exchange, unsettles him. "I guess not."

"I'm your first memory. Maybe your best in this town," K says, and then he laughs and tosses his head back. Suddenly Roger wants him to stay—suddenly he worries that the boy may be right. But he doesn't get the chance to plead his case. K turns and glides out of view.

Back in the main room Roger is relieved to spot Ricardo talking to an older man with bushy sideburns.

"Tonight, this is it," Ricardo says. "The action."

"Where are you staying?" Roger asks. "What neighborhood."

"I don't remember," Ricardo says. "Something with an S."

"Sandton? Me too," Roger says. "Do you want to share a cab back?"

"First I'm going to hit on that guy there," Ricardo says, pointing to a beefy blond holding up the wall across from them. "He looks Croatian. I'll either leave with him or with you."

Roger smiles. "I'll be by the bar."

At the bar the goatee refreshes his G&T. Roger feels dizzy, a recipe two parts elation, two parts jet lag, one part what-the-fuck-just-happened. Why did he stop the boy? It's not like he wasn't turned on. It's not like he hasn't had more than his share of backroom hook-ups, and the list of unknown-HIV-status men who've given him head could fill several pages. If it was just a gut feeling, then maybe it was a stupid feeling. Perhaps worse than stupid.

He knocks back the rest of his drink and pushes the questions out of his mind. Instead he thinks about plans. He should visit a museum, do a city tour. He should experience something unique and cultural. But he is tired, so tired. And he has no idea how he'll get back to the hotel. He has no driver, and the drivers in Johannesburg are more than drivers, they are gatekeepers. They tether him to safety.

Ricardo returns twenty minutes later, looking deflated. "Do you have a guy? My driver is asleep already."

"You have a driver?" Roger asks.

"Long story," Ricardo says. "Very helpful. Speaks Portuguese. He's going to take me on a tour tomorrow."

Roger asks the security guard to call a cab. While they wait, they have another drink, and the room, already spinning, speeds up. About thirty minutes later the guard tells them the cab has arrived. They exit and Roger spots the small vehicle by the curb, a car the size of a large turkey. A when-I-grow-up-I-want-to-be-a-car car.

"Welcome, welcome," the driver says, opening the door for them.

"We're going to Sandton," Roger says.

"Yes, yes," the driver says.

Once inside the driver turns to hand each of them a card. "Thalong is my name. Call me twenty-four hours. I take you wherever you need to go."

"We're making two stops," Roger says.

"Yes, yes." Thalong says, adjusting his mirror, Roger thinks, to appear more trustworthy. "Sandton."

Roger opens the window. He wonders if his eyes are as glazed as the Brazilian's.

"Good-time party boys? You want to go to disco?" Thalong asks.

Ricardo sits up. "You know where the action is?"

Thalong laughs a long, throaty laugh. "Tomorrow night. I make special for you. Good-time party disco."

"Oh yeah? You know where the hot men are?"

Thalong clucks, shakes his head. "I'm not gay, bobo," he says. "Some people they have problem with the gay but not me. Everybody is Thalong's customer."

"Good man," Roger says.

Thalong laughs. He drives tentatively out of Melville. Ricardo slouches against the door, ready to pass out. Roger scans out the window and takes in the streets, the sparse storefronts, the peeling signage, the empty lots. The hum of the silence is deep and menacing, and the few people loitering about remind him of stones. He's drunk, but apparently not drunk enough to fail to notice that something is wrong. They pass the same gas station three times. And then Thalong pulls onto the highway headed south. Green as he is, Roger knows that Sandton is north.

"I think you're going the wrong way," Roger says.

Thalong massages the back of his neck, looks at Roger in his rearview mirror. "Long day, man. I've been up twenty-eight hours straight. My boss is short drivers. He tells me I can go to sleep or I can keep my job."

"Sorry," Roger says. His hands search the back of the seat for the safety belt. "So are you from Joburg?"

Thalong laughs. "No, man. I'm a tourist. Like you. I come here to make money but this isn't my city. We're all tourists in this town."

Thalong gets off the highway at the next stop. He drives down narrow streets, past abandoned warehouses. Suddenly Roger feels himself sobering up, quickly. Was Thalong really lost? Roger pokes Ricardo awake. He needs someone to share in his horror, or else tell him to chill out.

"We're lost," Roger says.

"Don't worry," Thalong says. He pulls the car over at the next traffic light, beside three men leaning against a green Dodge Neon that has seen better days. "I'll ask directions."

When Thalong gets out of the car, Ricardo tunes back in. "Why did we stop?"

"He doesn't know where he's going," Roger says. "Do you have a lot of cash on you?"

Ricardo kneads the sleep out of his eyes. "I need a bed, man."

The night sky silvers, flirting with dawn. The men Thalong talks to wear brightly colored tracksuits. All of them seem preternaturally unfazed, like cows in pasture. Everyone is smoking. One of them laughs, and then Thalong says something quick, and suddenly everyone looks at Roger. Roger's heart quickens. The others chuckle and say "hello" playfully, and Ricardo sings a drunk hello back. Then Thalong slips back into the car, and the others wave as they pull away. Roger curses himself. The sting of his own paranoia irritates him. Taxi drivers get lost. He's read too many guidebooks, heard too many stories. He should know better.

For the rest of the ride Thalong drives more purposefully. Ricardo nods back to sleep, and Roger watches Johannesburg submit to a new day. When he sees the taut bushes, the ten-foot walls, he knows they are nearing Sandton.

They drop Ricardo off first. "Come with me, tomorrow, on the tour," Ricardo says, handing him the hotel's phone number. "Around two. We'll go to Mandela's house."

"Sure," Roger says.

Thalong turns on the radio. He taps his fingers against the steering wheel and whistles. Roger wonders if he's struggling to keep himself awake.

"Where you from, man?" Thalong asks.

"New York City," Roger answers. He never answers the more generic "United States." Not now, with W as President. Not two years into the phony Iraq War.

"New York, New York," Thalong says, like every other cabdriver in the world. "You like rap music? Biggie Smalls? Jay-Z?"

"I'm from Brooklyn," Roger says. "Like them."

"You from Brooklyn, bobo?" Thalong turns to look at him, his face lighting up and his teeth exposed, like Roger is a celebrity. "Brooklyn is the place, man."

"It's pretty cool."

"I want to go to Brooklyn, man," Thalong says. "Walk across your bridge and see the big statue."

"You should visit," Roger says, and then immediately regrets it.

Thalong nods, his smile almost a smirk. "Maybe one day."

Around three the next day Ricardo pulls up to Roger's hotel in the backseat of a natty beige Citroën station wagon. He looks refreshed and alert, all traces of a hangover absent. In the driver's seat is a rotund, avuncular old man with thick gray hair wearing large sunglasses scotch-taped at the bridge. Beside him is a wisp of a boy, bony and silent, about eight years old but lacking the curiosity one expects in a young boy. Both of them sit silently.

"This is Mansoor," Ricardo says. "And that's his grandson, Nisim."

Mansoor nods. Nisim fidgets with the door lock.

"So we have him for the whole day, for 300 rand," Ricardo says. About forty dollars. "Do you want to see Soweto?"

Roger nods; it's where you're supposed to go when in Johannesburg. Ricardo and Mansoor speak to each other boisterously in Portuguese.

"Does he speak English?" Roger asks.

"A little," Ricardo says. "He's from Mozambique, but he's lived here long enough you'd think he knew more English."

"What about the grandson?"

"It's his daughter's kid. She died of cancer a few years ago, and the father is working in some mine for the summer, so Mansoor is taking care of him."

"But he speaks English."

"You'd be surprised," Ricardo says. "It's a tight-knit community down here."

The drive is slow. Roger wonders if it's the car that refuses to go fast, or just Mansoor. He imagines the old man's not taking any chances with his grandson in the passenger seat. Mansoor chats at length in Portuguese, which Ricardo sporadically translates into English.

"He's going to pass by the downtown district, so you can see it," Ricardo says. "But we're not going to get out. And keep the windows closed, he says. He'll point out the important buildings to us."

"Is it really that bad?" Roger says.

"It's a Sunday afternoon, so the offices are empty. Mansoor says the only people on the streets are looking for trouble."

Roger adjusts to free himself of the vinyl sticking to his thighs. "I'm not used to this," he says. "I mean, I've been to Rio, and it's not exactly safe there either. But at least there are *people*. And you can walk around in the daytime, no problem. I'm just wondering how much of this is paranoia."

Ricardo laughs. "Was it paranoia last night in the cab?" he asks, rubbing his chin. "But listen, who knows? In 1975, the Mozambique people rose up to claim their independence from the Portuguese. They gave them twenty-four hours to leave the country with no more than twenty-two kilos of personal items. Everything else—their houses, their TVs, their cars—had to stay. Of course the Portuguese had it good in Mozambique for many years, which means lots of empty mansions left behind. A ghost town for the natives, who went inside these homes and didn't understand what they saw. They didn't know what anything *was*—the kitchen appliances, the electronics. These people didn't have refrigerators, or washing machines. So they stole the wood to make fire. They broke the windows to make pottery from the glass. They filled up the bathtubs with soil and grew tomato plants. Thirty years ago! Not ancient history. We were already alive."

Roger shakes his head. "So I guess the whites here have it easy, then."

"Not if you ask them."

"But should we ask them? After apartheid?"

Ricardo's eyebrows bunch together. "I don't know."

"At least this country seems to be moving in the right direction," Roger says. "They've legalized gay marriage here."

"That doesn't mean anything. Men are killed for being gay in the townships, and sometimes they don't even allow the bodies to be buried in a cemetery."

Roger feels himself shudder. "These things take time."

"Some prejudices cannot be broken," Ricardo says.

"But they're getting there," Roger says. He hears, as the words leave his lips, how emphatic they sound, how defensive. "They'll get there. One day."

Downtown is deserted. None of the buildings impress, and Roger wonders if Mansoor is only here because he believes this is what tourists want to see. Afterward they drive to Soweto. The day is bright and cool. The city stretches long and flat; there's something dead about the way it stretches, Roger thinks.

The traffic starts to slow and Roger spots several tour buses up ahead. The township sprawls around them, mind-boggling in its vastness. Houses extend toward the horizon in all directions. At first they seem like tenement villages, rough and grimy, but soon these fade into sturdier, modest homes, of brick and stucco. Out his window Roger sees two large water towers covered with murals of colorful, cartoon-like scenes of black people engaged in Progress. Trains, cars, pretty homes and prettier schoolchildren, smiling faces rushing to work, all spiraling around a central bubble framing what appears to be a black Madonna and Child.

Nisim fidgets with the radio until Mansoor gently takes his hand off the dial. Mansoor lifts a cigarette from his pack, raises it in the air, and looks back at both of them. Roger and Ricardo nod. Mansoor begins telling a story.

"He says four million people live here, just in Soweto," Ricardo says.

"Fucking hell," Roger says.

"He calls it the Johannesburg Zoo. When he takes tourists here he calls it 'going on safari.' "

"Wow." Roger turns to look at Mansoor, who is popping a cracker into Nisim's mouth. He watches the boy chew eagerly. Both the man and the boy are brown-skinned, likely Muslim given their names. "Not too fond of black people, is he?"

"It's just a joke," Ricardo says. "It's not all bad, though. He says the neighborhoods are different. There's a middle class and an upper class here, too."

They park the car in a ditch underneath an amarula tree. Roger looks around. Lots of dead grass and weeds, laundry left out to dry, children on rickety bikes. They walk down a few dusty roads toward Mandela's childhood home, a nondescript brick one-story filled with mementos and knick-knacks and tons of pictures of Mandela with celebrities and dignitaries. Honorary degrees and other accolades take up the remaining space on the walls.

Outside the home is a cluster of souvenir stands, where most of the buses are parked. Six people descend from their bus, plump middle-aged Europeans, all sun-screened, all Bermuda-shorted. The tables are littered with masks, colorful jewelry boxes, South African flags, salad tongs, tall, thin statues of pregnant women, hosts of giraffes and rhinos, busts of Mandela. Roger scans through the mix. Other than a few batiks, he finds the whole lot uninspiring. Still, he needs gifts to bring back home, and batiks are light and can be rolled up.

The souvenir peddler, a man with sunken eyes and a grave smile, pulls out samples for Roger to mull over. While Roger sifts through them Nisim approaches, leaving Ricardo and Mansoor by a nearby bench.

"I'll give you special price," the man says, without enthusiasm. Nisim picks up a wooden giraffe and is turning it in his hands.

"How much for five?" Roger asks, pulling out pieces he likes.

"Buy four get one free." The peddler reaches across the table and takes the giraffe from Nisim's hands. Nisim looks up, confused. "*Hhayibo,* little one," the man says, returning the giraffe to the table. "Careful."

"How about two free?" Roger asks. He looks over his shoulder, sees Mansoor and Ricardo smoking, lost in conversation. Nisim takes one of the colorful boxes off the table. The peddler looks at Roger, then back at the boy, and shakes his head. Roger smiles at Nisim uneasily, wondering if he should say something. He studies the boy's eyes, so absorbed by the box's clasp. He wonders what Nisim is thinking. A boy who should be in school, who lost his mother at such a young age, who likely can barely understand, much less converse, with the peddler. Perhaps he'll buy the boy that box.

"All five for three hundred rand," the peddler says, grabbing the pieces from Roger and beginning to wrap them, as if the decision's been made.

"One second," Roger says. The man's rashness irks him.

The peddler frowns and tosses aside the batiks. "I gave you a *good* price," he says, looking scorned. When the man turns back to Nisim, Roger can tell his anger is real. He jerks the box out of the boy's hand and Nisim, surprised by the man's force, lets go. The box falls and shatters.

"*Eish!* Boy! I told you not to touch." The peddler jostles to the front of his table, his eyes wide with fury, thrusting his face into Roger's. "Why do you let your boy break my things?"

"He's not my boy," Roger says, stepping back.

"Then who is responsible for him," the peddler says.

A few of the other salespeople shake their heads. The other tourists fan out to tables farther away. The peddler starts shouting in a native tongue: *Umfana omubi. Hamba.* Nisim is frozen in place. Only when Mansoor and Ricardo come over does he move to stand behind his grandfather.

"What's the problem?" Ricardo asks the peddler.

"The boy broke the box. Someone has to pay." The peddler points down at the shards littering the ground.

Mansoor crouches beside Nisim and speaks to him gently. Ricardo puts on a friendly smile, but the peddler isn't having it; he shouts and gestures to the others around him, looking indignant. Ricardo exchanges words with Mansoor. Roger can't understand anything. His head is sweating.

"*Oi,* Roger." Ricardo looks at him flatly. "Did you see? Nisim says the man grabbed the box."

Roger shakes his head. Mansoor and Nisim gape at him, dense stares that bore into him. He wonders if it's wise to take a side, to escalate things.

"Two hundred fifty rand." The peddler holds his two hands out in front of him, one with two fingers up, the other with all five. "You will pay me, please."

"I'll pay for it." The words spill out of Roger's mouth. "I should have been watching him."

Ricardo's face twists with disgust. "What are you talking about, man?" He turns to the peddler. "Listen, my friend, that box isn't worth fifty rand. And we aren't going to pay because you broke it."

"I broke nothing, man." The peddler's nostrils expand and his eyes bead. "The boy broke it. You must watch your children. They can't go around and break things or else you pay."

"Roger." Ricardo says. "Did Nisim break the box?"

"It was no one's fault," Roger says. "It fell."

"But he grabbed the box," Ricardo says, pointing to the peddler. "Yes?"

Roger shrugs his shoulders and out comes a thin, nervous laugh. "It's all right. I can pay for it." But before he can reach inside his pocket Mansoor grabs his hand, squeezes Roger's palm with both of his own, squeezing it like a faith healer squeezes the legs of a lame man before commanding him to walk. "No one pays," he says. The first English words Roger has heard from his mouth.

Four other peddlers have joined their circle. Three fold their arms across their chests, and two are mumbling. Roger can't make out a single word, and isn't sure he wants to. Their looks unnerve him. They are peering into his soul and find it lacking. He wants to get out of there, before they get angrier, before they pounce.

"Arrivederci," Ricardo tells the peddler. "Have a nice day, man."

"You are not going to pay?" The peddler throws up his hands and spits on the ground.

"No," Ricardo says. "Not one rand."

"You are raising the boy in a bad way," the peddler says.

"I'm not his father," Ricardo says.

"Then who are you then?"

"It's not your business," Ricardo says.

"You are together," the peddler says, his face practically glowing with the revelation. "The two of you. Gay people."

Roger feels his insides collapse. He is both afraid and ashamed of his fear. He thrusts his hand into his pocket and pulls out a bill. "Here's one hundred rand," Roger says. "More than enough."

The peddler stares at the note. "Why do you come to Africa?" he asks. "To give us diseases?"

"Enough, Njani," another of the peddler says. "You are scaring our customers."

Roger stretches the note taut, holds it up to the man's face. "Are you taking the money or am I putting it back in my pocket?"

"Put it away," the man says. "I don't need your dirty money."

Roger smiles. "Have a fantastic afternoon," he says. Ricardo, Mansoor and Nisim have already walked away, past the buses. As he scurries to join them Roger tries to contain his emotions. He is angry. More than angry. He is disgusted, indignant. The clouds in the sky feel heavier, *cloudier.* Colors—on clothes, on buildings, on buses— that had seemed bright and cheerful now seem garish and aggressive. The air feels stale, the whole area reeking of cheap sentiment and despair.

Mansoor holds tightly on to Nisim's hand and mumbles under his breath, words that Roger knows are curses, racist curses. Nisim looks pensive and glum. Roger wonders if he understands what just happened. He wonders how Mansoor will explain it to him.

"Oi, let's check out the memorial," Ricardo says.

Roger shudders. "Shouldn't we get out of here?"

"Are you kidding? This is the safest place in town. Their livelihood depends on tourists."

"You still want to visit, after what happened."

Ricardo laughs. "The man grabbed the box, didn't he?"

"He did," Roger says. "And then Nisim let go."

Ricardo shakes his head. "That jerk. Come on."

The nearby children's uprising memorial consists of three

tiers of shallow ponds that ascend to a memorial block carved in burgundy marble. Stones litter the ponds, some sunk to the bottom, others breaking the surface and forming abstract patterns. Beyond the memorial rise several free-standing slate brick walls. Roger approaches the block to read the inscription: "In Memory of Hector Peterson and all other young heroes and heroines of our struggle who laid down their lives for freedom, peace, and democracy."

"Nineteen-seventy-six," Roger says. "A year after Mozambique."

"Right," Ricardo says. "It took twenty more here."

"I can't even imagine," Roger says. He looks around, sees Mansoor squatting beside his grandson, pointing to an inscription by the pond, telling him something. Something important, from the look on his face.

"Mansoor likes it here," Ricardo says. "He left Mozambique back in '75 too. He wasn't rich or a diplomat or anything, but he just didn't think he'd be safe there anymore. So he came to South Africa and then the uprisings started and he thought he'd have to leave another country, but then those didn't succeed, so he stayed and raised his family here. Funny story, right?"

Roger winces before checking himself. "So essentially he's happy the uprising failed and apartheid lasted longer."

Ricardo laughs. "You're funny. I think he's just happy he didn't have to move again."

"The world is strange," Roger says.

"Yes," Ricardo says. "You'd prefer things make sense. Americans are like that."

Roger stares at Ricardo. "Aha. I see. Americans. And the rest of the world?"

Ricardo laughs. "You want me to speak for the rest of the world?

Listen, Roger, if it makes you happy, go back and give that asshole a hundred rand. Or buy a few batiks. I'm sure he'll gladly sell them to you. But you can't buy them all. Or maybe you *can* buy them all, or even organize a fundraiser for a batik collective, or sponsor a child to go to Batik University, and of course you should do all of those things, but not because the world is going to make any more sense."

He laughs again, reaches up and gives Roger's shoulder a friendly squeeze. Roger forces a smile back. A friendly ribbing, no harm done. It would be childish to get upset about it, and yet he is.

Walking back toward the car, Ricardo suggests a bite and Mansoor holds a napkin against Ricardo's back, drawing a path to a nearby restaurant for lunch. "There are swings nearby," Ricardo says, when Roger asks why Mansoor won't be joining them. "We'll meet back at the car in an hour."

They are the only white people at the restaurant, and Roger's first thought is that it's a good sign, because the food is likely to be what the locals really eat. His second thought is, this is a tourist trap—not a single one of these places is really authentic. And his third thought is, what if it isn't safe? What if the peddler is after them? And his last thought is, what if my digestive system can't handle strange ingredients, will the doxycycline be enough to kill any suspicious bacteria?

"You need a beer," Ricardo says.

"At least two, actually," Roger says.

The Brazilian starts cracking peanuts between his teeth and smirking, likely imagining the action he hopes to get later that night. Roger sighs. He's tired of being the good-intentioned sad-sack New Yorker, forever second-guessing himself.

A young, ravishing girl with a red bandanna holding back her hair approaches to take their order. She wears the credulous stare of a newborn kitten, and when she chuckles, which she does with every question he asks, her cheeks push up against her nose. In a few minutes she returns and puts down his order in front of him, and as she does so she blushes and says, in a thick English, *Impala stew. I hope you like it.* Roger is struck by the bounce in her eyes, how modest, almost embarrassed, she is to put the plate down in front of him. He senses a certain anxiety in her expression, and it surprises him—that she actually seems to care, that she's worried he might not like it. And somehow, this anxiety touches him. He wants to eat the entire plate now. He wants to lick it clean and lift it up, ask for seconds. He wants to see her smile back at him.

"*Oi,* Roger." Ricardo snaps his fingers. "What's with the stupid grin?"

Roger lifts his beer, attempts to chug it down. "Just looking forward to my safari next week," he says. "So I can see what an impala looks like when it's alive."

Body and Mind

It fascinates him, all the things he can do without ever getting up from the bed: turn off the lights. Close the blinds and the curtains. Set an alarm, check voice-mail, order room service, switch from TV to DVD to WebTV. He can even phone in Keno numbers and charge them to the room.

Andy spreads himself out, foraging through a bag of Cheez Doodles. He's adjusted the thermostat twice and yet the air in the room remains bone chilling. It's his first time in Sin City. Hunter comes to Vegas several times a year on business, and when the Wynn sent him a comp for four nights, he parlayed it into an early anniversary present.

On the TV: *Notes on a Scandal.* Young Steven Connolly is coming on to Sheba Hart, played by Cate Blanchett. He keeps calling her "Miss." Andy and Hunter have seen the film several times. They bonded over the campy drama during their first month of dating. *Of course she'd risk her marriage. Look at him!* Andy said. *So he's sixteen,* Hunter said. *He's worth some jail time.* Andy's eyes narrowed impishly. Later that night they fucked like wind-up toys whose bezels had been turned to snapping.

His phone buzzes: both he and Hunter are on Grindr, and BiggRigg9x10 has sent him an opening "hey." BiggRigg's picture has a face, which is a plus, but his stats say forty-three, outside of Hunter's age range. Hunter is seven years older and still maintains a stricter cutoff than Andy does. Andy sometimes wonders what will happen when he gets to that cutoff date, if Hunter will trade him in for a newer model.

The bathroom door opens, and he catches a glimpse of Hunter's hairy thigh in the hallway mirror.

"Sorry." Hunter sounds defensive. "The WiFi doesn't work when it's closed."

So now he's priggish just because he doesn't want to see his boyfriend taking a dump. "BiggRigg said hello to me," he says.

"Is he sexy?" Hunter asks.

"I think so." Andy grabs the remote to turn up the volume. Judi Dench has just been introduced to Cate Blanchett's much older husband and Down-syndrome son. The narrative voice-over is deliciously cruel.

"He's old," Hunter says, dismissively.

You're old, Andy thinks. "I like older guys," he says instead.

"I know," Hunter says. "Let's keep looking."

They're about to celebrate four years together. Andy got his iPhone several months after Hunter did. *Now we can window-shop together,* he joked that night. Hunter grimaced, but the comment wasn't meant to be cutting. And Hunter was the one who brought it up a few weeks before their trip: *Should we go on Grindr in Vegas?* It was a sensitive topic, considering Andy's infidelity the year before. Hunter was being mature about it, all things considered. They'd recently started talking about three-ways again, vaguely, like one talks about adoption or moving to a new city. Andy wanted to believe the suggestion meant Hunter was moving on, so he smiled, and paused—a bit theatrically— before he took Hunter's hand and said *Sure, why not.*

An ad for Absolut pops up on the bottom of the screen. Someone's rich, Andy thinks. By arranging people according to distance, Grindr cuts straight to the chase: Gay men want dick and they don't want to travel, or at least they want the traveling they do to be in proportion to the magnificence of said dick. Then again, he and Hunter met on a chat site. *So you dig Asians?* he'd asked Hunter, early on in their first chat. He had to, since it wasn't unusual on these sites to find white men writing nasty tercets like "No fats, femmes or Asians." Turned out Hunter had dated several Filipinos.

He sends out two hellos: to Homotextual, to IMNneedofcock, both younger than him, yet more manly than Hunter usually likes.

Are you alone? Homotextual writes back. Andy smirks; both he and Hunter put "Couple looking for 3rd" as their status line.

I'm with my boyfriend, he writes. *He's on too. NYCBeast. Where r u?*

@ a bar off Harmony, Homotextual writes back. And then, a minute later, after presumably checking out Hunter's photo: *I can be there in 10.*

Andy wonders about being online while in a bar, if one doesn't defeat the purpose of the other. Then again, it's just after 2 a.m., and the options at the bar are likely whittling down to troll territory. "What about Homotextual?" he calls out.

"I'll check," Hunter says.

"He wants to come over," Andy says, flipping through the stations. *Who's Afraid of Virginia Woolf?* is on AMC. It's a hard call; Elizabeth Taylor has great lines. But Judi Dench is about to fondle Cate Blanchett's hands. He switches back to *Notes.*

"Hold on."

Andy hears an odd tapping coming from the bathroom. Hunter is limping. Andy guesses his leg must have fallen asleep from sitting too long on the toilet. He laughs, then sighs, as Hunter fumbles with his pants.

Sex with Hunter used to be great. Hot. Smoking hot. Raw. Three, four times a day. Moments when time stopped. Moments when he felt like he was part of one grand, pulsating engine of lust. Belts. Handcuffs. Dildos and *I'm gonna breed you, you dirty fucking cumrag*. They crossed lines. He liked it when they crossed lines, when Hunter smacked him, spit on him, said obscene things, things that shouldn't be said outside of a bedroom.

And then it slowed. Not all of a sudden. The flood became a river, then a stream, then a trickle. Sex became stale. Worse, a chore, like laundry, like clipping toenails. He worried for a while. Hunter was losing interest, Hunter no longer found him attractive. But it wasn't that simple. He didn't initiate either; it was more of a mutual decision.

The lack of passion left him feeling disconnected, undesirable. When he hooked up that first time, he hoped to get these thoughts out of his system. A few others followed, all random guys he found online. Shortly after, Andy confessed, hoping to spark some dialogue. Which he did. Healthy dialogue. Meaningful dialogue. Hunter said: *I understand.* Hunter said: *We'll work through this.* And they did; the sex not only resumed, it got hotter. Nastier, as if Hunter had something to prove. Andy wasn't about to complain. The sizzle was back. A brief, beautiful burst. And then.

"Let's pass on Homotextual," Hunter says. He comes out of the bathroom, sits down on the opposite bed. Andy types his regrets and they share a quick, flat smile of acknowledgment. Hunter, still so lovely to look at. Rugged and masculine, a man one pictures in flannel.

It's not like they've stopped getting along. If anything, the affection between them has grown. They're like lesbians now, experiencing the inevitable bed death. Why did affection have to be the death knell of lust? What is it about hugging Hunter that makes Andy's dick limp? Or rather, not limp, but awake for the briefest spell, like a bear that peeks out of his cave only to decide his winter isn't over. He told his friend Kevin about it one night over too many drinks, and Kevin said: *Maybe you shouldn't be together then.* Andy laughed. Single people always thought they saw things more clearly.

"Hey," Hunter says. "Check out Sexxyboi26."

Andy watches Hunter's face, the way his eyebrows raise and his lips turn inside his mouth. There's something forced and hollow about this expression. Hunter types furiously into his phone, and then he laughs: short, sharp tremors of breath. It unnerves Andy, this laugh. He hates the familiarity of it, the *freedom* of it. So Sexxyboi is interesting, so he's Prince Fucking Charming. He doesn't get why Hunter shot down Homotextual, who's clearly hot enough. No doubt it has something to do with that laugh.

Then he checks. In the photo Sexxyboi wears a baseball cap and jeans. He's shirtless and thin, white, mostly smooth, aside from the treasure trail leading down to his boxer briefs, poking out from underneath. He has a tattoo of a leprechaun on his right arm. His eyes are gray and his lips chewy, like fresh taffy. His expression isn't just vacant, but suggestive of a deep, piercing emptiness, the kind of look fashion photographers elicit from models on billboards advertising fragrances. Sexy, like a Popsicle can be sexy: refreshingly sexy. The kind of guy who hand-washes his car, who holds the hose between his legs and lets the water soak his t-shirt.

"Looks great." Andy smiles, eagerly. He thinks Hunter wants him eager.

"He's in the lobby," Hunter says.

"Invite him up," Andy says.

Hunter stares back. "You sure?"

"What do you mean? Should I not be?"

"Of course not," Hunter says. "I'm feeling this'll be a good thing."

"Are you going to fuck him?" Andy says. "I want you to fuck him."

"Okay," Hunter says. He looks down at the floor. "Do you want him to fuck you?"

"I don't know," Andy says. "Do *you* want him to?"

"Do I look fatter to you?" Hunter gets up and stands by the full-length mirror, needlessly sucking in his gut.

"You look sexy," Andy says.

Hunter sighs and stares at himself. Andy takes two bottles of vodka from the mini-bar and puts them on the desk. He rinses his ass in the sink and dabs some cologne on the back of his neck while Hunter throws dirty clothes into their luggage, straightens the towels, finds the lube in his toiletry bag and slips it into the nightstand drawer. They feed each other breath strips.

They stand, face to face. Hunter takes a deep breath. Andy does too, and Hunter's eyes widen. They're nervous; it's normal to be nervous. He wants to say something before Sexxyboi gets there. Maybe not say something, but *do* something: a gesture, an affirmation of his love. *Four years.* Andy thinks back to moving day. Suddenly Hunter was always there. Suddenly he'd turn around and Hunter was adding vitamins to the pantry, creams to the medicine cabinet. Was this alright with him? It was frightening, and then it wasn't. It was ordinary.

There's a rapping at the door. Andy watches Hunter fix his hair one last time in the mirror. Hunter's fingers fumble on the doorknob.

He straightens his back and just as he takes another long breath, Andy wonders if he should stop him. He didn't think Hunter would be this anxious. He wonders where he should place himself: Standing by the window? Sitting on a chair, the bed? No, not the bed.

I can't tell you not to have sex with someone else, he'd told Hunter that night, months after his confession. *I just want us to be emotionally monogamous.* Hunter nodded repeatedly. *Of course,* he said, as if picking up on a subtext Andy wasn't sure he was implying. It hadn't been a suggestion, or a license, or a warning; Andy just wanted them to be realistic. He has little empathy for the women on daytime TV talk shows, crying about their cheating partners. Don't they get it? Men like variety. It doesn't matter if you're the juiciest steak in the world; even unrepentant meat-eaters want a pizza now and again. He loves Hunter, and he still fucked around. And who knows, maybe Hunter fucked around too. With someone younger or someone with a thicker cock or even someone who just smelled different. It didn't matter, so long as the love between them stayed strong.

Hunter opens the door. Sexxyboi leans against the frame, one hand behind the trucker cap on his head. He's taller than Andy pictured him to be, taller and bonier. Still, sexy; *ridiculously* sexy. He doesn't respond when Hunter offers his hand. Instead he looks past Hunter to Andy, his mouth opening to a squiggly, mischievous smile.

"Marcel," he says, finally shaking Hunter's hand.

The tension in Hunter's face snaps into relief, and Andy realizes that what seemed like anxiety before was more likely enthusiasm. Hunter introduces himself, then Andy, who waves from his seat by the desk, not yet willing to get up. But Marcel makes the move anyway.

"Pleasure to meet you." Marcel shakes Andy's hand with both of his own. "So you boys are from New York? I've lived there."

"Whereabouts?" Andy asks.

"Here and there," Marcel says. He puts his hands on his hips and eyes Hunter quizzically. "You seem familiar. Have we met before?"

Hunter's eyebrows arch. He clears his throat. "I don't think so."

Andy gauges Hunter's expression, the quiet surprise in it. He thinks of stoplights, how red lights seem stern and serious, and green lights almost seem to be smiling at you. Hunter's face is a yellow light, he thinks, not sure whether to slow down or hurry up.

"Can I fix you something?" Andy heads for the vodka.

"I'm good," Marcel says. He looks at Hunter and sighs. His eyes canvass the room, and then lock on Andy's; it's a pushy, puzzled look, like he's trying to determine Andy's place in the universe. Andy wonders if Marcel is on something, a mood stabilizer or enhancer.

"Take a seat," Hunter says.

Marcel heads to the bed. "You guys play together often?"

Hunter and Andy turn to each other. "Sometimes," Andy says.

"Sometimes," Marcel repeats. "It's good to spice things up."

"Yeah," Hunter says, forcing a grin.

"That's why I'm here." Marcel claps his hands. "To spice things up."

"We're glad," Andy says. The TV is still on. Andy grabs the remote, considers turning it off, but instead lowers the volume. Judi Dench is promising to protect Cate from harm.

"So you're an Oriental," Marcel says, nodding at Andy. He reclines on the bed with one hand twisted behind his back, the other lifting up the front of his t-shirt. The word, followed quickly by the offered peek of Marcel's abs, unsettles Andy. He takes both in and lets them simmer.

Hunter laughs, tensely. "He's not a rug."

Marcel shakes his head. "Well, I can see that. He's as smooth as they come."

"I'm Filipino," Andy says. He sits down beside Marcel, the vacuous stare from the photo somehow more menacing in person. He wonders if Marcel's comment is meant to trouble him, excite him, or both. He's not sure why exactly, but the cloudier his thoughts get the more his body longs to find out what's next. He takes Marcel's hand into his lap and starts drawing circles up the man's sinewy forearm and taut biceps. Marcel doesn't resist.

"No one says Oriental anymore." Hunter's voice is slow and low. He studies Andy's expression, searching for an accomplice to his offense. *But I'm not offended,* Andy thinks.

"I'm confused," Marcel says, looking first at Andy, then at Hunter. "The Philippines are in Asia, right? Where are Filipinos from?"

Andy laughs; Marcel isn't confused. Andy looks at Hunter, nods at the empty space on the other side of the bed. "Sit down, Hunter," he says.

Hunter doesn't move. Andy lifts Marcel's shirt higher, revealing sleek muscles and creamy nipples, dusted with a few tufts of gossamer hair. Andy is aroused. He knows Hunter must be too.

"Oriental refers to objects from Asia." Hunter shakes his head. The words sound labored, schoolmarmish. "People are Asian."

Marcel smiles at Andy, revealing dimples. Dimples that make him look naive or stupid, Andy isn't sure which. He takes Andy's hand and puts it on his belt buckle. "So are you Asian? Is that where you're from, pumpkin?"

Hunter walks behind Andy. He reaches over and takes his boyfriend's hand off of Marcel and squeezes Andy's shoulders, firmly, protectively. Andy looks up, irritated. It's not like Hunter to get worked up over silly comments. It's not like him to refuse to take a joke.

"He's from Queens," Hunter says.

"Filipinos are from Queens?" Marcel asks.

Andy chuckles. Marcel's being an ass. Marcel pokes him playfully in the stomach and laughs too. Still, Andy is certain they're not laughing at the same thing.

Andy shoots Hunter a placating look. "Relax," he says.

"I think my uncle is Filipino," Marcel says. "He's a rabbi in Forest Hills."

Andy reaches for Hunter's hand, which is wet and tight. He wants to ease his boyfriend back into the moment. What does it matter what Marcel says? Hunter's jaw is clenched. He's tapping his loose hand against his thigh. He's angry, and Marcel isn't picking up on the cues—or maybe he is. Maybe Marcel wants Hunter angry. Maybe Marcel wants Hunter to fuck the anger into him.

"Wait, he's Ashkenazi, though," Marcel says. "Wouldn't Filipinos be Sephardic? Because of Spanish ancestry? I feel so dumb."

Marcel bites his index finger. His eyes are too big for his face, innocent, dewy eyes that remind Andy of cartoon deer. But Marcel isn't innocent. Marcel has a swagger. Marcel lounges on their bed without being invited. He takes what he wants, says what he wants, in the manner of a gambler who's grown used to winning. *Let him call me Oriental,* Andy thinks. *I want to be Oriental tonight.*

"I wouldn't know." Andy puts his hand back on Marcel's crotch, looks up at Hunter and sighs a let's-get-on-with-this sigh. "I'm not Jewish."

Hunter's eyes tilt to Andy, then retreat. "He's not 'from' Asia. He wasn't born in the Philippines so it's not accurate so say he's 'from' there. He's from Queens," he says.

"This isn't necessary," Andy says. He looks at Marcel, whose smirk is more jovial than angry. Andy studies the smirk. He thinks he understands now: Marcel is playing a game, and Hunter is the prize.

Eric Sasson

Marcel is jealous; he wonders how a man they just met could already be jealous.

"Right. So he's Oriental and from Queens," Marcel says. "I get it now."

"Your use of the word Oriental is just plain stupid at this point," Hunter says. He cups his forehead with his right hand and rubs his temples. Andy wishes he was moved. He wants to be touched by the gallantry on Hunter's part, but he isn't. Because Marcel is playing. And since Hunter *has* to know that, then maybe Hunter's playing too.

"Take off my shoes," Marcel says. He's staring at Hunter, but Andy knows he's the one being addressed. He doesn't need to be asked twice. He slides down the bed, and lifts Marcel's right leg in the air, languidly slipping the man's loafer off of his foot. Marcel's sock is damp at the heel and toes. The soft, buttery scent of sweat fills the air. Andy shoves his face into the man's foot and inhales. He opens his eyes and looks at Hunter as he sucks on Marcel's toes. Hunter stands rigid, frozen in place. He looks like a wounded dog. No, not a dog, a wolf, a wounded wolf staring into the eyes of the giraffe it tried to attack and which had kicked it, hard.

"Let me ask you, Hunter," Marcel says. He seems indifferent to Andy's kink, indifferent as a queen to the vassals performing her daily pedicure. Instead he makes for Hunter's thigh, just within reach of his left hand. "Is Oriental only Chinese, Japanese, and Korean?"

"The term Oriental is offensive to Asians." Hunter's voice is quavering. Still Andy ignores him. He decides to brave Marcel's other foot. He takes a sidelong glance, sees that Hunter is hard, sees that he wishes he wasn't.

"All the Orientals I know don't seem to mind," Marcel says. "But then again, they're from Asia, not Queens."

"They *do* mind. They just don't tell you. Ask them."

Marcel laughs. "I don't speak Oriental though."

"No need to continue this." Hunter walks toward the door. "You should leave."

"Should I?" Marcel says. "Really? You want me to leave?"

"No," Andy says. "Please stay, mister. Me so horny. Me love you long time!"

Marcel laughs. Hunter turns white as an envelope. "Jesus Christ, Andy," he says.

"He wants me to stay," Marcel says, a meaty vein in his neck pulsating as he stares at Hunter. "Do you want me to stay?"

"This isn't going to work," Hunter says, throwing up his hands.

"Why not?" Andy asks. Hunter is getting furious. And now he's going to call it off because of what, their dignity? Andy doesn't need someone protecting his dignity. He thinks about Hunter's laugh earlier, the look on his face when Marcel walked in. This strange look of disorientation, but also of regret, like Hunter had forgotten the events of a magical day and seeing Marcel had reminded him, brought back this rush of memories.

"Andy, can I please talk to you alone?" Hunter says.

Andy doesn't move. He can't remember the last time he was this turned on. He sees that Hunter is turned on despite himself and he imagines Marcel is turning himself on too. They're on the threshold of one spectacular fuck, one mind-blowing fuck that will sear into their memory and erase months of bad sex, and he could turn around, he could waver and negotiate with Hunter, but he senses, deeply, that this is not what Hunter wants, to pseudo-save him from this asshole who may be a real asshole but who was more likely just playing one.

Instead he unbuckles Marcel's belt. He rips open the button fly, tugs Marcel's pants off of his legs, and pulls on the elastic band of his boxers. Marcel is large, punishingly hard. And yet quivering, almost shy, now that he's naked.

"Are you happy?" Marcel looks up at Hunter with eerie surprise, his smirk practically hostile. "Are you getting what you want?"

And then Andy knows.

He's not sure exactly how he knows, if it's the catastrophic chill in Hunter's eyes, directed at Marcel, or the spastic flaring of his nostrils. Or is it Marcel who tells him everything, Marcel whose deer eyes are suddenly not so cartoonish after all. Andy proceeds to deep-throat him; he watches Marcel's mouth droop in shock, his eyes clouding, not with pleasure, not exactly shame. Andy stares into those eyes as his head bobs back and forth, and thinks of the white sheets artists place over their canvasses, to delay the moment of surprise. Marcel's eyes are a white sheet and Hunter and his dithering another white sheet and Andy has lifted too soon; the work wasn't ready, apparently. They needed more time.

And once he knows, he can't stop. He *won't* stop. He's going to oblige, perform his part spectacularly. He gets up from the bed, strips down naked before them. He sees his reflection in the mirror beside the television, his soft, smooth, brown skin, his small nipples, his frail arms. Not a man's body. A boy's body. A body meant to submit.

"Andy, please," Hunter says.

Andy shushes him. "Get undressed, Hunter."

He asks Hunter to pass him a condom. When he insists, Hunter doesn't refuse. Andy reaches for the lube from the nightstand, squirts a few drops, and massages it into his hands. He lubricates himself from behind and throws the condom onto Marcel's stomach. Marcel stares at the packet and looks across at Hunter. Hunter nods and Marcel opens it, quickly ripping the foil with his teeth. He slides it over his cock.

Andy straddles him. The heavy murmur of their breaths is interrupted by the murderous screams from the TV, audible despite the low volume: Cate Blanchett is finally tearing into Judi Dench, finally accusing her of all that's coming to her. He rides Marcel and thinks of how long it's been since he's ridden Hunter. He thinks of Stephen Connelly, and his devilish chivalry, his infernal magnetism and how tough it is, even after several anniversaries, for someone to resist the cruelty of beauty.

He rides. Marcel is pounding back, unforgiving. Andy closes his eyes and imagines floods and fires, supernovas fading, dying beautifully. When he opens them Hunter has taken off his pants. He masturbates right by Marcel's face, slapping his cock against Marcel's cheeks in a way that makes Andy laugh whenever Hunter does it to him, a laugh that Andy knows irritates Hunter. He wonders if Hunter is as happy as he is now. He wonders if he's making Hunter happy, finally. He wants to see beyond Hunter's façade and make the inside of Hunter happy, the part that must hate him. The part that will not forgive.

But there's no point in thinking of happiness, or forgiveness. There's no point in understanding, because now there is only this moment, this final act, this searing, mind-bending, scorching, and insanely pleasurable moment, hotter than ever before, absurdly hot, *inhumanly* hot. They switch positions, everyone fucks, everyone is fucked, and when Andy asks both of them to penetrate him at the same time, they do. And when he asks Marcel and Hunter to call him a chink, a gook, a dog-eating faggot, they supply even more adjectives; they coin new phrases. They can't settle for less now, this is the only way it can be.

Once everyone is spent, Andy lies between Hunter and Marcel, who have both turned away from him to face opposite walls. He stares up at the ceiling and listens to the thrum of their breaths, feeling the weight of the silence. Soon they all shift; it's not possible to remain on a bed after a moment like this, not possible to bask in a pleasure so brittle and fleeting. Marcel heads to the bathroom. Hunter searches for the remote; *Notes on a Scandal* is long over. Now it's *Sleepless in Seattle*. Hunter and Andy hate *Sleepless in Seattle*. Andy sits up and stares into Hunter's eyes. He stares hard, like staring might provide insight, like staring might express his feelings.

He thinks back to the first time they had sex after his confession. Hunter had entered him raw, right on the living room floor, and when he yelped, Hunter had covered his mouth, told him to shut up and take it. He doesn't know why these images consume him. Perhaps Hunter understands this better than he does. Perhaps he really has provided the perfect anniversary present. These thoughts echo in his brain, even above the din of his anger and disgust.

When Marcel comes out of the bathroom he slips into his jeans and shirt and adjusts his hat. "That was quite an adventure, boys," he says.

Hunter looks away and Andy attempts a smile. Neither says a word.

"I'd like to say I wish you both the best." Marcel claps his hands. "But I don't." His eyes fixate on Hunter. His lips tremble then open to release a croaking, jittery laugh. "You're perfect for each other," he says, no longer attempting to disguise his sarcasm. He tips his hat and heads out the door.

Hunter gets up. He grabs the Cheez Doodles and shoves a few into his mouth before resealing the bag and putting it on the dresser. He washes the mess down with some vodka.

"Sit down," Andy says.

But Hunter doesn't. He paces the room, rearranging tourist

brochures on the desk. Andy knows conversation won't settle him. But conversation isn't optional now.

"Please sit down," Andy says, and this time Hunter stops, and sits, on the far side of the bed.

"How long have you been seeing him?" Andy asks. He slides closer, reaches for Hunter's hand. He's the one who should need comforting, but instead, this: Hunter on the verge of tears. Hunter about to collapse into a ball of yarn, unraveling, unraveling. It's Hunter's world that's been shattered.

"I didn't think he'd be so cruel," Hunter says. He pulls down on the lids of his eyes, his defeat complete.

"Do you love him?" Andy asks.

Hunter's lips tremble. "I love you," he says. But Andy is unmoved. It sounds more like a justification than a statement.

"Yes," Andy says. *That wasn't the question,* he thinks.

"I won't see him again," Hunter says.

"I think he loves you," Andy says. "Despite everything."

"I don't give a shit!" Hunter's face is a blubbery mess. Andy wonders whether he should cry too. He wonders if he can. "How could you . . . why did you let him say those things to you?"

Andy sighs. Was Hunter serious? "*You* say those things to me. You call me bitch, humiliate me. I wanted you to do those things to me."

"It's not the same."

"No," Andy says. "Maybe not."

"So what, are you leaving me now?" Hunter asks.

"If you did this," Andy says, "haven't you already left?"

"You left first." Hunter grinds his teeth, his face darkening, his eyes penetrating and sober. "You cheated *first*."

"I know." Andy tries to hold Hunter's gaze. "You said you forgave me. And since then, I've asked for one thing."

"But you can't ask. You don't *get* to ask." Hunter stands up. He grabs the remote from the bed and throws it across the room. Andy watches the batteries spill out and bounce on the carpet. He follows Hunter's pace with his eyes, wanting to understand his anger, wondering if he should share in it, or just accommodate it. But it's too brief: in a few seconds Hunter is sitting beside him. He cups Andy's cheeks, his eyes feral and desperate. "Listen, I don't love him. I swear to God I don't."

He pushes Hunter away. "I asked for *one* thing."

"I know." Hunter begins to whimper. "I'm sorry. But it was good, wasn't it? It was *really* good."

"It's over," Andy says. He turns away, walks into the bathroom. He's still naked. Hunter's phone rests on the vanity. He picks it up, opens Grindr, notices several messages pending. He sighs, puts the phone down and stares at himself in the mirror, at the vessel containing him. A needy vessel. Greedy and possessive.

He wonders if he'll really leave Hunter. He wonders if, in a few hours from now, while he's asleep, Hunter will stir him awake, and beg him for forgiveness. And when he refuses, when he insists that he hates Hunter and wishes him dead, perhaps then Hunter will stop crying. Perhaps Hunter will stop listening and take him by force, and then, suddenly, the lust will return to haunt them again, that fierce, primordial lust, that all-consuming fire which will scorch them, swallow them, remind them that they are alive.

CRUISING

Having sex in the steam rooms of cruise ships is our God-given right. We feel this is true as soon as we board and are reminded of all the ways the ship will attempt to erase us. Some might argue that it is you who have banished us there, but we don't mind; after all, the danger of being discovered quickens our pulse, makes our brief trysts thorny and memorable.

We cum quickly. We have to, lest one of you inadvertently opens the door and walks in on us. Still, it's not like you don't know what's going on. Perhaps some of you are naive, but most of you aren't. It's evident in the hesitant, almost coquettish way you walk by the fogged-up door, your hands slowly gripping the handle, giving us time to readjust and perform a transparent artifice for you. Dare we say that some of you want to see what we are doing? Not that you want to join us, exactly. More that you want to feel what it's like to experience such things that your narrow definitions of yourselves don't allow for. If you didn't want to see something, you could simply not go at all.

Of course there are those of you who don't want to sacrifice your right to enjoy steam to a bunch of sex-crazed perverts. These would be your words, not ours. Although to be fair, they may not be your words. Your words might be gentler. You might say: I understand you need a place for yourselves, but this cannot be it. The ship's public spaces are not to be abused. *Children* could walk in on us, even if technically they aren't supposed to be there at all.

We understand; really, we do. Despite the persistent rumors, we aren't interested in your children. We aren't interested in your brothers, cousins, uncles, not unless we *are* your brothers, cousins, uncles. We aren't interested in you at all, really. We might find you attractive, but we're not persuaded by such fripperies. We need you to want us in order for us to want you back. And when you don't, we don't pursue. We're quite content sticking to our own once we find ourselves.

We'd like to ask those of you who are angry at us to consider a few truths. Not those of you who hate us, because we won't get through to you. It is the ambivalent majority of you that we address. Imagine how we feel watching you do the Macarena. Imagine us in the audience during the Love and Marriage game, imagine those of us who are or know men who can also say they've been together forty years, and imagine how it feels to know that we will never be asked to the stage to participate. Imagine, because we don't have to imagine, what we see when we look at the couples everywhere, massaging sunblock into each others torsos, holding hands as they circle the promenade deck, dancing fox-trot to the soft nostalgia of the Stan Jones Quartet crooning "It Had to Be You."

You are everywhere. You are the welcome-aboard mai tai, the formal portraits taken with the crew at the Captain's Reception. You are the children splashing in the wave pool, huddling around the ice-cream machine, genetic extensions of yourselves, living trophies that testify to your unquestioned license to procreate. You are the Mr. Sexy Legs contest judged by three fifty-seven-year-old grandmothers from Champaign, Illinois. You are the anodyne comedian asking how many honeymooners are in the room and then asking why, met with commensurately insipid laughter. You are the large, centrally located sports bar, where you watch football or basketball or baseball depending on the season, but certainly not tennis, certainly not figure skating qualification rounds. You are the bingo, you are the cleavage-and-cologne-infused nightclub, you are the thong bikinis and the t-shirts with slogans proclaiming "The Man The Legend" with arrows pointing in different directions, you are the rat tails and the Aloha shirts and the Budweiser. You are definitely the Budweiser.

You are not, however, the entertainment. You are neither the singers nor the dancers, not the lighting designers or stagehands or costume coordinators. You do not teach the morning Pilates class, you do not give the ballroom dance lessons to the timid couple from Dubuque, you are not the sommelier expounding on the blackberry notes in the Pinot Noir at the wine-tasting seminar, nor would you teach anyone, ever, how to make a floral arrangement. And while you are the bingo, you are not the person calling out "and after" when announcing B4 as the next ball. You are not any of these people; we are. And if you are, then you are the girlfriends who stand next to us at bars agreeing with us that the man in the guayabera by the red couch is the finest man in the room, *hands down, girl*. Because if you are, then you know what we are thinking and how we are feeling, and you are secretly rooting for us in the steam room, you are egging us on to have threesomes and foursomes and all-out Caligula orgies with sound effects and confetti and trumpets. We love you, and had genetics or God been more forgiving, we could have shared our love for each other instead of for the guayabera man shimmering by the red couch, because he will disappoint us—much as we disappoint you—by not loving us the way we feel we are meant to be loved.

So you see we are all around you, mostly invisible to you, and if not quite invisible then barely detectable, like a faint stain on the back of a button-down shirt that you wear anyway, because the stain is inconspicuous and not worth thinking about. We are mostly invisible to each other, too. Consciously or not, we repress our brighter hues to blend in better with your muted colors. We try not to dress too dandily, yet there is only so far we will go; we still sport our fitted tank tops and Diesel trunks to the pool, and the tapered pants we wear to dinner may yet betray us. When we recognize each other outside of our encounters, we offer stolen winks as we pass by, silently assessing each other's families and loved ones. Sometimes we spot each other playing roulette in the casino, testing fragrances in the cosmetics shop. We are the ones who choose Whitney Houston songs at karaoke, instead of Jimmy Buffett. We linger longer in the gym, lift heavier weights, run faster miles, unabashedly join the step class.

Perhaps you're wondering why we would subject ourselves to you if we are so discomforted. Perhaps we shouldn't go on your big boats at all, or if we do, then perhaps with others like us so we could hold hands and fox-trot and even watch football together, although with somewhat different side commentary than you engage in. To this we say, why should we have to? Why can't we join our large families for sixtieth-anniversary celebrations, or tag along with our girlfriends for five-night escapes from the snows of February? What if some of us are older and still married to some of you, and what if we love you and we love our lives and maybe even the kids we've had with you and why would we ever want to fuck that up when we could simply let off some steam instead? What if we are not from the big cities or even the medium-size towns leaning against colleges, what if we are not from the north or the coasts, what if the one road that runs through us has seven churches and we are faithful members of these churches? If you are all we know, all we see, every minute of every

Eric Sasson

day, then how can you ask us to go off on our own, with people who we do not really understand or relate to?

Even those of us who hate those of us who pretend and play nice for you try to be compassionate in these instances. We want us to stand up for ourselves and live our lives with dignity, but we understand that life for us has always been a never-ending rainbow of grays and we are hardly ones to be casting first stones. Besides, we're not really concerned, once we enter that sticky room, about each other's situations; we all have *situations,* and we come here to escape from these situations, thank you very much.

Even those of us who hate those of us who insist on having sex in steam rooms understand that the world is hardly fair, and sometimes unfairness is met with rebellion, like teenagers breaking curfews and drinking Jaeger shots at their friends' parentless houses on weekends. These of us think that we must stop behaving like teenagers, and instead act like the respectable adults we want you to accept us for. Steam-room sex only hurts our cause, this group reminds us. We cannot expect to assimilate when we persist in behaving like the Other.

Perhaps, says the other side of us. Perhaps we don't want to assimilate. Perhaps we'd prefer tolerance. Perhaps we'd rather you accept our differences instead of asking us to be like you. Beauty and truth can only exist in the differences. We like you as you are, even if we find many of the things you do to be silly and ordinary. It must be nice to revel in the banality of the supermajority. But let us not oversimplify. Each of you—at least most—has experienced being the Other at some point in your life.

And we are hardly innocent of the crimes of exclusion. If anything we are guiltier. Even when our options are limited by location and population and of course the randomness of time and circumstance, even then we are excluders. Some of us only like smooth men, or muscular men, or thin men or men under thirty, and we ignore those who do not fit neatly into our categories. Even on a cruise ship, we want our expectations met.

Yes, there are those of us who slip in to the changing rooms, and because we are beautiful, or young, or both, we get noticed right away. We are pursued by a multitude of eyes, watching us undress, boring into us as we open our lockers and take sips of water as if these actions are somehow more meaningful because we are the ones engaging in them. We are followed into the steam, gazed upon like magnificent, unfathomable works of art. We notice how towels peel away around us, how legs begin to separate. Hands restlessly slide to their owner's inner thighs, and then further still, as we are assessed, as our eyes are met with the beseeching expressions of vassals appearing before their lords after committing petty crimes that might amount to their deaths. If we are satisfied with what we see, we shift, we adjust. We even smile, although we may not be seen, through the dense humidity of the steam. These seconds of ambiguity only make us more desirable. We choose, and there is no complication.

But we are not all young and beautiful and exquisitely defined, despite what some of you think. We age and we have bellies. We are bald and hair grows out of our ears and our penises can often be small or unshapely. And then, we are those vassals. We are the Waiting.

The Waiting can be found in the locker room at any time of the day, doing what our name requires us to do. We Waiting are biblical in our dedication to our craft, we are Sarah in her 98th year, still holding for news of Isaac. Beauty and youth having forsaken us, still we hope that somehow the sparkle of our one virtue, patience, will eventually bring forth salvation. Most of us do not expect to touch, or be touched. We are happy to just watch, to savor moments vicariously.

We might, if allowed, reach over and fondle a nipple, or stroke the unattended penis, but we understand that even this may be fleeting, unreciprocated, or restricted. Still, we wait, all day if necessary, for a bone to be thrown our way. And if the bone does not come, then we return tomorrow, and begin our waiting again. We lumber, back and forth, along the slippery tiles of the shower area, rinse ourselves repeatedly, stare at ourselves in mirrors (briefly). We grab new towels, we sit by the lockers waiting for new possibilities to enter, men who might show us mercy. We ignore those who ignore us, bringing their legs together and holding their towels close, staring off into space as we try to win their attention. We sit across from them and suddenly we are not all in the same boat, figuratively speaking, we are each man for himself. We are frustrated, but we understand. We have our role.

It's not like the sex is satisfying, anyway. None of us actually have sex, per se, unless we are lucky or foolish or both. The riskier of us will give each other head, but most of us are content with a handjob under the circumstances. You may ask: Why not take it back to the room? Why not come to terms and experience something more substantial? To this we reply, you share our rooms, and you may not approve. And even if you did approve, many of us do not want to go to a room. Doing so would require conversations, explaining why or how we are here in the first place. Doing so would infuse meaning into a wonderfully meaningless thing. Doing so might very well make us not want to have sex with each other at all. There are times in each of our lives (including your lives) when we all must engage in something shameful and ridiculous, so that we can remind ourselves just who we are, crude, pitiful creatures who end up as dusty afterthoughts in the ground, living on in the memories of our loved ones for a few more years, and then oblivion.

Life is too short not to be ridiculous. Which is why I have sex in the steam room. Sex with the married fertilizer wholesaler from Marietta, Georgia, whose wife is having a seaweed wrap. Sex with the Romanian insurance agent/deep-sea diver, his chest hairs trimmed, his bald head pointy and impatient, his lust-filled bleats escaping despite his attempts to muffle them.

Sex with the assistant head waiter, a Brazilian flirt (they're all flirts) with porn-video-cover locks and a sinewy body, parading his engorged cock around the locker room as if he were about to stick it into the ground and lay claim to a new moon. I see him, and even though I am ostensibly there to work my abs, I quickly undress to join him. The moment is absurd and particularly real; I've stepped into a dream, and as I play my role, I imagine concurrent dreams running alongside my real one, the dreams the rest of the ship is having:

While I shower myself off two seventeen-year-old girls sit by the pool, braiding each other's hair. They consider ordering mango sours.

I push open the sauna door and he looks up; his eyebrows say everything that needs to be said. Seven floors down, a woman fidgets at the guest services desk, complaining of an ant infestation in her room.

I sit across from him, release my towel so that it falls to the side. I spread my legs while an eleven-year-old calls out to his new friend across one of the Ping-Pong tables on the sports deck, begging for a do-over because the wind knocked his sunglasses off midshot.

His penis rises in the hazy space between his legs. His eyes dance down to it and then back up at me. He watches me watch him, while a frustrated mother from Columbia sits across her bulbous-cheeked

Eric Sasson

daughter in the Voyager Café, imploring the girl to eat something, *anything,* besides Tater-Tots for lunch.

Aroused, I glance cautiously toward the door. The silence beyond stills me so I cross over to sit beside him. I look over his Adonis flesh, his inhuman cock. My lips quake, desiccated by my own hunger, as two stateroom attendants on deck three talk about their girlfriends and the home-cooked meals waiting for them when they finally return after five months on the ship.

His eyes lock on mine, his right hand weighing the span of his penis. My hand reaches down. I stroke. The dewy air suffocates and excites my breathing. Just then, four middle-aged Persians seeking refuge from their wives gather in the Havana Nights Cigar Club and set up an impromptu backgammon tournament. Ironically, they chomp on Dominicans.

He reaches over. I surrender to his hand and he to mine. Our moans are soft, sparing, primary. At the martini bar, a husband with a comb-over orders two key-lime cosmopolitans while his wife fiddles with the daily cruise guide. The silent art auction begins in twenty minutes and they will bid on a Peter Max.

My other hand reaches for his chest. I grab at his skin as if grabbing for a life vest, as if expecting to be saved. And Captain Sven Swenson—why are all cruise captains Scandinavian?—gives his afternoon update, informing us of our precise longitudinal position, wind speed, the distance in nautical miles to our next destination. His speech is repeated in Spanish by Carmen Sanchez, the foreign guest hospitality coordinator.

Our eyes bounce back and forth, from each other to the door. Soon we no longer care; soon the door isn't even there. He takes my nipple in his teeth. I clutch his damp hair in my hand, holding his head against me. I smell him: shampoo, sweat, lust. In the solarium, a thirty-six-year-old redhead with a mole on her left cheek lounges in the shade, reading Junot Diaz's new novel, because unlike the friends she's traveling with, she refuses to get sun damage and read silly paperbacks just because she's on vacation.

I bend down to take him inside my mouth. He holds my head and fucks my lips for ten seconds that seem even shorter. I am both there and not. I choke my cock with my hand. My mind screams *What are you doing* and *Don't stop* at the same time, as a thirty-nine-year-old divorcée leaves the New York Deli on deck seven, squirts some Purell in her hands from one of the automatic dispensers conveniently placed throughout the ship before heading over to test her mettle at the rock-climbing wall.

I want more, more, but when I reach down again, he jerks me up. He spreads his legs wide and pumps himself ferociously until I see the release. I watch it dribble and spurt, too quick, I think, too quick, but I know it must be this quick, there is something heroic about it being this quick. The door rematerializes and soon I am quick too, soon my towel has already cleared up a mess I've never really made.

There is no lingering in the moment. Certainly no caresses, or words exchanged about what just happened; only a nod of the head, a "see ya around" with one foot already out the door. This is not disappointing. Sentimentalizing the moment would cheapen it.

Eric Sasson

Does this information scare you? Repulse you? Do you feel the gap between us widening? Must there even be a gap? Do these things not happen under the same sun? Are we not, all of us, nothing but tiny patches in the infinite quilt of time, different but essential parts of the fabric?

What do we seek here, with this confession? What do we stand to gain by sharing this with you, what, if we already have the tolerance of so many of you, could we add, with this gratuitously diligent exposition? Is it just our selfish desire to see ourselves as real in your eyes, our vanity begging for an objective witness? Or do we sense that something in our story might connect with you, something small, most likely, something we probably wouldn't even notice but you do, and maybe for a second a spark of recognition alights, and you add to the recipes of your understanding one further ingredient. What if, inside of you, there is more of us than either we or you care to admit?

Because in many ways we are similar. We too like the salty sea air, the cloudless skies. The boat tilts port and starboard while we sleep, and like you, some of us find it lulling while others find it nauseating. We too disembark at the Islands' ports, in Oranjestad and Philipsburg and Charlotte Amalie, where we cattle into overpriced taxis to the beach, haggle with the locals who make us hats from palm leaves, Jet-Ski and sunburn and drink dubious drinks made of indigenous rums, buy duty-free cigarettes for our friends back home. We too pretend not to see the poverty behind the tourist trade, as if our sunglasses had filters on them.

We split eights in blackjack when the dealer has a five, we play the bonus in three-card poker, and few of us understand craps but most of us wish we did. Vidalia onion tarts, chilled pear soups, blackened tilapia, cherries jubilee: like you, we have eaten them all, sometimes in the same sitting. We too pretend to go to the midnight buffet just to "see the ice sculptures" and end up gorging on roast-beef sandwiches and chocolate truffles. You will see us at the mandatory drill, reporting to our muster stations, our life jackets appropriately fastened. We enter the win-a-cruise raffles, we buy last-minute gifts at the cheesy $10 blowout sale on the final night of the cruise, the same night when we too slip our waiters their tips in preaddressed envelopes. We take too many photos, drink too many mojitos, charge far too much to our onboard accounts. We wave, at the other people, on the other boats, dressed like us, waving back at us, at the Sail Away Deck Party.

So allow me to offer up some reconciliation, an attempt to cross a divide that may exist but perhaps doesn't. Because there is one thing that at one point all of us who are cruising experience on a ship: we stand out on the deck, at dawn or dusk or on either side of the in-between, and we look out at the infinite blue with patches of white rolling into the horizon, we see the panorama of nature's perfect canvas, and we all—you and he and she and I, the we that is you, and the we that is us, all of us—are left breathless at how beautiful and unknowable the world is, how it has been so since forever past and will remain so for forever future, and how there is nothing, truly nothing we can do but gape and ponder, but only for a few seconds because if we think too long it will suffocate us. How incredibly insignificant we all are, how insignificant and glorious. Face to face with the naked bravado of the sun, with the serene self-possession of clouds, it's hard to imagine that our peccadilloes matter so much, be they in steam room or stateroom, the screening room on deck two or behind the bar of the Viking Club on deck fifteen.

In the end, we are on vacation. So go ahead and sip your rum runner. Shuffleboard's on deck three. The iceberg awaits us all, but then again, so does the shore.

Eric Sasson

REMAINS OF A ONCE
GREAT CIVILIZATION

In the daytime, the loneliness is less painful. At altitudes this high, the brutal sun can be deceptively comforting. The sky clear and pure, like a rare gem. The thinness of the air relaxes him, and the other tourists, snapping photos in the *Plaza de Armas,* provide companionship with their exposed maps and naive grins. Even the incessant pleas of the peddling locals, sometimes children as young as five, soothe him. Because they are familiar. Because they want so little, sometimes nothing more than a *No, gracias* and a smile.

It is at night when the anxieties come. When the sadness bears down upon him, along with the twilight chill in the air, entering his chambers and refusing to let him be.

Winter in July, in Cuzco, Peru. Connor returns to the city at 9 p.m., by backpacker train from Machu Picchu, after hiking the Inca Trail for two stress-free, exhilarating days. It had been he and three couples: Tom and Claire, from Galway; Steve and Bridget, from Sydney; Gustavo and Inez, from Sao Paolo. Tom and Claire and Gustavo and Inez on their honeymoons; Steve and Bridget five years married. The seven of them, and Diego, their guide, native of the Sacred Valley and fluent in Quechua.

Diego, rounding out the digits.

Diego, filling up the extra space across the table where Marcello, his lover of three years, should have been.

Diego, boyfriend substitute. (Terminally macho Diego would certainly take offense at such a characterization; it was he, after all, who insisted that the rainbow flags flapping so proudly on the tops of Cuzco's buildings were symbols of the city, and not—certainly not—of gay pride.)

On the train track, he and the married couples exchange stiff good-bye hugs. "Pleasure meeting you," he tells them, repeating the words with every handshake, backing them up with a smile. He will not see these people again, nor does he care to. They are oblivious to him. Love has cocooned them from the world. Before they separate, he recognizes it on their faces: pity.

At the Hotel Royal Inka Dos, a bellhop unburdens the bag from his shoulders. Beatriz behind the counter searches for his reservation on an old computer.

"You are with your friend, yes?" she asks, innocently enough.

"No. My friend is on the four-day Inca trail. I only went for two days."

"Ah, *si*." Beatriz nods her head. "So tonight you need a single room. Only."

"Yes." And then he repeats: "A single room."

"And your friend? He is coming back?"

"Yes. In two days." He says it loudly. "We will need a double again in two days."

He imagines himself repeating this story, again and again, to the waiter at breakfast, to the tour guides on *Calle Espaderos*, to the woman who sells him his bottled water. To his friends and family back home in New York, who will wonder about his photographs:

Why are there no pictures of the two of you at Machu Picchu??

"Come with me, Connor," Marcello kept insisting, all the way up to the night before their separation. The words always spoken softly, like a seduction.

"I want to know why," he said, "two days aren't enough. I want to *understand.*"

"I've been dreaming of this trip for years." Marcello closed his eyes and chewed on his lips, his face goading Connor to realize the fantasy with him.

Connor kept his eyes open. "You've been dreaming of camping in below-freezing temperatures? Of having to burn your toilet paper after shitting in the woods? Of mosquitoes bathing in the sweat of your unshowered body before eating you alive?"

"I dream of approaching the mountain," Marcello said. "With you by my side. We'll reach Intipunku gate before dawn and watch the sun rise over the ruins."

Connor swallowed his irritation. Difficult to resist are the lilting notes of the snake charmer's flute. "Two days are enough," he repeated. "But go ahead. I won't stand in the way of your dreams."

Marcello sighed and grinned, just deep enough to expose his dimples. "I will miss you," he said, grabbing Connor's hands into his own. "Will you be alright?"

How warm his hands always are, Connor thought. "It's a couple of days," he heard himself say, with just enough authority to justify it in his mind. "I'll be fine."

"Of course." Marcello took hold of his cheeks and kissed him on the forehead. "We'll be fine."

When he wakes it is past ten, too late for the hotel's breakfast. He had no idea he had been so tired. Outside the door, he can hear the cleaning woman's restless humming. Once on the plaza, he locates a second floor café with a balcony. Most of the seats are taken, by other tourists; even the Spanish speakers are tourists, from Chile or Argentina or Lima. They are in groups, of two, of four, as many as ten. And there is only one waitress. It takes her a while to notice him, and even then he's forced to secure his own menu. As he waits for his food, he listens to other people's conversations: current events back home, upcoming tours, rafting down the Rio Urubamba, day journeys to Pisac and Ollantaytambo. He listens but does not attempt to participate. He wonders if the others notice him. They don't know that he too has opinions. He too has much to offer in the way of conversation, if someone were only to ask.

If Marcello were here, he would have struck up a conversation with someone at a nearby table. Marcello is the charming and adventurous one. Marcello is fluent in Spanish, while he relies on tentative present-tense mumblings. Their first night in Cuzco they had dined at Fallen Angel, a gay-friendly restaurant. Within minutes Marcello had chatted up the men beside them, a mixed Spanish-American couple currently residing in Santiago. Marcello made the men laugh with flirty comments and clever quips. Connor smiled along, participating when he could, in the open spaces provided for him.

He wonders what it is that holds him back. Marcello doesn't pause before speaking; Marcello initiates whereas he is cautious. Is he afraid? Afraid that his thoughts will come out as uninformed, or blithering, or even worse, boring? He has always been fearful of boring people.

There's not much to see in Cuzco, and in some ways he is grateful. He walks down Avenida del Sol to Q'oriqancha, once the richest and holiest temple of the Incan empire. Only a few walls remain, the rest decimated by the Spaniards, who built the Church of Santo Domingo

Eric Sasson

upon its ruins. The church, while pretty and delicate, seems ordinary. But the dark granite blocks of the Incans—these silent, brave stones—fascinate him. He runs his fingers across their flat contours. He reads about the earthquake of 1950, when most of the church was demolished; only the Incan stones stubbornly refused to give way. He wonders what the natives knew that their European conquerors did not.

After an hour in Q'oriqancha, he has the rest of the day to himself. The sky is relentlessly bright. He sits on a bench and watches giggling schoolchildren pass him by, money-changers clumping thick wads soliciting US dollars, banker-types on cell phones, other tourists. A grandmother with kind eyes approaches him, her face marked with ridges like the pit of a peach. Her fingers place a gray sweater onto his lap. The stitching is imperfect, the alpacas in the pattern stumpy and somber. But the fabric is so soft. *"Con mis manos,"* she says. *"Compra, amigo. Compra."*

Her eyes lock onto his. He has learned to harden himself against the street peddlers, but he cannot resist this woman. With little haggling, he purchases it. Today, he tells himself, he will shop. He'll buy gifts. The time will pass this way.

He meanders through the cobblestone streets and back-alley stalls, observing, contemplating, touching, negotiating. He wants to occupy his mind with thoughts other than Marcello, and where he is at that moment. He imagines Marcello has reached the terraces of Wiñaywayna, a site seven kilometers away from Machu Picchu. He knows Marcello's itinerary. He's sure Marcello has bonded with the other group members, over songs sung around an evening campfire or intimate tales revealed in tents before falling asleep. Marcello's tour is more grueling, presents more opportunities for shared experience. Marcello will make friendships, friendships Connor did not make with the married couples on his posh, hotel-bound two-day tour. No one fell down a well or found a snake. No one got drunk and pissed all over himself.

He wonders if Marcello has brought up his name. Perhaps Marcello has chosen to be single. Perhaps he is flirting with married Brazilians or bi-curious Croatians, refusing to acknowledge the cowardly lamb he's left behind, his stubborn other half. He wonders but cannot answer his own questions. The thoughts weigh down his mind, and when they start to hurt, he closes his eyes and allows the white heat of the midday sun to caress his face, sedating him, bringing him peace.

When he wakes it is half past eight. The room is cold. He had returned to the hotel three hours earlier, and is once again surprised to see how heavy his body has become, how needy. He showers quickly and searches his Lonely Planet for a dinner suggestion. He knows himself: he will choose someplace quiet, inconspicuous. Somewhere he can sit through his meal without the prying looks of strangers. But then he thinks of Marcello and realizes he doesn't want to define himself so narrowly. It's not every day he is in Peru. He will eat someplace fun and fabulous. The guidebook suggests Macondo.

Cuesta San Blas is narrow and steep. He ascends the street, adjusting his eyes to the leaner certainties of the moonlight. The city seems emptier, and the few people who pass by do so in haste. The evening air penetrates him. He's happy for the scarf and hat he's wearing.

The people inside Macondo look warm and relaxed, the menu adventurous and appetizing. He wants to enter but cannot spot a table small enough to seat one. He doesn't want to embarrass himself, be turned away for being too few. So he continues to walk but cannot think of where to go. His hands are cold. The hour is late and he doesn't want to fret over alternatives. He returns and enters.

He's seated upstairs, in an attic really, with ceilings so low that everyone is forced to bend down. The space is whimsical and funky: orange walls, stacks of pillows doubling as chairs, exceptionally low tables, indigenous lamps and sconces. He's placed between two tables, one occupied by a large group of Americans, the other by what seems to be a trio of German women. He stumbles into his pillow-chair and feels everyone staring. He smiles, reasonably, self-effacingly.

"Not so easy getting settled," the boy closest to him says, with a lazy Texas drawl.

"Sure ain't," he replies, surprised at his choice of words.

"The food's great here," a woman at the large table mentions.

"Glad to hear it," he mumbles, avoiding her eyes. Half of the Americans are staring at him. He is a curiosity. He will not speak to them if they feel bad for him. If they feel obligated to be gracious.

He should have given in, joined Marcello on the four-day tour. Wouldn't it have been better in the long term? But no, he couldn't. Not again. Marcello always got his way. He had a right to stand his ground. He had an obligation to himself to not always be the one who compromised. Why couldn't Marcello understand that? Why was it that just because Marcello's smile rose easier to his lips, that words bounced more readily off his tongue, that decisions always had to favor him?

Their separation offended him. Not just because Marcello was so amenable to it, but because it made him look like the spoiled one, the stubborn one. Because the story will never be: *Self-absorbed Marcello goes off on his own.* It will be*: Connor needed a bed. Connor wanted a shower. Connor can be a bit childish sometimes.*

His food takes a long time to arrive. He doesn't have much to do, except look around, listen to the Americans talk, to their painless laughs and free-flowing commentary. He listens, and Diego rises up in his mind. Diego with his scratchy, staccato English, his tall tales of Incan superiority, his scripted stories of Hiram Bingham. Bingham, professor at Yale University, found Machu Picchu in 1911, a lucky fool who stumbled upon a lost civilization in the jungle on his way to an entirely different place, drunk on sugar-cane liquor and coca-leaf tea, falling over himself and tripping over hidden stones. He wonders what Marcello would have made of Diego's tales. Marcello would have appreciated them. Marcello could find the good in everyone.

The waiter is a lanky boy with patchy blond hair and a wide, forgiving smile. Peruvian, no doubt, but of Spanish descent; no indigenous blood coursing through his veins. There's a playfulness in his eyes, a sympathy when he looks over, which is often.

When Connor's meal finally arrives, the upstairs area has cleared, and he's been left alone. The waiter puts down his dish in front of him, apologizing for the delay in a bouncy, broken English.

"How long are you in Cuzco?" the boy asks, sitting down beside Connor. He has large hands, which he lays flat on the table. Connor wonders if it's a cultural thing, this dispensing with formality.

"A few days," he replies. He immediately launches into his story: he's not alone, he's traveling with a boyfriend, his friend is on the four-day trail, he'll return tomorrow night.

"But tonight you are free," the boy says. It was more than just an observation. "You are free to dance away the night."

Connor is captivated by a feral luminosity in the boy's eyes; his irises are still and yet fickle and indistinct, like twin moons intermittently shrouded by passing clouds.

"I guess so," he says. "I didn't think about going dancing."

"Well, what did you want to do?"

"I don't know." He is uncomfortable. The question is too direct.

"But of course you know what you want. What you like."

He cannot deny the boy's gaze, the rhythms of his voice, constant and lulling, like the sound of water tapping against stones at the bottom of a waterfall. Connor's head is groggy; his eyes can only find focus on the floor. "I thought I was going back to my hotel room, to be honest."

"Ah. I see." The boy doesn't even attempt to hide the disappointment in his expression. "You are a quiet person. I understand."

He gets up, and walks away.

Connor is shell-shocked. Is he really being seduced by this waiter, a boy several years his junior? Not him. He doesn't belong to that club, that coterie of men who are picked up in bars, at train stations, on elevators. He's the invisible one, the last person suspected in a line-up.

He doesn't have reference for his feelings. He is excited, very excited. He's ashamed to be so excited. He knows he shouldn't continue to talk to this boy, but he wants to. He wants to have a real conversation with him. To forge a bond. He imagines Marcello sitting underneath a tree, sharing stories with a cruel simplicity to a gathering of foreigners hanging on his every word. He looks at the four walls where he has been left behind. Why should he be alone? Why shouldn't he have experiences too?

When the boy returns, Connor orders a tea. The look they exchange lingers for several seconds. When the waiter returns with the tea and the check, he stretches himself on the floor beside Connor.

They make small talk: where are you from, where are you going. The invitation to proceed is not subtle. Connor senses no innocence in the boy's repose, his increasingly determined stare.

"You have a great smile." Connor places his index finger on the boy's dimples.

"You should smile more," the boy replies, caressing Connor's mouth with his hand. He slides up his t-shirt, nonchalantly. Connor spots the freckles mottling the boy's abdominal area, so exotic and mysterious to him, like the stars of the southern hemisphere. He pictures the Australian flag in his mind; he wants to find the Southern Cross on the boy's chest. He imagines losing himself in the unfamiliar lights of lives lived billions of years ago.

"What you thinking?" the boy asks.

"About you," Connor says.

"What do you want to do?"

"I don't know."

"*I* know." The boy doesn't flinch. "You want to have sex with me."

It's not up for debate. "Yes. I want to have sex with you."

"I stop work in an hour. Where is your hotel?"

Connor gives him the address and directions.

"I will be there at eleven thirty," the boy says.

"Okay. I'll wait for you right outside the door."

"Thank you. What is your name? I'm Javier."

"Connor."

"See you soon, Connor."

Connor tries to hold back his excitement as he walks back to the hotel. He has picked up a man in a restaurant, in Peru of all places. *I do not pick up men in restaurants,* he thinks.

For forty minutes he paces the room. He tells himself he doesn't have to go downstairs. But he showers anyway. He puts on cologne, fusses with his hair. At 11:20 he sits on his bed. His breathing is irregular. He recognizes something new inside, something that tells him that even though there will be no parity in this indiscretion, no compensation for past wrongs, he will not stay in the room. Because he is tired of four walls.

At 11:25, Connor stands outside the imposing doors of the Hotel Royal Inka Dos. The streets are menacing and empty, the darkness reminding him of the Victorian London alleys of Jack the Ripper movies. Taxis pass by sporadically, tooting their horns at him, surprised to see anyone outside alone at this hour.

At 11:35 Javier has not come. Nor at 11:40, 11:45, 11:50. Shadows whirr by on peripheral side streets, casting curious silhouettes on walls, shapes he longs to recognize but cannot. At midnight, hollow, spent, the tips of his fingers throbbing, Connor paces up and down Calle Santa Teresa for the last time. He rings the buzzer of his hotel and heads back up to the room.

The next morning he wakes, and his first thought of the day is *Marcello will return tonight.* His second thought is *That asshole Javier stood me up.* The second thought stings far greater than the comfort of the first.

Why does he care? Men are flakes. Latin American men are notorious for not keeping appointments. So why is he so angry, sweaty with anger? It can't be the sex. He'd have sex with Marcello later that night. *I just want an explanation. I want to understand why.* It amazes him, over breakfast, how willful these thoughts are. He has to free himself of them. What's he going to do, confront the boy? He could. Javier has told him his work schedule. He has little else to do that day, besides more shopping. Would it serve a purpose? *You'll have an answer,* he tells himself. *It may not be a good one, but it'll be an answer.* He thinks of Diego, and the answers the tour guide had supplied on the tour, half improvised, half regurgitated history.

At 1 p.m., despite the solidarity of his fellow tourists, despite the familiar buzz of the locals petitioning for his dollars, despite a sun so cheerfully resolved to never yield its spot in the sky that it forces him to squint in fear of going blind from its brilliance, Connor finds himself on Cuesta San Blas, a few doors down from Macondo. He'd hoped that the feelings would have diminished by now, but instead they had plagued him all day. Even when he tried to visit a museum or archaeological site, somehow his mind would bend in a certain direction. Did the Incan people know they were going to be conquered? Were they aware of their impending downfall and decided, sheepishly, to flee deeper into the jungles to avoid capture? Well, he wasn't going to flee. He was going to face down his opponent.

At 1:15 he spots Javier walking down the street in the other direction. The boy looks fresh, well rested, a sporty messenger bag slung around his shoulders.

Connor is nervous. He's unfamiliar with confrontation but cannot afford to miss this opportunity. He lurches himself in front of the boy, awkwardly.

"Javier," he says. "What's up?"

Javier is struck by the ambush but quickly recovers. "*Hola, Connor! Que tal?*"

"So what happened?" He wastes no time. "You were supposed to meet me last night. I waited for you outside. It was cold. I wanted you to come."

"I'm sorry," Javier says, shrugging.

"I don't understand." He's loud. His anger is obvious. "Why did you tell me you would come and not show up?"

"You need me to explain?" There's nothing resembling remorse in Javier's eyes. "You have a boyfriend."

"But I don't." The words catch in his throat, like medicine too bitter to swallow. "I don't have a boyfriend."

"Yesterday," the boy says. "You did."

"I did. I did say that?" The words rush out of his mouth. "But you said you would come."

"It was a little flirtation," the boy says. "Why ruin it?"

"It was supposed to be more," Connor says. "You tricked me into thinking there'd be more."

"Sometimes, there is nothing more," Javier says. "Sometimes when there is nothing more it is beautiful."

"What is beautiful about it? You left me alone. In the dark."

"Close your eyes," Javier says, "And picture us last night in your mind. Do you like what you see? You were happy then. Just think about that instead."

"You were supposed to be there," Connor insists. "You left me alone."

"I have to work now," Javier says. Connor senses the boy's patience ebbing, along with his smile. People are passing by, and they are observing. "We can have sex later if you want. I am open."

Connor is furious. So unceremonious is the boy's offer, so careless, like an offer of a cup of coffee. "Not *later*. I can't later. I waited for you. Last night."

"*Disculpame,* Connor. I have to work now."

Javier turns around. There is no use in continuing. The conversation is over.

Later that night, Marcello returns, with a lifetime of experience in his broad smile. His hug is fierce. He showers Connor with kisses, all genuine.

"I am a changed man," Marcello says. "I have so much to tell you. But first, I must clean up. We're meeting my new friends at eight."

"Of course," Connor replies.

"It was everything I imagined. Everything and more. How I wish you had been there!"

"I was there," he says. "Just not with you."

"You know what I mean," Marcello says. "And what about you? What do you have to tell me?"

"Not much, I'm afraid."

"And the last two days? How have you been, all by yourself in this strange place?"

Connor shrugs. "I've just been."

"Anything exciting happen?" Marcello searches frantically through his bag for fresh clothes.

"Nothing at all," Connor says. "But tell me your stories."

"Of course." Marcello is beaming. "So much to tell! Where do I begin?"

After midnight, when they return to the hotel room, after jugs of *chicha morada,* bottles of *Cuzqueña* beer, *ají de gallina, cuy*, pizzas, and *postres*, after a symphony of stories related by Dutchmen and Israelis and ordinary folk from just outside St. Paul, Minnesota, stories about the legendary four-day Inca trail, stories about his lover and what a special guy he was—this Marcello fella, what a charmer—after all this, Connor finds himself lying on a hard bed, beside his boyfriend. Marcello's arms envelop him; he is too tired for sex. A good-night kiss will suffice until the morning, when the hunger will return to his boyfriend's lips, and their lives can resume again. Until then he will lie there and think, think about the lies he's told to keep himself going, the justifications he's built to stop his world from collapsing around him. The dimmest light, no matter how faint, is better than no light at all.

So much is unknown, Connor thinks. The Incas built walls without mortar, without cement, perfectly aligned. The slowness of time slid across these mathematically confounding walls of the Sun Temple, from one window to the next, so that one clear morning, in an ancient September, when the sun rose, and the light shone precisely through the window, the people knew their world was reborn again. They knew it was time to start building, to tend to the fields, to stop sleeping.

Cuzco is shaped like a puma. This is what Diego told him, as they stood on the terraces overlooking the remains of a once great civilization, in the dusk hours, when the light was struggling to remain above the mountains. Winay Picchu, young mountain, is also a puma's head; Machu Picchu is a condor with its wings outstretched. The Urubamba River in the valley below circles around like a serpent. Diego's fingers traced the animal shapes in the air, but Connor could make out only shadows—formless shadows cast by the afterglow of a powerful, fading sun.

The puma. The condor. The serpent. He couldn't make out the shapes. He didn't comprehend these symbols, these testaments to a nature long since dissolved, swallowed up by the jungles of time.

What he saw were the mountains, the ruins, the river.

The mountains, the ruins, the river. They were all he could see.

REASON TO DOUBT

Thomas looked out onto the sweep of asphalt stretching before him as it cut through acres and acres of cornfields singed by brutal August heat. He had thought his month at the writers' residency just outside of Minneapolis would be an escape from the humid torture of New York City. Weather had stopped making sense years ago.

He'd borrowed the car from the residency director and was driving to the home of Harriet St. Clair, a woman who lived about eighty miles south and who he hoped would be the final interview subject for his book. Carl, the director, had called him in March to offer him the spot. "Someone needs to expose that malarkey," Carl had said. "We'll be glad to have you here." A quiet month away from home, enough time to assemble his sludge of information into a cohesive, damning narrative. All expenses paid, to boot.

Harriet St. Clair claimed to have been abducted sixteen times. Thomas imagined he'd get enough material on her to fill up an entire chapter. Over the phone she sounded tart and self-possessed, less spooked than the usual brand of abductees he was used to speaking with. She went through her pitch, fairly run-of-the-mill stuff. He had politely cautioned her that it was his job to remain skeptical and hers to sell him. She didn't seem worried, and he didn't elaborate on the purpose of his research. He had prepared well for this battle, and was looking forward to blindsiding her.

His phone rang and Boomer's name lit up the screen.

"Hey. Tennille and I are somewhere in New Jersey."

"Great," he said.

"We're driving straight through," Boomer said.

"Not what I'd do, but okay," he said.

"Tennille has an appointment Monday morning, remember?"

Boomer had managed to get his friend Tennille an interview for a job in Florida, and apparently they had hired her over the phone. How on earth that could happen in this economy, he didn't know. Just like that, she was going to uproot her life in New York and move down south. "You could still make it if you spent the night in South Carolina."

"Stop worrying," Boomer said.

"Okay," Thomas said. But he wasn't going to. "You must be excited."

"Nervous. I just hope I get the classes I want."

"I hope so too."

"I'll call you later," Boomer said. "Love you."

"You too."

Thomas put the phone down and stared at the blistering monotony of the fields sandwiching the road. It wasn't a good month to be away. But how could he have known, back in March, that Boomer would move out while he was gone? Two years together and suddenly his boyfriend was relocating to Florida. The situation for teachers in New York had grown desperate. Almost a year after pursuing leads, Boomer gave up and took an offer from a school in Boca Raton, where he'd lived before moving to New York. The job paid well and the benefits were considerable. *Plus,* he'd told Thomas, *I'll have the whole summer to spend with you.*

Coincidentally—or not—Boomer's ex Kayden lived in Boca. Thomas had met Kayden a few times on weekend visits to Florida, and was disquieted by the younger man's pretty eyes and languid smile, the breezy, sarcastic banter that ricocheted between him and Boomer. When Boomer explained that he and Kayden had broken up because Kayden had "deep-seated issues," Thomas tried to act reassured.

It'll just be a year, Boomer insisted, that weekend before Thomas left for the residency. *I'll move back, I promise.* And Thomas nodded. What was he going to say, don't go? He supposed he could have supported them both for a year. But then he imagined the strain that would place on their relationship—he coming home after a hard day's work at the newspaper office to Boomer rearranging their spice rack or color-coordinating their towels, feigning enthusiasm as he kissed Thomas while silently resenting him for making him give up the job—and knew there was no way he'd say no. Boomer had to make this decision himself.

Thomas flipped through the stations on the radio. A lot of chatter on the air, which didn't surprise him; Minnesotans loved to talk. He hoped for some change in the scenery. An endless supply of county roads. White A-framed churches so ubiquitous they couldn't serve as track markers, anchoring towns small enough to fit inside snow globes. He remembered Harriet's directions over the phone, lefts and rights and railroad tracks and gas stations and a stone bridge she described as "ornery." He'd listened politely, MapQuested the entire thing later.

At County Road L, he made a left onto a gravel path through a thicket of wild growth. The sunflowers hugging the road seemed freakish and depressed. He was looking for Bartholomew Pass, but when the odometer said he'd gone three miles, he decided to turn around. Back at the main highway, he pulled out Harriet's directions and noticed a reference to "Maggie's Tomatoes."

He wondered about people living knee-deep in the middle of nowhere and their seemingly universal distaste for signage. No doubt the isolation played tricks with their minds. Two minutes later he saw the corroding gate that led to the St. Clair property. Harriet had told him to unlock it and let himself in.

He turned up the driveway, figuring she had several acres. It was vast and fallow, with several enormous white beeches; the lack of upkeep seemed almost deliberate. The grass was not manicured and the plantings seemed stiff, almost bored. He passed by a small pond thick with algae; two turtles sunning themselves on a rock jumped into the murky water as soon as they saw him. A shame to force them into such a mess.

Things weren't much better when he pulled up outside the battered, glum house, although the flower beds surrounding the porch seemed better tended. He imagined that with this effort Harriet St. Clair managed to forgive herself, or at least remind herself of her limitations. No one in the world was getting any younger.

He headed up the creaky steps and rang the doorbell. She was expecting him at six, and he was a few minutes early. He assumed older people appreciated that over tardiness. No one answered. His phone began to vibrate.

"We're in Delaware," Boomer said. "The car overheated."

"Shit. Are you're okay?"

"I'm fine. But Tennille's pissed. She asked me if I did a check-up before I left."

Thomas couldn't restrain a sigh.

"I forgot," Boomer said. "I'm sorry."

Thomas could hear the lock being turned on the other side of the door. "No need to apologize to me."

"The guy says I just need a tune-up and we'll be done in half an hour."

"I've heard that before."

"Well, I'm going to hope he's right," Boomer said.

The front door opened. "Me too. Listen, I have to go."

He hung up the phone. Harriet St. Clair wore khaki overalls and a bright yellow t-shirt. Her red hair had been pulled back into a bun but several large wisps had escaped to frame her long, narrow face. Her arms were covered with liver spots that reminded Thomas of agates.

"Mr. Moreland?" she said. She seemed to be focusing beyond him, and for a moment Thomas thought she was blind.

"Yes, Ms. St. Clair, pleasure to meet you." He extended his hand and she reached for it. Her grip was meek yet she bore a full smile and her eyes met his with force, a disparity that left him guessing: she could have been forty-seven or sixty-seven or anywhere in between.

"Please come in." She led him into the living room. "I'll be just a minute with the tea."

He canvassed the neat, compact room, the picture frames and modest furnishings, searching for telltale signs of crazy he knew he wouldn't find. He had studied all the major cases, including John Edward Mack's landmark 1992 study, and they all agreed on one thing: how profoundly *ordinary* abductees seemed, how indications of psychopathology were no more prevalent among them than in the general population. At least Mack had enough good sense to conclude the experiences were spiritual and psychological in nature, unlike Hopkins, Streiber, and those other hucksters, who insisted on the physical reality of aliens. And Ronald Sprinkle, that coot—beginning his study skeptically and then insisting that *he* had been abducted by aliens as a child. Nice going, Doc. Thomas knew the human instinct to believe was deep-seated and compelling. He understood: your average person can only handle so much exposure to the flirtations of paranormal experience and human frailty; gradually defenses go down, empathy kicks in and you are lulled into believing. But these men were supposed to be *scientists*.

He had done extensive research on Harriet St. Clair before his visit. He'd hardly been the first to take interest in her story, although he hoped to be the last. Sort of obscene how much information he could glean from the Internet, although less obscene when he considered how transparent she seemed to be. She had no qualms about submitting herself to several tests with a wide variety of doctors and analysts. These tests revealed very little out of the ordinary. But Thomas dug a little deeper.

She returned with a well-stocked tray. "Do you take milk? I wasn't sure about sugar or honey either so I just brought out everything." She laughed.

"I take it straight, thanks."

She sat down on the love seat across from him. "So how has your research been going?"

"Terrific, so far. I've interviewed several people."

A genial smirk crept up on her face. "Something tells me you didn't believe many of them."

"If I just believed them, Ms. St. Clair, I wouldn't be doing my job."

She stirred honey into her cup. "A dose of skepticism seems healthy. I imagine a few of them might be confused. It's so easy to be confused, don't you think? It seems like the natural order of things."

He reached inside his bag for the recorder. "I strive to lessen that confusion, myself. May I?"

"Of course." She began her spiel: her abductors were Greys, the small-bodied, smooth-skinned creatures with enormous eyes and heads that were particularly common among the abductees of the northern regions of the United States and Canada. Her narrative ran through the common elements of capture, examination, loss of time and return—although she had been offered a tour of the extraterrestrials' vehicle once, which she claimed to have politely refused. The beings had not conferenced with her; their communication was strictly telepathic, "in fairly serviceable English," she said. They ignored her respiratory and cardiovascular systems but were quite preoccupied with her reproductive system. He was taken by how unemotional and matter-of-fact she was; she relayed these abductions as just another trip to the library.

"Fantastic stuff," he said. "Very vivid."

"Well," she said. "It's what I experienced."

"I think you believe that," he said. "But wanting to believe in something doesn't necessarily make it true."

Harriet St. Clair sighed, like she had heard this angle before. "You asked to see me, Mr. Moreland."

Once again, his phone vibrated. He detested the interruption; it made him seem unprofessional. He wanted to ignore the call. But Boomer was edgy and didn't handle setbacks well. Harriet seemed to read the dilemma on his face. "You might want to answer that," she said. He shut off the recorder and excused himself, walking out to the foyer.

"The car broke down. Again." Boomer sounded exasperated.

"Where are you?"

"I don't know. Maryland? We haven't even hit D.C. yet. It keeps overheating. I may just scrap the car."

Thomas closed his eyes. Boomer had a tendency toward melodrama, and it was his job to talk his boyfriend back down to earth. "Are you kidding? There are 35,000 miles on it."

"It was on *fire,* Thomas." Boomer was shouting. "There was smoke coming through the vents."

"Okay, calm down. Can't you just go to a mechanic? Get it checked out?"

"Tennille has an appointment on Monday. And I have to report on Tuesday."

As if these were reasons enough. "Well, shit happens, right? I mean, I understand it sucks, but you have to deal with it."

"I don't know. We'll see."

Thomas paced the foyer. He pictured Boomer poking his head under the hood, staring at the parts like a paraplegic stares up a flight of stairs. Neither he nor Boomer understood the first thing about mechanics. "You need that car."

"I need to make it down there alive."

"Don't be sarcastic. I know that. But let someone take a look at it. You don't just abandon a car."

"We put in new fluid twice now. Tennille says she's going back home."

"What? You *got her* that job."

"She doesn't care. She's looking into flights on her phone."

"Before you even *try* to get it fixed?"

"It's Sunday. Nothing's open."

Something is always open, Thomas thought. "I should have had the car inspected before you left."

"It's my car. Why would you have done that?"

"I don't know." His face felt flush. He didn't know why he cared so much about a car, and yet, he did. He wished he could tell Boomer to just turn around and go back to New York. But he couldn't. Instead he let his silence work for him.

"Listen, we'll look for a mechanic, okay?" Boomer said. "I'll call you later."

"Okay." Thomas hung up the phone. Before returning to the living room, he stepped out onto the porch. He needed two minutes. Two minutes of engagement with the flat simplicity of southeast Minnesota to remind him where his head needed to be. Boomer was capricious, immature. The whole story made no sense. Who even considers scrapping a car just because it overheated? If Boomer had no car, he couldn't get to work, but since he needed to get to work, he'd have to buy another car. Which meant Thomas would have to lend him money, money that was supposed to be reserved for their mutual monthly visits back and forth between New York and Florida. Which meant an even greater strain on their relationship, or possibly an end to it.

But he had no time to dwell. He had a book to finish, a subject to dissect. He took a deep breath and returned inside the house. Harriet was still sitting on the love seat. She had picked up sewing needles in the interim and was busy knitting what looked like a miniature hoodie. She smiled up at him as he restarted the recorder.

"For my cat, Agnes," she said. "She's around somewhere. You should only see January if you think this is bad."

"When was the last time you were visited, Ms. St. Clair?"

She put down the needles and raised a finger to her mouth. "So this is 2010. . . . I'd say about five years ago. I could tell they were getting tired of me the last few times, so I can't say I was surprised."

"And why's that?"

"I was forty-six. They liked me better when my organs were fresh. Typical of men, don't you think?"

"So you think they were male?"

"I imagine they were sexless but I still think of them as men somehow. Probably because of all the probing."

"Can you recall any discrepancies between the abductions? Do any of the sixteen stand out as different to you?"

Her eyes shifted to the ceiling and then back to him. "It was *that* many, wasn't it? Hell, I could barely recall the details all that well when they happened, let alone this many years later. I don't know if I'm meant to, frankly."

"Have you discussed these encounters with a therapist?"

"I was asked to, by my ex-husband, but I refused. Other than with you research types I don't discuss these things much at all."

Thomas leaned in closer to her. "By research types, Ms. St. Clair, you mean advocates of certain theories with a vested interest in fitting your experience into their narrative."

Harriet paused to take a long sip of her tea. "Do you place yourself in that category, Mr. Moreland?"

"And you've undergone hypnosis."

"Yes."

"With the results being confirmation of the abduction story with elaborated detail."

"For the most part, yes. The hypnosis contradicted some of my memories, but I have to say, minds are fuzzy things and I'm resigned to expect contradictions."

"Of course, it's the extent of these contradictions that I find troubling, Ms. St. Clair. Your husband died many years ago, am I right?"

"*Ex*-husband, Mr. Moreland." She looked him straight in the eye. "George died in 2003."

"2004, I believe. And you have no children, and few living relatives."

"I have a sister. In Arizona."

"Ms. St. Clair, you've heard of confabulation?"

Harriet smirked. "You're not the first to use the term with me."

"You've told others your husband watched a lot of science fiction movies."

"In the living room, yes. While I was watching *Ally McBeal* and *Seinfeld*."

"I understand he was quite the storyteller."

She chuckled. "Much better at telling them than listening to mine, I'm afraid. George wasn't much of a believer. More of a tolerator. But I suppose even tolerance has its limits. He liked to ask questions too; it was only natural given the circumstances. He'd come up with what he called a 'reasonable explanation' for every scenario I described, down to the last detail. The bright lights were army planes landing at the base nearby. The fact that I'd woken up in another room, just sleepwalking. He even traced a history of schizophrenia on my mother's side, and insisted that my visitors were just manifestations of my subconscious mind dealing with the trauma of my mother's untimely death."

"And none of these explanations resonated with you."

"They did not." Harriet looked up at the ceiling. Her eyes widened and her body tensed, as if a memory had seized her, a nerve of regret suddenly pinched. "I only wish they had."

"Did you know that your blood analyses repeatedly show a statistically significant amount of dimethyltryptamine in your system?"

She placed two fingers on her lower lip. "I'm afraid I have no idea what that is, Mr. Moreland."

"It's a naturally occuring hallucinogenic found in several plants but also produced by the body, usually in minuscule quantities. In your case, at several times the level considered normal."

Harriet shifted in her seat but didn't break her smile. "And I suppose that's meant to tell me something, right?"

Once again, his phone rang. He should have turned it off, instead of letting it vibrate. He couldn't pick up. Not now, just as he was about to corner her. He let it go to voice mail. Harriet stood up, excusing herself to the bathroom. When his phone vibrated once more, he slid out to the foyer.

"Listen, I'm real busy right now," he said.

"I'm at the mechanic's," Boomer said. "He says I need to scrap the car."

"What? You can't be serious."

"It sounds terrible but Derek's being really nice about it. He's going to drive us to the airport later."

"What the hell is wrong with it? And who's Derek?"

"The mechanic. I don't know. Something about the thermometer melting into the engine and slowing the pistons down? You know how much I know about cars. Anyway, Tennille is flying home and I'm catching a flight down to Florida."

"But I don't understand. The car was *fine,* Boomer."

Boomer sighed. "It's not fine, Thomas. It's a wreck."

"So why don't you just rent a car?"

"Are you kidding? That will be way more money than a flight from DC."

"Boomer, come on. Shouldn't you at least get a second opinion?"

"Listen, I got Kayden on the phone with the guy and he said the guy's probably right, it's junk. He's got an extra car he can lend me until I buy a new one."

Aha. Kayden. So now Kayden was loaning him a car. How thoughtful, how considerate of Kayden to concur with the mechanic's explanation and offer Boomer his car. Kayden to the rescue. "And how do you know Derek isn't just trying to scam you?"

"You're not here, Thomas." He could hear the sting in Boomer's voice. "You have no idea how nice these people have been to us. He even offered to help me out with the hotel if we decided to stay the night."

Thomas felt a nagging throb running up his spine and catching in the back of his skull. No. This wasn't the story. It was only a cover for some other story, one that Boomer was conveniently leaving out. "How can you take his charity? *I'll* pay for your hotel room."

"I didn't say I was letting him pay, I just said he offered."

Thomas shifted the phone to his left ear. His neck was sweating and his stomach burned. The heat was unbearable enough, and now this. He looked up and saw Harriet St. Clair studying him with her rheumy eyes. He felt exposed and furious: utterly useless. He should have turned down the residency. He should have been there when Boomer was moving out, he should have helped him, guided him, seen to it that things would turn out right. He hated his guilt, hated that Boomer had helped justify it.

"I had no idea you were so naive," he said.

"How am I being naive? Some people are just nice."

"Not that nice. Mechanics especially."

"You're just a cynic." Boomer was getting testy. "You never had any faith in me, either."

"So is that it? You had to take a job in Florida to prove I lacked faith in you?"

"I tried for months to get a job in New York. You know that."

"Do I?" Thomas said. "Or is that just what you wanted me to believe?"

"If you'd just told me to stay," Boomer said, his voice trailing off.

"But you didn't."

"I couldn't. You had to make this decision yourself. What about your stuff?"

"Derek says he's going to mail it down to me."

Thomas looked at the receiver. No, this was too much. Thousands of dollars of stuff! Insanity. People didn't do this. They rented cars. They didn't trust this way. Even Boomer wasn't this gullible. Something else was going on. "I have to go, Boomer. I just can't talk about this right now."

"Fine. I'll call you from the airport."

Thomas hung up the phone. He looked at his hands; they were shaking. He had raised his voice. Harriet had surely noticed, and now she was going to have the upper hand.

But when he turned around Harriet had still not returned. He sat down on the couch, taking sharp breaths. Pointless, inconceivable naïveté. Who takes the word of a stranger just like that? He felt lightheaded and dry. The hum of the fans was tepid and uncertain, the blades turning simply to pass the time. The entire room was a relic, overbearingly quaint, insufferably matronly. Figurines and cozies and lithographs of springs and sunsets. He felt suffocated by the forced cheer.

Two years. What had he and Boomer accomplished in this time? All the humps they had gotten over, but maybe these were nothing but molehills. Maybe, faced with mountains, their relationship would cringe and back off. With each passing month, he tried to quantify a makeshift list of their accomplishments as a couple: successfully romantic Valentine's Days, a consistently passionate sex life, the moving in, the comfortable patterns that settled between them which indicated the normalization of their lives. But these seemed like temporary assurances, pledges written by sky-writing planes, brilliant for a moment but soon to disperse. Could their bond withstand the stipulations of distance? Or was distance just a way for Boomer to manifest his ambivalence, to say without saying that things were getting stale, or cold, or worse?

Several minutes later Harriet returned to the room with a pitcher of lemonade and a plate of finger sandwiches. She placed the tray on the coffee table, poured him a cup with ice and picked up a sandwich with a napkin and offered them to him. "Cucumber and egg salad," she said. "I imagine all this talk might have stirred up an appetite."

He looked at her hands extending the sandwich to him, then up to her clever eyes, diligent in their attempt to mask both his discomfort and her own with an extra helping of dogged hospitality. She patted down her overalls before sitting down again. He needed to get back on track. And yet Harriet's eyes, her increasing politesse in the face of his increasing skepticism, disoriented him, almost as if she had heard his conversation with Boomer and decided to test his cynicism further. Of course, she had *not* heard the conversation. She knew nothing, and he was simply projecting, conflating one situation with the other. Things had been so clear. Why was he allowing them to muddy?

"I think I may have to go," he said, uncertainly.

"Was it the phone call?" she said. "I didn't mean to interrupt."

"You weren't interrupting. It's just . . ." He stopped himself. He wasn't going to confess to Harriet St. Clair. "There are things I just don't get."

"It's hard," she said. "There are so many things to *get*."

"They're not going to return, are they?" His lower lip trembled. "You're not expecting another visitation?"

"Expectations are slippery enough with human beings, Thomas."

"And you've never wondered why, of all the billions of people on this earth, *you've* been chosen for these visits?"

Harriet looked beyond him again. It was uncanny, her ability to seem so far away, to be taken by things she couldn't see. "I don't know if I've been chosen, Thomas. It could've been anybody, I suppose. Maybe I've just been more accepting of their presence than others have. I never questioned it or fought it much. Although I'm not one for spreading the word, either."

"So they never divulged any secrets to you? They never gave you a message of hope to share with the universe?"

Harriet laughed. "None that I can recall, Thomas. Although they were always very kind. Kind in their disposition. Kind enough to bring me back."

"You classify all that probing as kindness?"

She searched his eyes with her own. "Your conversation was unpleasant."

"Don't worry about me, Harriet."

"Oh, but you *are* worrying, dear. I can see it. Do you want to talk about your troubles?"

It was time to go. He wasn't going to let her talk to him like she was his favorite aunt. He could feel her pity. It distressed him that she could sense his emotions so plainly. He stopped the recorder and slipped it into his bag. "I think I have enough, Ms. St. Clair. You've been very gracious."

She nodded her head. "Not at all, dear. Let me see you out."

She got up from her chair, humming as she walked toward the front of the house, a chirpy, untroubled melody. He hadn't succeeded in ruffling her, and she was lording her serenity over him. They reached the door and he extended his hand. "Thanks again," he said. But she did not take it; instead she looked at his hand as if looking at a small, wounded bird. Her eyes traveled up to his face and stared into him, pulling at him, her gaze heavy with the gravity of regret, and for a second Thomas thought she was about to confess something, finally admit to him what she couldn't admit even to herself.

But she said nothing. Instead she leaned in and embraced him. A hug both fierce and tender, as if he in fact had confessed and she was forgiving him for every bad thing he'd ever done in his life. "I haven't been much help, Thomas."

"Not at all, Harriet," he said, unsure of where to put his hands. "You've been kind."

She didn't let go of him, and he could feel, in her grasp, an unsettling sensation traveling through him, a feeling of distance and extreme closeness at once, both gentle and overpowering. When she finally let go she held fast to one of his hands. "You and I are more alike than you know, Thomas. George kept trying to talk me out of everything but I kept insisting. *No, George,* I said. *It's the truth, George, I swear. All of it.* Only after he left me did I realize that he'd have understood me better if I just let him explain things his way. If I allowed him to hold on to his fears. Sometimes I wonder if we're supposed to just *accept* things," she said.

He separated from her, in what he hoped was the smoothest way possible. He didn't know how to respond. All he could manage was an awkward half wave and a grunt, as he walked back to the car.

He listened to his footsteps crackle against the dry grass, the persistent thrum of cicadas disturbed by the heat. The sun was beginning its descent, and the shadows the beeches cast against the ground seemed gangly and grotesque. He stepped inside the car and looked back at the house in the rearview mirror, the porch and the siding grizzled with years of neglect. He understood why aliens would choose this spot as their target and why the woman living there would welcome them.

He pulled onto the highway, the stillness of dusk approaching. He never liked the in-between hours. They always filled him with dread, and the drab Minnesota highway wasn't helping. Why had he let her off the hook? He had sixteen—sixteen!—case studies that proved that people with unusually high levels of dimethyltryptamine almost always experienced what was typically classified as "out-of-body"experiences, not once but *regularly*, experiences so horrifyingly real so as to fool the patients themselves into thinking they had in fact happened, so lucid so as to hoodwink even the most stringent of polygraph tests.

No matter. He felt even more certain now that his project would be finished. He would finish it without any mention of Harriet St. Clair and her fantastic visitations. His book didn't need her.

Several minutes into these thoughts his phone rang.

"The tickets are booked," Boomer said. "I'm boarding in an hour."

"I'm not going to understand," Thomas said. "I don't think I want to."

"So what, you're going to stop speaking to me over this?" He could hear something in Boomer's voice. Was it pain? He wasn't sure.

"I don't know," he said. "I might. Good-bye."

He hung up the phone and threw it down on the seat. His chest felt tight, and he kept imagining himself reaching for the phone, calling Boomer and apologizing. But no, he couldn't do that. His life would go on without Boomer. He couldn't be with someone like that. Not anymore. He didn't need to know how the story ended because he would end it here. It didn't matter if Tennille made it to her job, if she actually ever had one. It didn't matter if Boomer kept or scrapped the car, it didn't matter if the mechanic really was a stand-up guy and shipped each and every last item down to Boomer, it didn't matter if Kayden was or wasn't waiting in Florida, waiting to rekindle the flame. He didn't need to know any of these things, because he had reason to doubt. And having reason to doubt was his faith; it was reason enough.

People believed kindness addressed so many things. But it didn't. Minnesota nice was a cliché for a reason, a tenderness that masked all sorts of animosity. And he was going to expose this animosity. Oh yes, the aliens were kind in Minnesota! And they landed here and left without a trace, because heaven forbid they be more direct, heaven forbid they give us a tangible, concrete proof of their existence.

Thomas accelerated. Night was bringing a dependable blue to the sky. He couldn't wait to get back to the house and work on his project.

THE COMING REVOLUTION

I want to tongue kiss a boy in a straight bar in St. Petersburg, Russia. Not a noble pursuit or a fulfillment of a lifelong dream; not even something that would be close to the top of a list of things to do, should I ever bother to make such a list, which I won't. But right now, yes, I want to feel my spit crevassing around another boy's gums, on the dinky, dimly lit dance floor of a bar not too far from the Nevsky Prospekt, or perhaps Ligovsky, but certainly near one of the major canals of the Venice of the North, in the country that gave us Pushkin and Stalin, Tchaikovsky and dancing bears.

I want the boy to be Russian. I want him to look Russian, act Russian, dress Russian, speak only Russian, except for seven words: "You're hot. Will you kiss me, please?" His lips: Molotov pink. His eyes: blue as the Smolny Cathedral. His skin, fairer than any Romanov's. He should smell Russian, but not like a Russian, who could very well smell of vodka or sour cream or herring or all three; no, he should smell like the *idea* of Russia, a fragrant wind swirling through centuries and philosophies, across oceans and dense, frigid continents, the pungent bouquet of accumulated contradictions.

I want to kiss him because I can't. Well, I shouldn't say "can't." I can, but at the risk of violence. Or perhaps not violence, but at the very least interference, interrupting our kiss at a moment not of my own choosing, which wouldn't be satisfying, really. If I'm going to kiss a Russian boy in a bar in Petersburg, it should be a long, drawn-out kiss, cursive and purposeful like a river, maddening and endless like the daylight of the late June sky. Together we could feel an all-consuming *perestroika*, a dazzling surrender of our breaths to each other's lungs. We could, but I imagine we won't; what we will feel is hands upon us, disapproving hands with hairy knuckles prying us apart and screaming at us (unintelligibly to me, although I'm sure I'll understand) words most foul and not particularly tourist-friendly. What we will feel is the thrust through an unmarked door, the repel of instant judgment, the slicing murmurs of people who can no longer enjoy themselves because we've upset their natural order.

Now if I were a woman, this wouldn't be an issue. The Russian service industry accommodates lesbians quite smoothly, which, to be fair, is sort of true everywhere else in the world as well, but particularly true in Petersburg, where the women are demonstrably more beautiful than the men. Even in my most generous moments (and when I'm really horny, I can be quite generous) I cannot deny the fact that the two tricked-out-on-eyeliner Avril Lavigne-esque Natashas currently sucking face to my right make a far more aesthetically pleasing sight than your average Boris-and-Dimitry homo bear hug. But is it fair to base decisions on aesthetics? Are we going to ask ugly people not to make out at a bar now? Will we "face control" the lame, the zaftig, the large-nosed and zitted, the shiny-foreheaded, the gap-toothed? Besides, aesthetics are subjective, and many of the above leave some people breathless with anticipation. And even if I were to round up a pair of incontrovertibly gorgeous men to perform a pulchritude-pleasing lip-lock, this still would not win over the masses.

Several questions pop up in my mind about this. As the straight population begins to get more and more queer, and more men are brazenly requesting their girlfriends to shove things up their asses, be they as tiny as pinky fingers or as large as strap-on horse dildos, I wonder if such perversions have spread to our manly-men comrades of the former Soviet Republic. Closet prostate queens have probably existed there (everywhere) for millennia and beyond, but are these football-and-vodka-obsessed beat-on-my-wife-for-sport types really beginning to get vocal about their need for back door exploration?

Not that we really have in the States yet, honestly, outside the big cities. Case in point: Walking to the club this evening, I hear one of my fellow countrypeople from Dallas make a comment about how she would never bring her husband to Russia after she got married. So I make a comment back about how he would have less to worry about than she did, as the Russian men aren't exactly break-up-my-marriage material. She agreed and then added that *apparently* Russian women were very attractive.

Apparently? *Devotchka,* please. Are girls from Dallas so afraid of appearing to be gay that they can't even call other women attractive? If remarking on the attractiveness of someone of your own gender instantly renders you a fag (or at least a hetero-of-questionable-integrity) then the world has truly not evolved.

Does the Avril Lavigne reference date this piece? Maybe I'll remove it. Here's why I won't, though: I'm optimistic. I'm optimistic that by the time people no longer know who Avril Lavigne is, my entire story will already be dated. By this I mean people will read it and say: Boys didn't kiss each other in bars in St. Petersburg? Really? Aww, prejudice. How precious. I'm optimistic that even in a place like Russia, where the hairs on the furry-backed men grow hairs, where there are high-heel marathons for women, where sexist stereotyping is the air you breathe (not that I'm breathing anything different), that even in this regressive backwater enlightenment will soon rear its rainbow head and allow for fairies to skip arm-in-arm.

Because I have seen the future, and it is metrosexualized. Boys have feelings now, which they wear on the sleeves of their fitted Ted Baker button-down shirts featuring more than just a hint of the following colors: magenta, lavender, sea foam. Boys accessorize: their belts match their shoes, their titanium frames are purchased to bring out the hazel accents in their eyes. They skin-cream, they floss, they pluck, they trim, they fashion-magazine, they latte, they suppose (instead of guess), they wonder (instead of think), they perhaps (instead of maybe), they watch quirky television shows with female lead characters while sipping microbrewed beers accompanied by artisanal cheeses accompanied by condiments such as white watermelon mustard or sour cherry fig compote. They know the difference between a halter top and a tube, a mule and an espadrille.

But do I want to kiss a metrosexual? If he is capital *H* Hottie, yes. If he is drunk and seeking escape, no. If it's part of his journey toward self-acceptance, yes. If he is using me to get his girlfriend jealous, no. If it's full-on with tongue, yes, yes, hell yes. If it's on the top of his head or the part of the cheek where his grandfather also kisses him, no. If it means I'm a naughty home-wrecking homo seeking to seduce young impressionable God-fearing straight boys to join the dark side by the simplest flick of my tongue, a thousand times yes. If Putin himself would be upset, yes, but with an asterisk, which stipulates that I am not subject to polonium poisoning at any moment for the rest of my trip and beyond. If he needs to confirm he is straight, no. If it's out of pity for me because he understands how hard it is to want something as hot as him and never be able to really get it, no. If it makes him hard, yes, but only if it makes him happy-hard and not confused-hard, only if he doesn't start to have an instant orientation crisis on the spot.

Eric Sasson

If the moon is red and we are midnight cruising on the Neva and the glittery bridges are about to rise up and the drunk Russians in the boat alongside us are toasting us with Putinka and I reach for him and he doesn't hesitate and some of the Russians boo but some of them cheer, less loudly, yes. If his breath smells of Bokharov, no. If it smells of Baltika 8, spicy and sweet like a good microbrewed white beer should, yes.

If he is hesitant, no. If he is at first hesitant but then loosens up, because he suddenly realizes my lips and my mouth and my very being excite him, yes. If he's a bad kisser, no. If he's a bad kisser whom I can make better, maybe. If he's a bad kisser because he's only kissed women and now, oh now, he understands what it means to kiss and be kissed, what it means to feel deep primal sloppy lust, hell to the yes.

If he smells like Drakkar, no. (But what self-respecting Metro would smell like Drakkar?) If it is so good we need to get a room, yes. If it is so good I start to fall in love with him, start imagining us in Mars Field feeding each other grapes and start sending him cryptic notes about our superclose friendship and then even more cryptic haikus that upset me when he doesn't manage to decipher them, no.

Forgive me: I'm a man of stipulations.

HONNE / TATEMAE

Subject: Tokyo

From: RadBrad@hotmail.com
Sent: 12/4/07, 10:05 am
To: RyanDavis@hotmail.com

Ryan,

Konichiwa, bro! Jill and I arrived yesterday. Free Internet in the lobby—sweet. Actually the hotels here have free WiFi in the rooms, but Jill told me that if I brought my laptop she was going to use every minute I spent cooped up online noshing on fifteen-dollar strawberries in the department stores of Ginza. I'm allowed an hour a day.

It was good seeing you a few weeks ago. Of course, under different circumstances it would've been better, but still. You looked good. Diane too. It's been a long time. *Twice a year I see my boys together.* Remember how Mom used to say that to us? I'm glad you told me to keep in better touch with you. I was feeling the same thing and didn't know how to express it, so when you pulled me aside and said that, I was a little moved. It's strange what funerals can do.

I just want us to be brothers. Of course we always have been, but you know what I mean. That's why I'm going to write you a little from each place I visit. I know you and Diane have wanted to come here together. You should. Jill and I planned it for months. Took us forever to coordinate eighteen days off but I really think it's going to be special, sort of like a second honeymoon. Sometimes it's hard to find the energy to focus on each other. You know how it is; everybody's got the same problems. It'll be good for us, having this time to ourselves. I could use the distraction, to be honest.

Anyway, last night we headed out to Shinjuku, which is sort of like Times Square on crack. I felt like I'd died and entered Neon Sign Hell. Nah, it was cool. It's Tokyo! It's the future! Get this—the toilets here, even the public ones in the train stations, are totally automatic: the seat goes up and down when you push a button, and it's heated, and there's even a built-in electronic bidet! I'm not shitting you. You press a button, sit back, and enjoy. Betcha Dad would've liked that, right? Mom too, although she'd have probably blushed and pretended not to notice.

Remember that trip we took in 1980? How Mom insisted we come along? The Japanese fascinated her. *They're so advanced!* she'd said. *So proper, so meticulous. We'll all go!* And then when Dad gave her his I-don't-know eyes, remember how tight she got, how she clammed up and started folding and refolding the lace doilies until finally she spat out: *Thirty trips a year, Harold. You can bring us this one time.*

I can still picture Mom's face as we wandered around the Seibu department store. How stoked she was watching that woman gift-wrap the lacquer tray she brought home for Aunt Millie, like she'd seen the Virgin Mary herself in the paper pattern. *They understand how important appearances are,* she'd said.

Gosh we had some good times. Gorging ourselves on shabu-shabu. Sneaking off to Roppongi when Mom and Dad were asleep. Remember those lunatic sailors who squirreled us into that bar and bought us sake all night? We were pretty close then, don't you think? I kinda miss that.

Anyway, keep in touch. Let me know if there's something you'd like me to bring back. And if there's anything you want to talk about . . . it's kinda odd being here with Mom dead only three weeks. But Jill's right—Mom wouldn't have wanted us to cancel the trip. Besides, she lived a pretty good life. Outlasted Dad a good what, seventeen years? She's in a better place now, don't you think? I don't know if you noticed the last time you visited but when I was there in October she seemed, I don't know, troubled. She kept looking at me like she wanted to tell me something. Her eyes were anxious but they were also kinda cloudy and distant; I couldn't make out what they were trying to say. I asked her about it but we both know how pointless that was. *Everything's fine, Bradley,* she insisted. And then that textbook smile popped back onto her face and her eyes cleared up as if the question itself was all she needed to restore her peace.

Maybe she knew what was coming. Or maybe it was more than that. Maybe there was something she wanted to tell me. I should have pushed a little. It's gnawing at me that I didn't push her, that there was something she needed to say and I didn't give her the right to say it.

Geez, I'm getting all morose. Sorry for the heavy questions. I guess I'm still in the mourning phase. I'm sure you are too. I'll write more in a few days.

Hugs from your brother,
Bradley.

Subject: Kyoto
From: RadBrad@hotmail.com
Sent: 12/7/07, 1:34 pm
To: RyanDavis@hotmail.com

Hey bro! We're in Kyoto now. The ladies working at the hotel all wear baby-pink kimonos, and when we checked in one of them hauled our bags onto a cart and wheeled them to our room. I tried to help but she wasn't having any of it. Tiny little thing, but Christ was she strong.

Kyoto, man: Temples everywhere, with wild fucking names. Kinkako-ji. Kiyomizu-dera. Sanjusangendo. Jill is ecstatic. I have to hand it to these people: they really know how to make things look beautiful. It's almost like the ancient Japanese predicted photography. These places are postcard-perfect, what with five-story pagodas and reflecting ponds and Japanese maples in every color of the fall handbook, stone bridges and waterfalls and God knows what else.

I know what else: Japanese *women.* Everywhere we go, the women are wearing short-shorts and cowboy boots, even in December. It's like an ocean of these perfect, smooth legs. *I guess it's okay to look like a prostitute here,* Jill said, giving me the eye. *Different culture,* I said, shrugging my shoulders like I hadn't noticed. But man, it's impossible not to notice! They may not have much in the chest department but the legs, man. The legs! Even the teenagers wear these Catholic school miniskirts, fitted white shirts and bobby sox and penny loafers. Hey I'm no perv but it's hard not to get distracted, you know?

Jill doesn't seem to agree. We haven't been getting along great these past couple of days. This morning we passed by these two geisha and I asked someone to take a picture of us with them and Jill insisted she didn't want to be in it. Did you know there are less than a thousand of them left in Japan? Jill read that in our guidebook and she was like, good riddance, it's about time they stop the sexual slave trade. And so I gently disagreed, saying it was a fascinating cultural phenomenon and part of Japanese history, to which she replied that of course I'd say that, because the idea of women obediently servicing my every need held great appeal to me, and then she asked if I thought it'd be nice if back in America we still kept a few African slaves around just for tourists to take pictures, which I thought was a low blow, frankly.

We didn't speak much the rest of the day. I wasn't used to this kind of outburst from her because it's not like we fight like that at all, it's more like—well, it's more like Mom and Dad, actually. I guess I've picked up my cues well. Ever since the funeral Jill's been asking me a lot of questions and getting upset when I don't answer them. Right before we turned in for the night she reached over and took my hands and stared into me something sharp. *I know you need some time,* she said. *But maybe we should talk about it.*

I froze at that moment. I didn't know what to say so I looked into those rainy gray eyes of hers, and I nodded my head and just let out this useless *unh-huh.* Then she repeated the unh-huh and I repeated my unh-huh and she looked down at the ground and started laughing, and when her head popped back up I could see her eyes rolling to the ceiling, but not out of frustration, more to stop the tears that were about to form, tears because we weren't communicating. We were supposed to communicate on this trip; we were supposed to reconnect.

I need to ask you something, Ryan. I know you told me not to overanalyze in your e-mail but do you think Mom was at peace with herself when she died? I wonder sometimes because, well, I just wonder. You can think an awful lot about things in seventeen years. I know I have. I'm sure you have too. And some of the thoughts I've had aren't pretty. Some of them are making me wonder if I'll ever have a future with Jill, or with anybody. God knows I know how to fuck up relationships. Maybe you can help me out here? You and Diane seem pretty happy together. Are you happy? Are things alright? I know we always say things are alright. But Mom and Dad said things were alright too.

I expected a conversation before she died, Ryan. I think you know what I mean. Maybe you don't but I think you do. I'm sorry for bringing this up but maybe we ought to talk about it. Let me know.

Bradley

Subject: Osaka
From: RadBrad@hotmail.com
Sent: 12/12/07, 6:35 am
To: RyanDavis@hotmail.com

Hey Rye,

Did you get my last e-mail?? Not feeling too hot, bro. Think I may have caught something. You'd think that wouldn't be possible since all the sick people here walk around with face masks on. It's kinda creepy actually. Almost like a scarlet letter. Jill thinks they're being considerate; I'm not so sure. Maybe they're just worried *they* might catch something and wear the masks as protection.

Still, she's right, in a way. The Japanese are a considerate people. Maybe too much so. They don't like to say "no" here if they can avoid it. They'd rather say something like "it will be difficult" and you're supposed to interpret that as "no." All this to avoid conflict at all costs. Keep your cool, put the collective good above your individual needs, and always strive to maintain harmony. There are two concepts here that basically define Japanese society: *honne* (real value) versus *tatemae* (face value). They're really big on keeping up appearances.

Everything they do in public revolves around maintaining this sense of happiness and civility. What they do in private, however, is another story. Which means Satomi can be a raging sex queen with multiple partners coming in and out of her home every day and all of her neighbors will know about it but no one will ever *talk* about it. They'll just say she's a "hostess."

Kinda fucked up, if you ask me. It's like no one can ever express displeasure or disagreement. But what if you *are* angry? What if you need to let that anger out, and let that person know they made you angry? For instance, yesterday afternoon, Jill and I were checking in to our hotel in Osaka. They told us our room wouldn't be ready for an hour. Normally this wouldn't be a big deal. But you don't understand how inflexible they are here, how much they follow the exact letter of the law. If check-in is at 1 p.m., then you just *can't* check in before then. No exceptions. So when we show up at 12:55 and they tell us we still have to wait an hour I'm not okay with that, and I told the lady at the front desk how I felt.

Jill pulled me aside like I had just spat at the Pope. *Do not do this, Bradley,* she whispered. *You're upsetting her for nothing.* Which confused me, because I didn't think Jill was in on this conspiracy of goodwill. Her teeth were clenched and her neck had gotten so tense I could see little veins popping out, and for a second I thought of Mom, on the day of Dad's funeral, the way she kept zigzagging around, whispering things to the priest, to Aunt Jane, to us, through the tightest jaw the world has ever seen, almost as if she expected us to make out the words without her having to say them. I used to think Dad's funeral was really beautiful. I mean, of course it was terrible, and sad, but it was such a lovely ceremony, and such a sunny day, and the coffin was spectacular and the flowers were overflowing and everyone was so appropriately mournful, so rich with memories and funny stories about our old man who had died way too young. Just then, looking at Jill, I started seeing things differently. The word that popped up in my mind was: *whitewashed*. Dad's funeral had been whitewashed to make it seem perfect, and I don't know why, but that made me so angry, right there in the lobby of a hotel in Osaka, that I just had to get out.

I left her there, Ryan, and I stayed out until this morning. I wandered around the streets and when it got late I taxied over to Dotombori, the nightlife district down here. I swear, it's like a cartoon version of *Blade Runner*. Bars stacked one on top of the other, seven or eight stories of signs with the most random nonsensical English phrases (my favorite, outside a "love" hotel: "Let's melt our time slowly"), wacky storefront blowups of puffer fish and crabs and get this, Ferris wheels on tops of buildings. I found a karaoke place and got shit-faced on several bottles of Shochu. And hell, I'll admit it, third verse into "You've Lost that Lovin' Feelin'," and the ladies of Osaka were digging me. I had a gaggle of them circling me at the bar, feeding me pickled daikon and eggplant. And maybe I made out with one of them, who knows. But it's not like I fucked anyone.

I haven't gone upstairs yet. Who knows if Jill is even there. I'm not proud of myself but is it really such a big deal? I mean, sometimes guys just need to blow off steam. I don't know. Dad used to go out all the time on his own. He'd stay out after work so often we started making those bets, remember, about what time he'd make it home? We'd stay up just to see who won, no matter how late. *Your father has to be social. It's part of his job,* Mom would say. *It's what puts these steaks on the table. It'll put you boys through college.*

Well, it sure did that. At least his life insurance did. I wonder what kind of witchcraft Mom had to perform to get Aetna to pay, how she managed to convince the doctors to write that her husband had died of cancer. She managed to convince her own son for so many years, so what's a few naive insurance agents?

Are you still laboring under that illusion, Ryan? That our dad was a good man, shot down too soon by cancer? That our mother was the noble widow, her perfect marriage tragically cut short? I don't think so. I think you've known for years. You're kinda like Mom, actually, in that way. Not that that's necessarily bad. I'm just saying.

Write back soon,
Bradley

Subject: Hiroshima
From: RadBrad@hotmail.com
Sent: 12/16/07, 8:15 am
To: RyanDavis@hotmail.com

Haven't heard back from you. I know you're busy, but write soon, okay?

Jill went back home on Wednesday. When I saw her that morning in Osaka, she was already packing. I tried to plead my case. *I just needed some space,* I said, putting on the dewy-eye routine and caressing her hair. She wasn't having it though. *You've been taking space for years now, Bradley,* she said. *This trip was about us trying not to take any more space.*

I can't really blame her. I've been a bad fucking husband for so long now. Have you been a good husband, Ryan? Diane is one fine-looking woman but is that enough to keep you from wandering? I'm not implying anything here, bro. Just asking.

I've been feeling miserable ever since I got to Hiroshima. This fever's really backing me up. Making up for past sins, I guess. I even checked myself into a hospital briefly. Did you know that the doctors here often don't tell their patients what's wrong with them? Instead they consult with the patient's family, allowing them to decide what's in his best interest. Which means the poor shmuck could end up going through all sorts of tests without a clue as to what's ailing him. They think it's better that way.

Sounds a lot like Mom. Remember when she found out how sick Dad was, how she took over his life? The woman had discovered her calling. Every time I stopped by the house she was on the phone, to this or that doctor, to Dad's brother in Atlanta, to Aunt Jane in Raleigh. Suddenly she was a Rolodex, an appointment calendar, an accountant, an advisor, a nurse. She made lists. Remember those lists? *Pills Harold has to take and at what hour. Foods Harold must avoid. Bills that must be paid by the 15th. Tax forms for Harold's stock distributions.* I think she enjoyed being in charge. Being able to control Dad.

Don't you think it was strange when she wouldn't let people visit him? Even we only got to see him sporadically. *Your father needs his rest,* she'd say. Or: *Your father doesn't want you to see him in his condition.* I didn't question her then. There was something about her conviction that didn't allow for skepticism. The woman knew everything, and if she said Dad wasn't in the mood for company, I trusted her. She was so certain she made me certain. But now I wonder: Maybe it wasn't Dad who didn't want us to see him. Maybe it was her. How cruel if that were true, if she had denied our father access to his sons on his death bed. I'm not saying it is. But it might be.

Anyway, I visited Peace Memorial Park and the atomic bomb museum today. It was kinda weird without Jill there—she would've loved it. Dude, they're not even confrontational in the *museum*. I'm streamlining, but essentially the story goes as follows: the Japanese bombed Pearl Harbor and the Americans needed to retaliate and also pay for the enormous costs of the bomb and keep Russia in line so they just went ahead and dropped it. Don't get me wrong, they play up the tragedy and it's really fucking sad, seeing photographs of what the city looked like a few days before and then a few days after, but they're so coolheaded about the whole thing. I know it's been over sixty years but I still kind of expected someone— a coat check lady, a guard, another tourist—to at least give me the stink eye. Tsk-tsk me. Say something. *Anything.* Of course I'm not responsible. But they can't really be fine with us. They just can't. We didn't stop at one bomb. We went for the second. It seems malicious if you think about it, and I know there's a shitload of context and the Japs were super-aggressive and bent on world domination and Christ they were awful to the Chinese and Koreans back then, too. So there's always perspective. But two bombs. You can't just move on from something like that. You can try, but I think you need to get pissed-off first. They never get pissed off here. Maybe they should.

Bradley

Subject: Nagasaki
From: RadBrad@hotmail.com
Sent: 12/21/07, 1:21 pm
To: RyanDavis@hotmail.com

Still not feeling so good, bro. And it's not making things any better that you're not writing me back. Maybe you're not getting my emails, who knows. But I don't think it's that. I'm sorry if I've touched a nerve. You said we needed to get close again, and that's all I'm trying to do here. I hope you understand.

The fever just won't go away. I take the pills but still it lingers.

I'm going ahead with the trip, though. We prebooked the hotels so I don't see the point in going back home. Besides, Jill will be there and she's probably still mad. Maybe it's better this way, to have some time away from each other.

It doesn't stop raining here in Nagasaki, this depressing, relentless drip that's more like a mist than a rain. Not that it should be sunny. Not that the rain isn't somehow appropriate. Still, the city's pretty cheerful. You can't believe how well these people recover, dude. It's almost as if the bomb never happened. Supposedly a lot of people in Japan are saying they don't want to dwell on it anymore.

I've been thinking back to the days right before Dad died. I know you probably don't want to hear about this anymore. But I can't keep quiet, bro, I just can't. Think back: Remember how Mom would turn off the TV when certain news segments came on? How she'd storm out of the room? I didn't think much about it then, watching those ACT UP people chain themselves to St. Patrick's Cathedral. *Goddamn animals,* she said, snapping the remote control and throwing it onto the couch. And who could argue with her? Who could even think about connecting dots we couldn't even see?

Why do you think that made her so angry, Ryan?

I'm going to tell you this because I can't keep it inside any longer. I've been wanting to tell you for so long, even before the funeral, but the guilt has been holding me back. We're good at holding things back, right? But I'm sick, bro, and I think this is part of it, this stress of not telling you. I don't know, maybe I'm reaching for excuses. But I don't care if I am anymore.

Remember when I asked if you noticed something was up with Mom the months before she died? How I thought she was trying to tell me something? Well, that's not the whole truth. Not even close.

I found letters. I was over the house, and Mom was downstairs making tea in the kitchen. She had already seen a few doctors by then, but it didn't seem so serious yet. Anyway, she had asked me to find the deed to the house for her. She told me to search the closets. Every closet, she said. She told me to, Ryan.

Letters. Seventy-eight of them, to be exact. I read them, each and every goddamn one, to the period after the final postscript. Did you know I was named after one of Dad's ex-lovers? I think she knew it too, and she let him do that to me. She let him mock her in that way.

She kept them! For seventeen years she kept them, when she should've shredded them, burned them in a bonfire that even Dad himself would have applauded. Why would she hold on to letters that other men wrote to our father? What sort of perversity is that?

You expected me to do nothing about it, sit back like a good Davis boy does? The Davises don't get angry; the Davises keep a stiff upper lip. No. Not anymore. I confronted her. I didn't care that she was a fragile old lady, I didn't think about what could have shaped her to reach her conclusions, all I could see was the betrayal, this sickening cesspool of lies that we've been swimming in for the majority of our lives. For once I understood why I was so angry, why I've been so angry for so long. Don't you ever wonder, Ryan, why neither of us have kids? Maybe there's something stopping us from committing to that.

Anyway, she was drying off some dishes and I just stormed in and threw the letters in her face. *He died of AIDS,* I said. My voice was cracking; I was eight years old again and just found out that Santa wasn't real.

She bent down to the ground, sweeping the letters with her hands into a pile, folding them into a neat bundle. All this time her face showed nothing. Not anger, not surprise, certainly not remorse. She was as calm as an old tree in a desert. *Your father had a lot of love in him,* she said, using a chair to help herself back up.

Sure, I said. *For other men.*

For me, she said. *For all of us.*

How can you say that! He betrayed you. Your marriage was a sham.

Her head shook and her mouth twisted into a small smile. *You don't know that,* she said.

You lied. To me. To Ryan. You could've told us. All these years. All these questions in my head. They've fucked with me.

You don't know, she repeated. *You don't understand.*

I don't understand?!

And then she caressed my cheek with the back of her palm and said, *You know, you're looking more and more like him every day.*

I couldn't believe she'd say that. I couldn't believe she was still unruffled.

Your whole life is a fucking lie, I said.

This, finally, gave her pause. I saw her take it in. I saw her eyes dilate, her lips curl, considering the meaning of what I just said. She stacked the letters onto the table and dusted off the top one with her left hand. *So now that the truth is out,* she said, *do you think things will get any better?*

She walked away from me then. She smoothed down her dress, turned around, and walked up the stairs. *I'm going to lie down,* she said, her final words that day.

It's hard not to feel responsible now. I guess it's crazy for me to think that that conversation killed her, but who's to say that it didn't? Who's to say it didn't accelerate the process? I tried talking to her on the phone a couple of weeks after that, and I sort of felt it, you know, felt she was finally going to let it out, finally ready to scream bloody murder if I only brought it up. But I don't know, I just couldn't. I should have, maybe. But I felt bad, because I thought I'd made her sicker. And now you're not writing me back, so I guess you think so too. I guess you blame me now.

Are you surprised by all this? Or do you just resent the fact that she chose me to find the letters? Really, Ryan, you can't be mad about that. Maybe she thought you knew all along, I don't know. Did you? Because that would explain a lot, bro. That would help me understand why you've pulled away all these years. Why you're not writing me back even now. Because maybe you knew too.

Maybe she was right. Now that it's out in the open, are things really any better for me? I'm still hoping they can be, Ryan. I'm hoping our mother was wrong. Maybe I'm just naive.

Did she just not love us enough to tell us? Or did she love us too much? I'm trying to understand what Mom gained from keeping a secret like that for so many years. How didn't it eat her alive? Why didn't she move on, remarry, rebuild her life? Because frankly I don't get it. And I don't forgive her for it. I can even forgive Dad more— who was gay in 1959? Who knew that AIDS was coming? Not that he wasn't a fucking bastard. But she survived seventeen years. *How?* How come she never got it? Did they just stop having sex? Did she live with him all that time and never, ever have sex?

She should have talked about it with us. She should have talked about it, cleared the air of the lingering resentment that hung over our house like a sulfur cloud. Maybe if we had I wouldn't have ended up like both of them, fucking around behind my wife's back and then pretending nothing is wrong. Or maybe I would have anyway, and I'm just finding excuses for my own flaws.

Can you tell me which one's right?

Me.

INNER EYE

Distance will not save them. Absence won't make the heart grow fonder or whatever other drippy cliché people bandied about. Communication issues won't resolve themselves. He won't suddenly rediscover the passion he once had for Gary. This trip is the beginning of the end. He knows it.

Tyler sighs. The tomato-cheeked man at the tourist information office scrunches his face and says, *The bus runs every thirty minutes, until ten p.m.* Tyler checks his watch, smiles and heads toward the airport's exit. Although he can easily afford a taxi ride into town, he decides against it, allowing himself to acclimate to his new surroundings.

Salvador is the third stop of his Brazilian cross-country journey. The first two had been no more than pleasant. São Paulo was fast-paced but flavorless. He zipped around its dense skyscrapers, its hodgepodge of parks and storefronts in a detached blur as Paulistas scuttled around him, distracted by their cell phones. Foz do Iguaçu offered him the natural awe of the waterfalls, wrapped in safe, Disneylike packaging. He boarded safari-ready buses, listened to canned voice-overs, strolled along designated paths, snapped photos, purchased glossy postcards for his friends.

Here, in the capital of Bahia, he hopes to discover a more

authentic side to Brazil. His mind runs through the guidebook's catalog: Salvador's scenic, playful downtown, its stress-free, fun-loving locals, its unique *comida Bahiana,* the lissome, sensual *capoeira,* the mysterious *candomblé*, fusion of African myths and Catholic doctrine. He wants to immerse himself in something exotic, something that might permit him escape from thoughts of home.

He has time to call Gary, but decides against it. He needs to come up with better answers to Gary's inevitable questions. They had planned the trip together, but Gary had backed out to prove his "responsibility." Tyler *is* responsible—he's an insurance adjuster. Gary's more of a dreamer, a storyteller; people hire him to read tarot cards at parties. A bartender one day, an acupuncturist the next. His imagination intoxicated Tyler when they'd first started dating two years ago. Misty-eyed conversations about a summer cottage in Charleston, cooking classes in the south of France. But these dazzling tomorrows never materialized.

Three weeks earlier, after much urging by Tyler, Gary had landed a public relations gig for a nonprofit children's group. Tyler wanted to postpone the trip but Gary insisted that he didn't. "Besides, you need to go alone," Gary said, pencil-thin eyebrows arching over mischievous eyes, a slapdash smile unlocking his dimples. Gary was the master of the ambiguous one-liner. Once, as they'd meandered through the hallways of a West Chelsea gallery, looking at sculptures with titles like *Untitled no. 41* that to him looked like nothing more than shiftless, unfinished formulas, Tyler had sighed heavily, to which Gary remarked that he suffered from a "curious lack of faith." A lighthearted jab and yet its sting has stuck with him. How many people suffering from a lack of faith set off solo to Brazil for three weeks? More likely it's Gary who suffers from too much faith. Gary, with his eleven subscriptions to underground homeopathic journals.

Gary, who dabbled in Kabbalah, then Wicca, with a stopover in Scientology in between.

The dry, hot air lashes at his face. He and four others stand waiting: A mother and her four-year-old son. A shaved-headed surfer leaning against a pole, a serpent tattoo crawling up his left calf. A middle-aged Asian man in a purple silk shirt, pushing a cigarette in and out of his lips.

Up until now the South American slackness he's feared has not surfaced. His journey has proceeded with painless grace, and he's wondered if perhaps a few complications would deepen his experience. Where is the crime that the guidebooks repeatedly warned him about? The prostitutes, the gang-bangers? Not that he wants to experience danger, just flirt with it. Have a few meaty tales to tell Gary.

Forty minutes pass and still no bus. For a while he sits, flipping through his guidebook. Then he stands, wipes his brow, walks in tight, deliberate circles. He flirts with the tattooed surfer, whips him with the strap of his carry-on bag, and has sex with him in the bathroom—all in his mind. He wonders, should the opportunity present itself, if he'd entertain a hayride with a local. It's certainly possible; likely even, considering Brazil's reputation. Has that prospect crossed Gary's mind? Tyler doubts it. Gary *trusted* him.

By 10:05, he's ready to storm the tourist information office and strangle the tomato-faced ignoramus. He wants to murder everyone around him. He curses himself for not taking a taxi earlier, and yet, now that he's waited this long, he *needs* to see the bus come. A litany of regrets scrolls through his mind: by now he could have unpacked, eaten dinner, knocked back a few *caipirinhas*. Instead he's shackled to this desperate question mark.

At 10:16, the bus sputters up to the curb. No one says anything. He's not fluent, but what's their excuse? Why don't they demand an explanation? Gary, had he been there, wouldn't have complained either. No, Gary would have skipped onto the bus, humming the tune of a catchy Brazilian pop song he'd heard in the airport lounge. Gary loves airport lounges, sharing with strangers his thrill of planes thrusting and alighting.

The driver, a shaggy-haired baby-face sporting a Montreal Expos cap, places his suitcase in the back. The air-conditioning is delicious. Slowly he feels himself emerge from his anger coma. The bus moves quickly. Tyler slumps in his seat and absorbs the view: mile-long stretches of sand, curls of foamy white breaking against the shore.

The scenery out the opposite window surprises him. Though it's late January, sparkly signs reading *"Boa Festa"* and palm trees with Christmas lights linger belatedly. High-rise condominiums with doormen, sleek, cavernous restaurants, men dressed in linen pants and women in tight, skimpy dresses. Only occasionally does he spot darker faces: a man selling sugarcane juice, a woman at a bus stop. If he blinks, he could be in Miami. He writes this sentiment down in the back of his guidebook. He needs to accumulate thoughts for Gary.

At a quarter to eleven, the bus pulls up outside his posh, beach-side hotel. He takes out the money he's set aside in his pocket and pays the young driver, who unloads his suitcase and tips his cap. Two bellboys rush over.

The lobby is vast, smartly furnished in neutral tones, brightly lit. The receptionist, a man named Reginaldo, is stumpy and uptight, a human trapezoid. His smile endeavors to find the friendly formality required of him, but it doesn't seem genuine. Tyler is unwashed. His shorts are ragged, and day-old stubble litters his face. He wonders if the man is embarrassed for him.

Tyler takes out his passport and reaches for his wallet. Only it isn't there. He searches his pants, then the numerous pockets of his carry-on bag. Still no luck. Reginaldo continues to smile patiently. Tyler checks everything again. After a second run-through, reality creeps in.

"I can't find my wallet," he announces, his voice squeaking.

"Your wallet," Reginaldo repeats, loudly.

"Yes! I can't believe this."

"Are you sure?"

"I've checked everywhere. It's gone."

"Perhaps you dropped it on your way in." Reginaldo calls over several of the bellboys, speaking quickly in Portuguese. "They will help you look."

Tyler scuttles outside without responding, the bellboys trailing behind him. Surely this isn't happening. Surely hell would freeze over before he, of all people, would lose a wallet. In thirty years, he hasn't lost a wallet once. Gary's the one who loses wallets, keys, ATM PINs.

It has to be outside. But even if it *was* outside, someone on the street would've noticed and grabbed it—he's in Brazil, for God's sake. The bellboys scrutinize every inch of the ground. He studies their expressions and wonders if they're genuinely concerned for him. Perhaps one of them had snatched it when he entered the hotel. Thieves never look like thieves.

He is fucked. So fucked. He returns to the reception desk delirious and coated in sweat.

"You have money to pay?" Reginaldo is typing into a keyboard.

Tyler looks at him sideways. Was this an acceptable question, given the circumstances? "Not all of my money was in my wallet. But my credit cards. My driver's license. My library card . . ."

"Perhaps you left it on the bus."

"I don't know," Tyler says. "I don't know anything."

"You can chase the bus if you want. The last stop isn't far."

Tyler can barely make out what Reginaldo is saying. He feels exposed, embarrassed to have to go through these ridiculous motions with a bunch of strangers.

"The driver will wait at the terminal before resuming his route. Take a taxi and find the bus."

"I don't know where I am," Tyler shouts. "I don't speak Portuguese."

Reginaldo snaps his fingers to signal over the largest bellboy. The man is oily and has thick eyebrows, yet his eyes are sincere and dutiful; they remind Tyler of the large agoutis he saw in the parks of Saõ Paulo, the way these oversize rats scampered for food with what looked to him like optimism. "Carlos will go with you. You will need some *reais* for the driver."

"I only have dollars." Tyler presses his hands into the counter. "My *reais* were in the wallet."

Reginaldo laughs. "The driver will not refuse dollars."

"Is there a point to this?" Tyler's hands reach for his temples.

"Your choice, *senhor*. It's not very far. I will watch your bags for you."

Tyler follows Carlos outside the hotel. The receptionist is trying to offer him hope, and still he can't help but despise him. He imagines Reginaldo and the other bellboys pilfering his luggage while he's gone, mocking his oversized toiletry bag, fiddling with his camera. He imagines them having a good laugh at his expense: the spoiled gringo has lost his wallet; beware, the sky is falling!

Carlos flags down a driver and explains the situation as Tyler jumps into the back and slams the door. His brain is on fire. Surely chasing after a bus is the stupidest idea. The whole taxi ride could be a ruse. Carlos and the driver could simply ride him to an abandoned warehouse, steal his passport and cash, beat him close to death or beyond, return to the hotel, and split the spoils. What exactly should stop them?

The taxi follows a road that soon veers away from the shoreline. The neighborhoods become denser the farther they drive, the orchestrated gloss of the ocean properties giving way to something more grubby and disorderly. Locals gather on street corners in bursts of colorful tank tops. Their catcalls blend with the music wafting from the taxi's radio and the painfully relaxed conversation between Carlos and the driver.

Tyler's stomach is tight. He feels disconnected from his body: he is in one world, experiencing his shock, and the rest of them are in the looking glass, joyously indifferent. His anxieties mean nothing to them.

"You are American?" Carlos asks, in drawling but serviceable English. He has wrapped his brawny arm around the back of the driver's seat to better face Tyler.

"I'm from New York."

"Big country." Carlos laughs. "Big city."

"Yes," Tyler replies. "But Brazil is also a big country."

"New York, New York," Carlos says. "The Big Apple."

Tyler looks away. He wishes this man understood he did not want to banter.

"First time to Brazil?" Carlos takes the cigarette pack out of his pocket.

"Yes."

On the dashboard, a bobble-head Virgin Mary bounces playfully. The driver, a thin man with tired hands who sings cheerfully along with the radio, stares ahead with indifference. Soon the taxi slows and pulls into a small bus terminus. Tyler knows from the pictures in his guidebook that he is near the Praça da Sé, in Pelourinho, the historic district of Salvador; he can see the city hall on his right. Three buses idle ahead of them. Otherwise the area is mostly deserted. The driver gets out.

"He will ask someone," Carlos says.

"None of these is the bus."

"We know. He will ask someone about your bus."

As Carlos exits the taxi and lights a cigarette, Tyler notices a small brown stain on his lapel. He imagines Carlos's wife in the tiny bathroom of their Spartan apartment, hunched over the sink, yelling to her husband that the stain will not come out. He imagines Carlos's face hearing this news: a slight nod, an imperceptible sigh, and then a quick return to the potatoes resting in front of him.

The night air is warm and dreamy. The vinyl seat sticks to Tyler's skin. At the far end of the terminal, the driver converses with three men by a booth. Carlos has crossed the road over to an old woman sitting on the curb, her face darker than the night, her frizzy, wild mane pulled away from her forehead by a blue headdress. She is cracking seeds between her frail front teeth. A small cooler rests between her legs, from which she pulls out an empanada. Carlos takes out his wallet, and Tyler visualizes himself back on the bus, sees the wallet falling out of his too-loose front pocket. He tries to remember how much money was inside. Most of it.

A sudden tapping startles him out of his thoughts. A sinewy, sepia-skinned African, his face too thin for his bulging, ice-white eyes, thrusts a wooden stick with several necklaces up to Tyler's window. The necklaces are made of shells and dyed stones; some have colorful pendants, others tiny plastic charms. None of them look well made. None could ever arouse Tyler's interest.

The man speaks urgently, jangling the necklaces. Tyler smiles, says *obrigado,* and waves the universal sign for no. Undeterred, the man pulls open the passenger side door and enters the taxi.

"Desculpe! Obrigado! Não!" Tyler shouts. He looks out to the taxi driver and Carlos, too distracted by their conversations to notice.

"Italiano?" the man asks, his voice higher than expected, his tone pleading yet gentle.

Tyler's left hand reaches for the opposite door handle but the man grabs his right.

"What are you doing!" he shouts, hearing his loud American voice. He looks down at his wrist. The man is attempting to wrap a turquoise ribbon around it. "I don't want it."

He tries to shake himself free, but the man holds him tight as a parent holds a child about to cross into traffic.

"Fita do Senhor do Bonfim," the man says. *"Para a sorte boa. Gratis."*

Tyler nods skeptically. He has read about the superstitions of the church of Bonfim in his guidebook, even planned his itinerary to coincide with the *Lavagem do Bonfim,* the annual procession where the *Candomblé* priestesses wash the steps of the church in a ritual cleansing. In the infamous "Room of Miracles," wax arms, heads and legs suspend from the ceiling like a human butcher shop. Supposedly the faithful arrive every day with crutches, glass eyes, even kidneys in tow, symbolic offerings to inspire divine intervention for their sicknesses. The poor, desperate yokels. He can't begin to imagine what could inspire such collective folly.

"Gratis," the man insists. "Free. Good luck."

The man's fingers are rough and dry. Tyler looks into his eyes and sees a determination that's both disturbing and soothing. He knows that his refusal would wound the man's honor, so he allows his hand to go limp. Satisfied, the man sighs and continues the ritual, wrapping the turquoise scrap once, twice, three times around. He draws a solemn knot, then another, with an artist's calibrated attention, a slowness that is significant. When he is done, he looks up at Tyler with a smile that bares a mouth full of dazzling teeth.

He slaps Tyler's wrist. *"Sorte. Good luck. Mantê-lo em seu pulso."*

Tyler nods, says, *"Obrigado."*

The man picks up his stick and shakes the necklaces in front of him. "You look for something? *Para sua esposa?* Souvenir. *Cinco reais.* No expensive."

Of course, Tyler thinks, this is what it always comes down to. The man's ersatz generosity was nothing more than a sales pitch. He canvasses the cheap trinkets and suddenly imagines Gary there, sitting beside him, massaging the necklaces between his fingers and asking questions. Gary would pick out several to give as presents to the waitresses at the bar where he used to work, breathlessly recounting the story behind each of them as he dressed the girls' necks with his souvenirs. Tyler sighs. He will not buy anything from this man. *"Obrigado,"* he says, forcefully. *"Não."*

He opens the door as a warning. But the man simply shrugs his shoulders. *"De nada, senhor,"* the man says, tenderly patting Tyler's hand. "Next time. *Boa noite.*"

Tyler watches the peddler hobble away to the other side of the road and plunk himself on the ground beside the cracked husk of an ornate, narrow door frame. He adjusts the necklaces on his stick but otherwise looks oblivious. Frenzied pigeons jostle around his feet for the remaining scraps of dough that the old woman has thrown. Carlos has crossed back to join the driver. The two street people immerse in conversation.

Tyler and Gary had spent their last night together in New York on the roof deck of Gary's building, among the wicker lounge chairs and oblong Formica table Gary had salvaged from an Avenue D Dumpster. Gary liked the roof deck, even in the middle of winter. *Easier to receive up there,* he'd say, and Tyler would ask, *Receive what?* And Gary would say *the universe* or some other abstraction and Tyler would shake his head and sigh.

Gary had brought up a bottle of pear schnapps and a couple of shot glasses. The January air was sharp and clean; Tyler felt its bite on his skin. They sat on the broken loungers, their butts scraping against the ground, and looked out into the patchy sea of an East Village dusk.

"Don't send me a postcard," Gary said. "I hate postcards."

"These chairs," Tyler said, adjusting his ass and sighing.

"They have character." Gary liked that word. Everything he owned had a story behind it. They clinked glasses. "Three weeks," he said, and Tyler could sense him pondering the weight of it. "Have fun, babe."

"Are you worried?" Tyler asked.

Gary downed the rest of his shot and looked up at the gloaming sky. "You seem to want me to be."

"I don't know," Tyler said, his eyes tilting up.

"Tell me something." Gary reached over to Tyler's side, searching for Tyler's hand with his own without looking away from the sky. "What do you see up there?"

Tyler looked up. The light was getting dim. He could make out clouds, a couple of faint stars. "You want me to say something poetic," he said.

"Just tell me what you see."

"You want me to carve out shapes. To see beyond what's there. Use my inner eye."

Gary laughed. *Pretentious shit,* Tyler thought.

"It's a simple question. Why are you getting mad?"

"Just tell me what you see and I'll agree with you, okay?"

Gary squeezed his hand extra hard: a sign. And then, when he turned to look at him, Tyler could swear there was something in his expression, something promising or else threatening, only it was getting dark, and he wasn't sure what.

"Just answer the question." Gary's voice was still calm.

"I see nothing." He shook his hand free and reached for the schnapps bottle. "Absolutely nothing."

Gary sighed. He put his arms behind his head and stared up, even more mesmerized. Tyler handed him a refilled shot glass.

"Here's to nothing." Gary lifted his glass to toast. He sounded both resigned and amused.

"To nothing," Tyler repeated.

Several minutes pass. Carlos lingers in conversation with the taxi driver and the other loitering men. Tyler wonders what the hell they're waiting for. The bus isn't here. It's gone, along with his wallet. He's tired, aggravated, grimy, and prickly. He has become an afterthought to these curbside gossips. When they return to the hotel he will complain to Reginaldo. He exits the cab and marches purposefully toward them.

"What's going on?" he asks.

"Oi!" Carlos says, looking down to Tyler's wrist. "I see you have been initiated."

"What are we waiting for?" His tone is strained, but he doesn't care.

"Make three wishes and don't remove it," Carlos continues. "When it falls off, your wishes will be granted."

"I want to return to the hotel." The others stare at him without comment, but he can sense, behind their serene expressions, a desire to say something. To scold him.

"Your bus has continued to Igatapipe," Carlos says. "The driver will return on this route once more tonight. So we are waiting here."

"I'd rather return to the hotel."

Carlos's eyebrows shrivel toward his eyes. "Are you sure? We don't mind waiting."

"I mind," Tyler says. "I'm through waiting."

"And your wallet?" Carlos's expression gets even dewier. It infuriates Tyler, this look. He's seen it before, on Gary's face, this patronizing resignation, this nauseating disappointment, as if he were a petulant seven year old demanding pizza for breakfast and Gary the wise father resisting. Judgment has been rendered. By refusing to stay, he is somehow letting Carlos down.

"My wallet is history. Let's go."

Carlos sighs and explains the situation to the driver. The driver flicks his cigarette onto the curb, nods his head to the others who offer their farewells. The three of them head back to the cab.

"You should visit," Carlos says, pointing to the scrap around Tyler's wrist.

"What?"

"The *igreja*. The Church of Bonfim. Interesting place. Many superstitious people."

"Without a doubt." Tyler sniggers. "It's on my itinerary."

He looks across the street. The wild-haired woman is still there, cracking her seeds, and farther down the road, walking away from them, the necklace peddler, his skin flickering like a phantom in the streetlight. As they enter the cab Tyler looks ahead, and sees the peddler, seemingly oblivious to traffic, lurching himself out into the street—an action so absurd it seems inconceivable. His brain attempts to process the inevitable sequence that follows: the honk, the agonizing shriek of brakes locking, wheels ripping into asphalt. The brittle silence of contact, the spin of the peddler's body into the air, then gravity, claiming its right, the crackle of shells and twirling pendants, the soft thud of a human skull against the ground.

They rush out of the taxi. Bystanders in the square mobilize into the street. The driver of the vehicle, a bushy man with discolored skin, leaps out of his car, shouting and gesturing obscenely. He swats his forehead with his palm and walks around the far side of his car.

The crowd multiplies. Carlos, wearing the most prestigious-looking uniform, motions everyone away from the body. The peddler lies facedown on the ground, his pose eerily relaxed. He may as well be lying in bed, Tyler thinks.

A cacophony of shouting fills the central ring. Tyler tries to inch closer but the taxi driver grabs hold of him, mumbling something that suggests moving no further. The drivers of the two cars directly behind the accident vehicle have rallied around the perpetrator in a show of sympathy. Tyler imagines them reassuring the man that his eyes have not played tricks; the African jumped in front of the car without provocation. To his right, the old woman has risen, pointing at the driver and cursing.

Tyler's heart beats faster. He feels unsettled, anxious, and also distant, like a sheet of plastic has been put up between him and the crowd. The discussions around him are heated and jumbled; he can make out so few words, other than *ambulância* and *polícia*. He wonders if the man is simply crazy. Did he not realize what he was doing?

Eric Sasson

Dazed, he decides to walk away from the commotion toward the illuminated square. A throng of cars slog in the resulting traffic. He scans down the line. About ten cars ahead, something so extraordinary. Could it be? It couldn't.

The bus. *His* bus. The same bus. The same driver wearing the brown Expos cap. Tyler closes his eyes and reopens them. Carlos had predicted it and still the sight disturbs him. He dashes nervously ahead, gesticulating with his hands. The driver is oblivious until he knocks hard on the glass.

"Desculpe me," he says, when the driver reluctantly opens the door.

"Senhor?"

"It's possible," Tyler says. "I may have left my wallet on this bus earlier."

"Ah, yes." A look of recognition rises on the man's face. "Mr. New York."

The man reaches over to his far side and pulls out Tyler's wallet from his bag. Tyler stares at it, confused, before accepting it. Seeing it in someone else's hand disorients him, as if he's not sure it belongs to him.

"I was going to return it tomorrow morning," the driver says.

Tyler's first thought is *Yeah, right* but then a second thought creeps into his mind. Maybe it's true. Maybe he can accept the driver at his word. He opens the wallet. Incredibly, his money is still there. He takes out two twenties and hands them to the driver.

"That's enough," the man says, taking one bill and smiling.

He thanks the driver repeatedly before walking away. The wallet feels heavy in his pocket, heavier than he imagined. He walks back to the accident scene. A few of the onlookers are gathering the man's necklaces, pooling them in a pile by his feet. The peddler is faceup;

Tyler wonders whether others have turned him or he managed on his own. The man's face shows no signs of pain. His large, absorbing eyes look up to the sky, and Tyler thinks of Gary, back home, and his own baffling, incessant stargazing. The joy this simple act could bring to his boyfriend's face was incomprehensible.

How could he have forgotten? Gary had also given him a bracelet once. They were sitting at a beach-side bar on Long Island, getting drunk on blood orange margaritas. It was their second date; Gary had convinced him to phone in sick from work. A gorgeous, salty day in June when the sunlight seemed to have no end. They were soaking up a lazy afternoon when Gary looked at him playfully and took the bracelet out of his bag, wrapping it around Tyler's hand.

"I don't wear it anymore," he said, as if justifying his action. "I thought you'd like it. A woman named Esmerelda sold it to me. The round stones are Tibetan good luck charms."

"Thanks," Tyler said, a little drunk, a little unsure how he was supposed to react.

Instead of talking he headed out toward the water. The sand was hot so he jumped in, offering his body to the dubious safety of the ocean. The water was offensively cold; he trod circles with his arms to warm his body. He dunked his head and when he reemerged, he could see that Gary had turned—fully turned—his chair to stare at him. He could feel Gary's eyes on him, not just staring, more like the water had carried Gary's eyes to him, had brought them along, like microscopic fish, up to his wet, exposed body. He sensed, in the glistening pause of that moment, a current travel through him, a sharp, indescribable joy.

It took three months before he felt comfortable enough to mention the bracelet. "That was weird," he said, over the intimacy of takeout Thai on the floor. "For a second date, I mean."

"I had a feeling that there'd be more," Gary said.

"You could have scared me away."

"I had a feeling," Gary repeated. "I went with it."

The peddler is chuckling. First softly, but then his chuckles give way to song, as if he's sensed the spectacle he's caused and has decided to ease the tension. Tyler can't make out the words, and yet the melody is familiar, like a lullaby.

The wail of approaching sirens signals the small crowd to disperse. Tyler finds Carlos and the taxi driver waiting for him alongside the curb.

"Where did you go?" Carlos asks him.

Tyler takes the wallet out of his pocket and waves it in the air.

"You found the bus," Carlos says. He and the taxi driver share a look and a short laugh.

"Is the man alright?" Tyler asks.

"He'll be fine," Carlos says. "The idiot. Look at him singing. He thinks the whole thing is funny."

"It's easier to sing," Tyler says. "Now that he realizes he's alive."

Carlos laughs. "Welcome to Salvador! At least something good has come out of tonight, yes?"

Back at the hotel, Reginaldo takes his credit card and the bellboys listen eagerly as he and Carlos describe the events of the past hour. His story is pithy at first—he's not sure what to say, or how much English they understand, but then Carlos chimes in with more details, and suddenly Tyler finds himself getting more animated as well, allowing for more specifics. He likes watching their eyes expand as he speaks. They share a laugh and Carlos pats him on the back.

Carlos gathers his bags and together they head up to his room.

After a small tour, the two men shake hands. Tyler hands him ten *reais* which Carlos accepts graciously.

He should be exhausted and yet he's not sure he can sleep just yet. He sees the phone beside the bed and realizes he could call Gary. Yes, of course. He'll call Gary. He has a lot to tell him now.

"Hey." Gary's voice is steady, reassuring. "What time is it there?"

"You knew it was me," Tyler says.

"I had a hunch. Everything alright?"

He feels a fresh rumbling inside his chest, something eager to get out. "I lost my wallet. On a bus. And then . . ." Tyler stops himself midsentence. This isn't the story that needs to be told. Not now, not anymore. That story would not explain how he felt. The simple, flat truth of a wallet lost and found wouldn't convey what he needed to tell Gary. "I bought you a necklace," he says instead, the lie swimming out of his mouth.

"Wait a sec, what about your wallet?"

"This local guy," Tyler says, and as he speaks, the man begins to take shape in his mind, tenuously at first, but then vividly. "With pumpernickel skin."

"Are you sure you're okay?"

Tyler pictures the man holding the necklace up to his eyes, so he can see it more clearly. "His wife makes them. It's citrine and turquoise and it has these tiny, translucent shells. He found the shells on a special beach, twenty miles north. They're pretty unique, Gary. They look like tiny planets."

Gary's voice is placid, honey soaked. "Sounds pretty special."

"I'll be home soon." Tyler hears himself out loud, amazed that these, of all words, are the ones he's chosen to say.

"I know," Gary says. "Listen. Tyler?" Gary's voice lowers. "The new job? Not looking so good, babe. I have this idea. Maybe start my own business."

Tyler laughs. "Sure. When I get back, we'll talk about it."

They whisper soft good nights and Tyler hangs up the phone. He looks down at his wrist, tugs at the ribbon, testing how secure it feels. Tomorrow, he tells himself, as he begins to unpack, tomorrow he will journey to the Church of Bonfim. He will wander the dusty streets of Pelourinho in the scorching midday sun, let the colors and smells of the sacred present invade him. He will search and search until he finds that man, his wide-eyed phantom, hunched over a stool, singing a recycled lullaby, crafting a necklace that did not exist until Tyler had described it to his boyfriend over a transatlantic conversation, which is really nothing more than electric currents traveling, as if by dogged faith, via wires, across distances unfathomable, back and forth, in an endless and instantaneous symphony of energy.

He will find that man, lift up his creation, and see, for the first time, what his eyes could not see beforehand.

THE WORLD NEEDS EVERY BODY

How typical that the flight from JFK to Fort Lauderdale on that Passover eve was full of Jews. Specifically, young Jewish couples with small children. Less typical, perhaps, that the couple seated next to Bernie appeared to be "Black Hat," sporting the clothes and accoutrements synonymous with the ultrareligious Orthodox sects that clustered in the nooks of certain Brooklyn neighborhoods. When Bernie approached his row, the young wife, her Finnishly pale hair held up in a black head covering, was balancing her donut-faced boy up on her lap like he was an oversize bowling league trophy.

She was in his aisle seat, already a bad sign. Bernie pictured the next three hours trying to fake his way through the series of smiles expected of those seated beside infants. He imagined small hands grasping at his eyeglasses, cute rhyming couplets of nonsense spilling out of the mother's mouth in the exaggerated singsong tone reserved for the newly born and mentally challenged. Worst of all, he imagined three hours of nonstop bawling, with a mother too tired or indifferent to do anything about it.

Just last year, when his parents declared themselves too old to attempt any more Passovers in Brooklyn ("We have elevators in Miami," his mother said. "You can wheel the shopping cart all the way to your car. Did I mention it will be eighty degrees?"), Bernie had reluctantly agreed to take a week off from work and celebrate with them. And on that flight he'd encountered a similar couple across the aisle, also Orthodox but a bit less obvious about it, all too eager to subject the entire plane to the coyote screeches of their two-year-old daughter. Bernie had watched the wife shift her child from one shoulder to the other, barely acknowledging the girl's caterwauls while her husband watched episodes of *Lost* on his portable DVD player, pretending his earphones drowned out the noise. The young student seated beside Bernie, a somber biomedical engineering major, finally got fed up and asked, as courteously as Bernie imagined anyone could, if the woman would be so kind as to take her daughter for a walk to quiet her down. The blood sucked out of the young mother's face; she decided to take offense for all mothers everywhere. "Fine," she said, making it clear it was anything but. "I'll take a walk. But just so you know, it's very insulting what you're suggesting." When the engineering major insisted she meant no offense and was only trying to study for a final, the husband, now free of his headphones, said, "One day when you're a mother, you'll understand. You just don't ask a woman to do this."

All the while Bernie said nothing. His instinct to tell this clown that you don't ask an entire flight to sit through your child's incessant screams was trumped by his instinct to mind his own business. Only when they were deplaning did he whisper to the engineering major: *You did the right thing.*

The young woman scooted over to allow Bernie to take his seat. Her husband boarded a few minutes later: a black yarmulke and the round, pasty face of his Eastern European ancestors. His beard was scraggly and uncertain of itself, the hairs still too inexperienced to grow neatly. Neither of them could have been over twenty-two.

Bernie sat patiently as they passed the child between them, and then the equipment to handle the child: the blanket, the bottle, the snack bag, the bib. He felt like he was in the middle of a supermarket delivery, stuck between the truck and the conveyor belt leading down to receiving.

The husband sat down but not before jam-packing the overhead bin; he apologized halfheartedly but made no attempt to fix it, ceding responsibility to the attendant. The plane door closed, followed by the turn-off-your-electronic-devices announcement. Bernie tried to read his book but his concentration kept drifting. The couple was quibbling about things left behind that should or should not have been brought. They both spoke uncomfortably fast, as if their words were in a race to see which ones would come out first. Why did so many orthodox Ashkenazic Jews speak so quickly? Was it survival of the fittest—since it was difficult, in their typically large families, to get a word in edgewise? Bernie himself was Sephardic, and while his parents were certainly loud and had brilliantly thick accents, they didn't speak nearly as quickly.

Despite the announcement, the young husband was still on his cell phone, delivering the precise steps needed to drop off a package at FedEx. The wife, meanwhile, kept repeating how much better looking her son had gotten now that he was bigger. "Yossi. Yossi. Shimon looks so much cuter, right? Right? A *lot* cuter. A million times cuter. He's aging like a prince. Right, my prince? You're my prince, yes, my prince!"

Bernie sighed. He decided to avoid eye contact with both the boy and his parents. It wasn't really considered rude to avoid conversation with the people beside you on a plane. After all, this was not a pairing of choice but of circumstance. Bernie had a particularly strong aversion to this couple, and not just because of the child, who was, truth be told, sufficiently cute and not all that noisy yet. If he had to pin it down, he supposed it had to do with their ostentatious Judaism, their in-your-face devoutness, which was for him, as a lapsed Jew and even more so as a gay man, somewhat offensive. Not the devoutness itself but rather their small and yet conspicuous attempts to break free of it and connect with the secular world. If the cell phone were their only transgression, Bernie would have probably let it slide, although for people who regularly follow rules, they could have done a better job of listening to the captain. But the wife was reading *Us Weekly,* a fix for celebrity junkies, full of the kind of spineless gossip and innuendo that her rabbi would strictly forbid as egregious examples of the "evil tongue." Worse than that, the husband had his own copy of a rag, an *InStyle* with Sandra Bullock in a bikini on the cover. The man had no right to look at women in bikinis, ever. To fully complete this irony, when her child reached for her magazine, the mother swiftly swatted his palm and said, "No, *bubbe,* you're not allowed to look at magazines like this." Bernie almost snorted. As if she was!

And then—dear God then—the mother had the chutzpah to take out a package of Godiva chocolate pearls and pop them into her mouth. Now Bernie may have been a lapsed Jew, but he certainly knew that as of nine o'clock that morning, all consumption of leavened products was strictly verboten. And while a case could be made that the chocolates were not technically *chametz*, there was no way—in hell—that they were kosher for Passover. Not a chance. And yet here she was, *in public,* eating them! And the husband said nothing. In fact, he munched on a few himself.

Bernie wanted to shout at them. The only excuse these all-or-nothing Jews had going for them was that at least they walked the walk. If they had the audacity to pooh-pooh all other forms of Judaism, not accept converts, claim themselves as the only purveyors of truth and

God's will, strongly condemn homosexuality, et cetera, then they had to—*had to*—follow their own code, at least publicly. Clearly these two were engaging in these obvious no-no's simply because they were traveling alone, without the watchful eye of parents or cousins or others from their clan who would've kept them in line. Little did they realize they had someone in the know sitting right next to them, taking mental notes of every bad thing they were doing, gathering these sins up to expose their hypocrisy once and for all.

It was this same hypocrisy that made Bernie hesitate to make the trip to Florida in the first place. His parents' excuses notwithstanding, the unspoken reason for celebrating Passover away from Brooklyn was the opportunity to escape the probing eyes of the community and relax. In Miami, the seder would be a speedy affair, not the four-hour slog they'd often be subjected to at their cousins' houses in Midwood or Little Neck. The kosher for Passover rules, while not exactly relaxed, would allow for Starbucks coffee and gum and other items without the official seal to remain in the house. And there would be none of that "no electricity" business; his father wasn't about to give up a basketball game on ESPN just because it was a holy day.

But why not go full out, then, Bernie wondered. Why not have the seder—even two seders—and then just say fuck it on day three and get a Croissan'Wich from Burger King? For what were they maintaining this charade, other than their dubious sense of tradition? Even if he hadn't told them outright, his parents knew he wasn't about to keep the rest of Passover once he flew back to New York. They knew it, but they pretended not to know it, which made him think of the way they dealt with his sexuality, asking the barest minimum of questions, extending no formal invitations to his boyfriend to join them, and yet still not making a comment that in any way might come across as offensive. It was like they enjoyed their middle-of-the-roadness too much—as if somehow their moderation made them more reasonable, neither crazy strict like the Orthodox nor wanton and untethered like the reformists.

When the captain announced that they were second in line for takeoff, Bernie purposely trained his eye on the husband, to see if he would bother saying the *Tefilat HaDerech,* the prayer said right before traveling. No dice. Apparently Sandra Bullock's marital woes were more important. Bernie decided to whisper an impromptu prayer himself, something small and simple about safe takeoffs and landings and a moderate measure of turbulence, *nothing too scary, God, thanks*.

The plane took off and Bernie tried to disregard the quick suck of gravity in his stomach. The first and last twenty minutes of a flight, he knew, were always the most dangerous. Funny enough, the more he flew, the more frightened he became of flying. He wouldn't even dream of distracting himself with his book, or the in-flight magazine, not yet. No, he had to sit there and close his eyes and just try to relax. He thought of his father, a man often told by doctors in his youth to close his eyes and relax. They certainly needn't concern themselves with that now. The old man did nothing but relax these days. He'd sit in the apartment down in Hallandale, parked in front of the TV all day, every day, no matter how gorgeous the weather outside, a shift between recliner and couch his only stab at switching things up. *Everybody Loves Raymond* and *The King of Queens*. The History Channel and Fox News, and occasionally, Rachel Maddow, to spice things up. How could someone survive on such an endless stream of mindless diversion? Okay, the man was old, and tired, but could this be all there was left to live for? This, and tradition?

When Bernie opened his eyes he saw that the entire row to his left was looking in his direction. He pictured snot hanging from his nose, and then he remembered: the infant. You *had* to look at a baby in your row. You had to smile at it and gurgle and make noises, even if, like the man across the aisle from Bernie, you were a 260 pound piano-delivery type with muttonchops and a tattoo of two wolverines fucking on your meaty bicep.

Bernie pushed on the button and reclined so as to give row 19 a better view. Shimon's mother had lifted his little shirt and was making raspberries against his stomach. And Shimon was laughing. And row 19 was laughing with him. How novel of them all.

An odor wafted up the aisle, a mix of jet fuel and overcooked cabbage. The intercom buzzed and one of the attendants made the "We've reached ten thousand feet" announcement, but the passengers were well ahead of her, already playing with their electronic devices. Several had even gotten out of their seats in anticipation of the "The seat belt sign has been turned off" announcement, which wouldn't follow for several minutes.

Checking his watch, Bernie figured it was now safe to read. He took out his book. Yossi and his wife were discussing surprises. She didn't look very happy.

"You never surprise me with gifts," she said, holding Shimon out in Superman pose in front of her. "You can buy me earrings, you know. Take me to a nice dinner, instead of spending all that time with your cousin Hamish."

"He was depressed, Rachel," Yossi said. "I was doing a mitzvah."

"Your wife is the *biggest* mitzvah," Rachel said. "A wife deserves everything."

Yossi rolled his eyes. "What's wrong with those earrings?"

"You're a disgusting person," Rachel said. "Seriously, just disgusting."

But Bernie could tell her heart wasn't in it, because not two seconds later Yossi made a joke, which sent Rachel into hysterics.

Soon after, the beverage cart rolled down the aisle, the two flight attendants both sporting the fake-courteous smirk of workers who hated the people they were serving. Bernie badly needed some caffeine because his four hours of sleep were catching up with him. By the time they reached row ten, however, a spat of turbulence rocked the plane, bad enough to elicit a few "oohs" from the crowd and for Bernie to drop his book and close his eyes again. The captain announced a suspension of the in-flight service, and Bernie's left leg started trembling. It was not a good sign. Not good at all. His last moments on earth, spent beside an Orthodox couple and their baby, a couldn't-be-more-blatant reminder of the many ways he had failed his parents. If he hadn't been so frozen with fear, he would've laughed at the irony.

As abruptly as it started, the rattling settled down. Bernie took a deep breath and opened his eyes. The captain was simply erring on the side of caution, and service soon resumed. Yossi and Rachel were discussing a cousin's recent wedding.

"She should have picked something less ambitious," Rachel said. "I mean, she lost ten pounds but the dress needed her to lose twenty."

When the perky brunette approached his row, Bernie ordered a Coke Zero and some cookies. Yossi postponed his response to his wife to address her.

"What kind of snacks do you have?"

"Pretzels, peanuts, and cookies," the woman replied.

"I'll take pretzels," Yossi said. "And peanuts. One of each."

Rachel wanted water, preferably her own bottle, but if not, then in a cup without ice. *They don't clean their ice,* she whispered to Yossi, as the woman tended to their requests.

When the snacks were in Yossi's hand, Rachel grabbed them from him to inspect the ingredients on the back of the package. After microscopic perusal, she handed just the pretzels to Yossi. "You realize that Triangle K isn't kosher, right," Rachel said. "It's supervised by a reform rabbi."

"Who told you this? All the *hashgachot* are Orthodox."

"Please, Yossi, it's *common knowledge*. Don't argue with me. Eat the pretzels, but no peanuts. Sorry."

"If Triangle K wasn't kosher they would have sent everybody an email."

Rachel's eyes dilated into perfect circles of outrage. "You *can't* eat it, Yossi," she said. "Not in front of our child. I forbid it."

Up until now her sanctimony had only mildly irritated Bernie. But this, at last, was the final straw. He could not, would not, let this last remark go unanswered. "May I ask you a question?"

Rachel seemed surprised, and somewhat amused, that Bernie was addressing her. "I'm sorry?"

"Does it matter?" Bernie said.

"Excuse me?" Rachel was pouting. Yossi looked taken aback. "Does what matter?"

"Does it matter that it's Triangle K," Bernie said. He could feel something in him stirring, something vital, more energizing than the caffeine. "Because it's Erev Pesach, so you can't eat either of them anyway."

Rachel and Yossi passed each other a look of incredulity.

"You're Jewish?" Yossi said.

Bernie smirked. He wasn't dressed like they were, so somehow this allowed for their presumptions. "I am."

"Peanuts are kosher for Passover," Yossi said.

"Sorry, no. *Kosher for Passover* peanuts are kosher for Passover," Bernie said, proud of himself. "Airline peanuts are not. And pretzels are one hundred percent *chametz*."

Yossi laughed, nervously. Shimon's eyes stared at Bernie with a curious wonder. Rachel tried to distract him by cradling his head against her shoulder but the boy wouldn't have any of it.

"The holiday begins at sundown." Rachel looked at Yossi, her face a touch pinker than before.

"True," Bernie said, rubbing at an imaginary beard on his chin. "But the restriction not to eat *chametz* began around nine this morning. And you both know this. So let me ask, *since* you both know this, why do you even argue about these supervision details when the entire thing is moot anyway?"

Rachel's face tensed, like she was holding back a sneer. "I'm not sure why you care what we're doing."

Bernie nodded. "I care because he's wearing a yarmulke and you're discussing kosher rules out loud. So since *you've* decided to discuss this in public, I thought I'd comment on your apparent disregard for the laws of Passover while you openly argue about who is more holy. And while I'm at it, I hope you realize those magazines you're reading aren't exactly kosher either. They're frivolous. Immodest. A big sin to look at."

Rachel blushed, her gaze turning squarely toward her tray table.

"A regular Maimonides we have next to us," Yossi said.

"Hardly," Bernie said. "I just think that if you're going to be devout, then be devout. Otherwise you can't very well criticize a reformist supervision, can you? That's the problem with you Ultra Orthodox: you make all these decrees but as soon as someone's not looking you're doing your own thing. You can't decry abortion, rage against gay marriage, and believe you're somehow more 'chosen' than other people if you're—"

"I'm sorry," Rachel interrupted."But how do you know what we believe?"

"I know," Bernie said. "Trust me, I used to believe things too. But then I didn't see the point. From the looks of it, I've made the right decision."

"Is it because you're gay?" Yossi said.

Bernie shot up straight in his chair. "Excuse me?"

"That you stopped believing, is it because you're gay?"

Bernie shuddered. Had a rainbow flag suddenly appeared on his forehead? "I didn't stop believing," Bernie said. "And that's none of your business."

"You're right. It's not." Yossi smiled. "But we were discussing things, so I thought I might ask."

"It makes no difference if I am or not," Bernie said.

"I'm pretty sure it does," Yossi said. "Even if you want to think it doesn't."

"You're right," Rachel said, glaring at Yossi before turning to address Bernie. "Let's drop it. I'm sorry we've upset you. Thanks for pointing things out to us. We should have been more careful."

"It's okay," Bernie said, shocked that the argument had ended so quickly, so gracefully. He had thought of a few more well-crafted sentences to foist upon them, and now he wouldn't have the opportunity. Because Rachel had apologized. And Rachel looked embarrassed. And now Bernie *felt* embarrassed too, because he had embarrassed them, had forced them to apologize for their behavior. What was he doing, being so strident with a couple of strangers? A bunch of youngsters, no less, and here he was, so judgmental. He imagined his father later that evening, insisting that the seder plate be lifted for "Vehe She'amdah," or his mother, forcing everyone to cover their glasses of wine as her husband recited the ten plagues. And yet, after all that pomp and circumstance, right back they'd go, to TiVo-ed American Idol, to Scrabble online. What joy did they derive from this insistence on the minutest details?

Bernie felt the base of his neck itch. His mind drifted back to certain memories: how when he was seven years old, and his father, still spry and his head full of hair, had carried him on his shoulders all the way to temple on Simchat Torah, the most joyous holiday of the year. Bernie would stay until the end of the service, when he'd be guaranteed an amazing Technicolor bag of treasures: Tangy Taffies, Sugar Daddies, Charleston Chews. His bar mitzvah at the Kotel in Jerusalem, how proud his parents were when he went up to read the *parshah*, how he read for the other three boys who couldn't perform the mitzvah themselves. Their yearly Rosh Hashanah feast, how he, his brother, and his sister-in-law would gather around his parents' table, noshing on the strange combination of fish heads and leeks, sweet squash jelly and apples dipped in honey—gatherings that abruptly ended when his brother found a cushy job in Maryland two years ago.

Odd that these instances of observance would suddenly return to him, odder still that the memories, although festive, were only stinging him further. Perhaps because his parents had settled in Florida so soon after his brother's move. He'd often wondered about the timing—had they been too embarrassed to face their temple friends in New York with no one left to represent the family but a rapidly aging unmarried son? But then he thought of Yossi's speculation, and how the question had made him cringe. Who was it who was really embarrassed? And if all of this bothered him that much, shouldn't he be asking his parents these questions, instead of grilling the young couple?

Not long after, Shimon started screaming. Bernie blamed his iPhone; he had taken it out to distract himself and should have never tempted the boy with a toy. But Shimon wasn't looking at the phone. He was looking at Bernie. No, more than looking at him, looking *through* him, peering into him, and crying, crying, crying. Bernie hated the sound. The boy was lending his voice to the judgment Bernie already felt. He felt bad enough about his little tirade and now he had upset the boy too.

Yossi and Rachel were fumbling through their arsenal for a solution. "Give him the bottle," Yossi said. He looked puzzled, anxious.

But Shimon didn't want the bottle. He threw it to the floor. He refused the spoon with the applesauce; he tossed the blanket. Even when Bernie got up to let Rachel into the aisle, Shimon wouldn't stop screaming, a chilling vibrato that shook Bernie's insides like the pounding of a mallet against a giant bell. He had turned away from his mother to face Bernie, his pudgy arms reaching out in a concentrated skirmish of yearning.

Rachel tried cooing. She lifted the boy high into the air. Nothing was working. And then she looked down at Bernie, his book half covering his face.

"Will you take him?" she asked.

Bernie looked up to her. He pointed back at himself incredulously.

"Yes. He wants you. Will you take him?" And the look on her face was desperate, but also sympathetic.

Bernie hesitated. He looked toward Yossi. The man nodded his head. He looked back to Rachel, and back again to Yossi.

"Please," Yossi said. "It might quiet him."

Bernie knew he couldn't refuse them, not after all that had been said. But he wasn't good with babies. They unnerved him, upset his sense of balance. He remembered his young nephews squirming in his arms during his halfhearted attempts to embrace them, certain they could sense his ineptitude. And yet Shimon's bawls were only increasing, and Rachel looked insistent, more confident in him than he was in himself. More willing to trust.

He reached out his hands and let Rachel place Shimon between them. The boy was lighter than he expected. Lighter, but still substantial. Within a few seconds the screaming stopped, and Shimon's face opened from a purple-red ball of rage, opened like a flower blooming in rapid motion. Bernie could not stop staring at the boy's eyes. So large and bright, so much swallowing of the world ahead of him, so much less shame to squint about. Our eyes narrow as we get old, Bernie thought, because we can't take in as much as we used to.

Bernie stood up to let Rachel back in the row.

"He likes you," she said, her voice rising. She stared at her child with unbridled enthusiasm. Yossi, too, seemed rapt.

"I don't know," Bernie said. "I'm not used to kids."

"Neither are we," Yossi said.

Bernie watched as Shimon tried to make sense of his face. He wondered what the boy was thinking. Had Shimon sensed the uneasiness? It was ridiculous to imagine the boy as a peacemaker. It was stupid to give him powers of intuition his age simply didn't allow for. And yet, as Bernie and he poured into each other, he felt something. Something that he couldn't just dismiss, even if he'd have a hard time explaining it.

For what might have been three minutes, or five, or ten, they sat there, man and child, sizing each other up. Bernie tried to keep the goo-goo-gaga-ing to a minimum, but he couldn't help himself. And then the captain announced preparation for landing. He mentioned a recent series of tornadoes in the Miami area, said they might have to brace themselves for some rough patches.

Bernie closed his eyes. Shimon was still in his lap, resting against his right shoulder, and Rachel was rubbing the boy's hair. The bumps came, mostly mild, until one of them was sharp and sudden. Bernie felt his stomach drop.

He was breathing through his mouth when something reached for his right hand. At first he thought it was the boy. But when he opened his eyes, he knew it couldn't be. He looked down. Rachel had grabbed hold of him. She was squeezing his hand. Her palm felt clammy and warm at the same time.

"Turbulence is a great equalizer," Bernie said, and let out a chuckle. He didn't know how to react to Rachel's hand. Her touching him, in full view of her husband. A great sin, a fat, obvious transgression. Could Yossi see? Could he know what was happening and still say nothing?

The plane was going to land, somehow. Bernie looked out the window. All he could see was clouds. No water, no land. Just clouds—fleshy, gluttonous, difficult clouds. Only the pilot knew where they were. He had to trust that the pilot knew.

The turbulence continued, spurts of bumps that sent the plane rattling. Rachel continued to hold on to his hand. Bernie turned, pretending to look at Shimon's head resting on his shoulder, but instead caught Rachel's eyes, looking back at him with intent. Her face was peaceful, her eyes flat and hazy.

"The world needs every body," Rachel whispered. "Each and every one of us."

Bernie smiled. Was she patronizing him? Or was this just wishful thinking on the young girl's part? He wondered if he could disagree with her. He wondered if he could, just then, shake her hand out of his, say something back to that. But he couldn't. Instead, he just held on tighter.

THE MARGINS OF TOLERANCE

We used to have sex on the dining table. We used to drop to our knees in the kitchen, fuck like convicts against the bathroom walls. The curtains of our apartment in Chelsea would be only half-drawn in whatever room we were in, a mocking gesture toward modesty. It made Parker hot to think one of our neighbors might be watching.

But then we moved out to Paragon, New Jersey. Two months ago we settled into our charming house, with all the accoutrements: picket fence, backyard, trimmed hedges, cheerful neighbors. A house, because houses mean responsibility, maturity, normalcy. To be fair, a *gay* house, at least on the inside, with wainscoting and accent walls, Barcelona chairs and Lucite chandeliers. Paragon is known to be a bastion of liberalism, a community as averse to Bible-thumpers as any zip code in Manhattan.

So it shocked me when, within a few weeks, our fucking was sequestered to the bedroom. "It seems pretentious, don't you think?" Parker said when I made a comment about it. It was a Saturday night, and we were retouching paint on the molding. "Like we're trying to be these wild young studs."

But Parker had never been okay with sex in the bedroom before.

The new house had large windows in almost every room, practically floor to ceiling. "I love all the light," Parker said, when we'd scoped it out that first time.

We'd first discussed moving six months earlier. Parker took me out to Babbo, a fancy Italian place in the Village, and with a mouthful of beef cheeks said that it was time for us to settle down, become a part of the fabric of society. To which I replied that our fabric choices seemed appropriate enough thus far, as I arched a brow and took a sip of Amarone. *You know what I mean,* he said, revealing those sexy folds in his forehead that still bewitched me after all these years together.

Of course I knew what he meant. When you reach your late thirties, certain things are expected of you. Parker and I had already done the bar circuit, the clubs, the parties, Fire Island, Provincetown. We had tweaked, X-ed, G-ed, snorted, sniffed, passed out, blacked out, ménaged and beyond. Sometimes we still did, but four years into our relationship, we knew that, for the most part, this was behind us. Still, I had to wonder what was ahead. When Parker said settling down, was he expecting us to follow the model of straight society? Were we going to tie the knot now, raise a family in the 'burbs, scope out pre-K schools, and have bimonthly bowling nights with the Jensens and McGuires?

He asked me to come with him to inspect some towns near the GWB the following day, and I paused, swirling my glass a few times. Then I told him I'd love to. I may have been ambivalent, but I was moved. He was picturing the rest of his life with me. Which was pretty wild. Parker's amazing. How many times have I heard it from friends: *You're lucky to have Parker in your life. He's so solid, so responsible.* I've tried not to read too much between the lines. But they're right: Parker provides. Parker plans, and things turn out well.

He also makes seven times as much as I do. Which is probably why I always felt like I didn't have the same say as he did in making these decisions. I was concerned about falling victim to suburban malaise, but it reassured me that while Parker didn't discuss his tendencies much—his preference for being tied up, or the fair share of anal cream-pie and bukkake videos in his porn collection—it never stopped him from indulging in them with gusto. We also had a six-month rule, where each of us was allowed one night of outside-the-relationship sex. Condoms strictly enforced, no repeats, or follow-up hey-how's-it-goings. He never mentioned taking any of this off the table.

It didn't take long to get used to the idea. We found the right house, the next-to-last nouveau Victorian on a cul-de-sac lined with elms that radiated wisdom. The house had an enormous sunroom in the back, which would serve as my studio. Then there was the planning: I hate to admit to such a cliché, but we were two gay men decorating our first home. Needless to say we were beyond excited, and Parker's smile—if one can still call something that large and radiant a smile—was euphoric and infectious. Watching him as he directed the movers, assigning each box to its appropriate destination—it was like he had been waiting for this opportunity all his life. Parker had grown up in the suburbs; I suppose this was sort of a return home for him. I closed my eyes: the air smelled woodsy, sharp, and cool. Birds were warbling in the trees. I felt soothed, and still, somewhat uneasy. Was this just Parker's fantasy, or could I share in it? Manhattan was noisy, and messy, but what if I were just as noisy and messy myself?

Later that day, Barbra and Stan Shiner appeared at our doorstep. We had waved hello to them a few times before, when we had come to take measurements on weekends. Stan was a hulking man, certainly a football player in his day. He shook our hands vigorously and his smile

THE MARGINS OF TOLERANCE

was warm and mellow. Barbra was a bit harder to appraise. She was tall and thin, her sunken, dark eyes both probing and uncertain, as if they bored deep into your soul but weren't sure what they saw there.

She had a bottle of Merlot in her hand, which she handed to Parker. "It's not a pie," she said. "But then again, this isn't Georgia."

"We figured you two for red drinkers," Stan said.

"We don't discriminate," I said, inviting them in.

"Neither do we, trust me," Stan said, and then laughed at his own joke.

"I love your color palette," Barbra said, as her eyes scanned across our living room. "So soothing."

"Thank you." Parker beamed. We had argued about the seafoam green, and he'd won.

"So," Stan said, clapping his hands together. "You guys up for dinner sometime? We'd love to have you over. Barbra makes a mean Beef Bourguignon."

"How's next Tuesday sound?" Barbra asked.

"Next Tuesday it is," Parker said. I nodded along, and the Shiners wished us the best of luck getting settled.

"My, aren't they pleasant," Parker said, grabbing two glasses once they had left.

I laughed. "Far too pleasant." I had unwrapped a recent work, a painting I jokingly entitled *When Hell Freezes Over,* a Chagallesque collage that included, among other scenes, a female priest presiding over a wedding of two male rabbis. I wanted to set it above the fireplace.

"Hmm," Parker said, holding a finger to his lips. "I don't really see it there. Do you?"

"It's basically in the same location it was at the apartment," I said.

Eric Sasson

"Maybe we should change things up a bit," Parker said. "New house and all. Plus wouldn't *Midnight Picture Show* look better with the Nakashima bench and the womb chair?"

"It's my favorite piece," I said.

"Of course." Parker reached for my shoulder and kissed my cheek. "Mine too. I just thought it would showcase better in the study. Much softer lighting there. But hey, artist knows best, after all."

I smiled, but inside I was cringing. Softer lighting, my ass. Still, it *would* look better in the study. "No. You're right," I said. I sorted through my other canvases. *Midnight Picture Show* featured a drive-in theater with mostly straight couples watching *Brokeback Mountain.* Some of the couples were making out. The figures were natural, the hues soft, almost muted, as if to suggest how ordinary the whole scene was.

"So what do you think?" I said.

"Of course. Exactly there," Parker said. He was busy rearranging the fruit in a bowl on our dining table and hadn't bothered to turn around. It angered me, but I said nothing.

"So you're okay with dinner?" he asked.

"What?"

"With Stan and Barbra."

"Oh," I said. "Of course."

When people ask me what kind of artist I am, I tell them the fucked-up directionless kind. I get bored easily. Primarily I paint, but I've dabbled in sculpture, and collage, even anime. Last year I designed a video game, the first gay-themed RPG I'm aware of. In it, you choose from an assortment of characters—gym queens to yuppie HRC lawyers to librarian-chic lesbians—and follow their journeys as they fight discrimination, eating disorders, bitchy friends and drag queens hogging up the stalls at the Roxy. Last year a gallery in Soho offered me a spot in an upcoming show. The promotional materials were going to describe me as a "new-wave provocateur." Looking up the other artists, I knew I couldn't allow myself to be pigeonholed. So I turned them down. Of course Parker was disappointed. *Imagine the exposure,* he said. What he meant, but didn't say, was how could I turn down the money the show might have brought in.

As for Parker, he works in midtown as the operations coordinator of a company responsible for the inspection of new claims. When a detergent company claims, for instance, that its formula is "even sudsier!" Parker sends his workers out to make sure that the formula is, in fact, sudsier. Not too long before our move I noticed Parker began accepting lots of invitations to corporate gatherings: potluck picnics, after-work drinks, weekend brunches. It baffled me, since Parker usually complained about his coworkers, like bleached-mustache Paula, his boss, or Long Island Andy, who added a *W* to words like dog and song. I didn't get why he wanted to be accepted by people he didn't particularly like, and I teased him about it.

"Houses are expensive, Chase," he said, taking me far too seriously. "And I'm due for a promotion."

I didn't challenge him on that. Of course I got the schmoozing. But I'd been to some of these events and Parker was faking it, shooting the shit about sports and cars like he really cared. It made me wonder if he'd ever give people enough credit to meet him on his own terms. How did he even know all that effort was necessary?

The first week passed like a summer storm. When we weren't filling up bookshelves or grouting bathroom tiles, Parker saw to learning more about our neighbors. Lou was the manager of the deli three blocks over, and Molly our dry cleaner had a crush on Anderson Cooper. We had a Turkish restaurant not too far away, although the owners, apparently, were Armenian. There was something seductive about this newfound sense of community. I could see why Parker liked it.

Parker even stopped by the local Episcopal church and picked up a flyer about an upcoming bake-off. "The revenge of my white-chocolate brownies!" he said, while mounting a sconce on the wall above the sofa. I asked him if the church ordained gay ministers.

"I'm not sure," he said. "But even if they don't, they will, one day."

"Ah," I said, somewhat shocked that he had found his way inside a church. We had never visited one when we lived in Chelsea. "One day."

"They just need time to acclimate," Parker said. And then he flashed his dimples. "Look, Chase. They'll like us more once they see we're really just like them."

I looked at him sideways. We weren't those types of gay men, the TV-sitcom-kindhearted-next-door-eunuchs who made the world safe for faggotry. No, we were *not* just like them. "Since when do we want to be?"

Parker looked back at me, long enough for me to catch the glint of unease in his eyes before he adjusted himself. He was laughing as he grabbed me from behind and kissed me on the neck. "You know what I mean."

I put on a friendly smirk. I did know. That was the problem.

That Tuesday we headed next door to the Shiners with a rhubarb cheesecake from the local bakery and a bottle of Prosecco. Stan greeted us, and we men exchanged hearty handshakes. He took us on a mini-tour while Barbra, poking a newly coiffed head from out of the kitchen, said she'd join us in a minute. The house was inoffensive and tasteful the way only a furniture catalog could be. Clean lines, lots of safe, potted plants, the occasional vaguely ethnic tchotchke, with a serigraph thrown in here and there to add accent and color. On the coffee table, an old *Vanity Fair* with Ellen DeGeneres on the cover. I wondered if the gesture was purposeful.

Barbra came out with a tray of plum wine fizzes. We sat on their couch, which was, Stan assured us, made of recyclable materials, although he didn't specify what kind. We chitchatted for a while before Barbra retreated to the kitchen. Then Parker got Stan into a discussion about the Giants, and how his office had season tickets on the thirty-yard line and he could easily score a pair. Stan laughed and said the Steelers were his boys but that he'd love to go sometime.

I couldn't help feeling relief when Barbra finally popped out from the kitchen. "Dylan! We're ready for dinner," she shouted.

A minute later a boy slumped down the stairs. Dylan Shiner was tall and broad-shouldered like his father, but his pale skin and jet-black eyes were all Barbra. His haircut was choppy and asymmetrical, but his clothes were safely Abercrombie. When Barbra told us he was thirteen, Parker protested that they both looked far too young to have a teenage child. I was also shocked, but more because Dylan seemed older at first. Upon second and third glance, though, I realized my initial impression was misleading. Tall as he was, there was something small about him; he took up a lot less space than his body would have you believe.

"Parker and Chase just moved in next door," Barbra said.

"So how long have you boys been together?" Stan asked.

"Almost four years," Parker said, looking at me to confirm the number.

"That's fantastic!" Barbra said. "I hope this isn't too personal, but have you guys thought about going to Massachusetts and tying the knot?"

Eric Sasson

Parker's eyes widened. "We've thought about it," I said. The safest response, I told myself. Just vague enough to be true.

"Of course," Barbra said. "One step at a time."

I nodded my head, imagining us the latest in a series of diversity exhibits the Shiners were putting on for their son. Had they invited the African-American couple last week? Were atheists next on the list?

"Dylan, honey, Chase is a painter," Barbra said, resting her palm on her son's closed fist once we were seated at the dinner table. Dylan looked at his mother, and then at me, through the hair covering his eyes. His lips tumbled into a smile, although I wasn't sure if it really was a smile, because his eyes seemed angry. Not just uncomfortable, which I could understand, but actually angry. "Dylan also likes to paint," Barbra said, sheepishly.

"So what, Mom," Dylan said. "I also like to watch TV."

Stan laughed, and then punched his son in the arm. "He also plays guitar, and he's a yellow belt in judo. A regular Renaissance man."

"Right," Dylan said, rolling his eyes. I had to stifle a laugh.

"We encourage him to try new things," Barbra said.

"But hey, no pressure," Stan added. "It's all about options, right? Not like when I grew up. At his age, after school, I did my homework and played stickball with my friends in the driveway. Or maybe some Atari. You remember Atari? Not like that anymore. They're doing a million different things now."

I nodded but didn't say anything. The more they talked about him, the more Dylan seemed to recede, slumping in his chair as if about to disappear under the table. Of course I understood his frustration. I looked over at Parker, wondering if he was feeling as uncomfortable as I was, but his body language was all sunny skies.

"Dylan's thinking about taking art history next semester," Barbra said.

"He might as well," Stan said. "Probably lots of cute girls in that class, right, D?"

Stan laughed nervously. Parker joined in while Barbra looked down at her plate. I caught Dylan glancing at me, his look a puzzling cross between fear and anticipation. I tried to put on a reassuring face, my adults-are-annoying-don't-worry-this-will-soon-be-over face, but it wasn't met with relief. If anything, his stares became even more intense.

After dinner Dylan took off upstairs and Parker got Stan into talking property taxes, so I joined Barbra in the kitchen to help with the coffee. I could hear Stan guffawing through the door as Barbra took out our cheesecake and sliced four perfect triangles. She was curious about our kitchen remodel, asking whether we were going to install a backsplash and what I thought about heated concrete floors, and even though I usually adored remodeling talk, I was still peeved. Was this my role now, to retire with the wives to the kitchen between courses?

"Don't mind Stan," Barbra said, shooting me a look of concern.

I wasn't sure why I was supposed to. "I really like your dress," I said. I had noticed it earlier, but now had a better view of it: a Bavarian housedress, with yellows brighter than I imagined Barbra normally wore.

"Thanks," she said, reaching for the Prosecco. "I made it myself."

"Really?" I hoped I didn't sound too astonished. "The workmanship is exquisite. I adore the ruching at the sleeves."

"I shouldn't say myself," she said, refilling my glass. "Dylan helped."

She smiled, but I wasn't sure if it was a smile of pride or

disappointment.

"That's fantastic," I said. "You guys should go into business together someday."

Barbra took a large swig from her glass, looking up at the ceiling as she let out a taut, anxious giggle. "We'll see about that."

Suddenly the air in the room seemed heavier. "So tell me about Paragon. Any salacious gossip I should know about?"

"You didn't move out of the city for the gossip, did you?" Barbra said. "It's a cozy town. The people are friendly and relaxed. It's just easier here."

"Easier?" I said. "Easier than what?"

Barbra shrugged. "We lived in Gramercy a few years ago. Stan and I just felt . . . there's a unique danger to raising kids in Manhattan. It's not just the money. It's the expectations. The precociousness. Kids in Manhattan can be frighteningly blasé. Stan . . . didn't want that for Dylan. He convinced me the suburbs would be better."

"Hmm. That sounds familiar," I said, smiling. "So are they?"

Barbra looked down to her glass. "There's a real sense of community. It's different. It's nice. Stan's happy. Dylan seems to be adjusting well."

"What about you?" I asked.

"Me?" Barbra chuckled. "What's not to like? It's comfortable here. You'll see."

Her tone hardly struck me as comfortable. "But . . ." I said, wondering if I was opening a door I wasn't supposed to.

Barbra decided not to walk through it. Instead she held my wrist and gave it a sharp squeeze. "I'm happy you boys came tonight, Chase." She looked right at me as she tossed back her glass, her eyes searching mine for a tacit response. Then she lifted up the tray of cheesecake and coffee. "Shall we rejoin the men in the parlor?"

The next time I noticed Dylan Shiner staring at me I was pacing the sunroom one afternoon, having just thrown off my smock in surrender after another tiresome bout with self-doubt. Weeks had passed and I hadn't progressed on any of my new pieces, and now, standing by the full-length mirror leaning against the wall, I was hit with another blow. The person staring back was old. His skin seemed less vibrant than mine. There were purple purses under his eyes, and a pudginess around his midsection that was hard to reconcile, since if anything he worked out more often than he used to and ate far better. Who was this man and where had he come from?

And then I noticed it, reflected over my shoulder: a pair of binoculars. Another person besides me was checking this guy out. I turned around, but Dylan had already run off. I chuckled; his timidity was precious. I went about my business. He could just be trying to catch a glimpse of my work, I told myself. Unlikely, but possible.

The next time I saw him, I was in the den doing butterfly curls on our Soloflex, an early Christmas present from Parker, who was worried that now that the gym wasn't two blocks away "we would get too comfortable." (I didn't remind him that *his* gym was still two blocks away from the office.) None of my pieces were hanging there, and when I looked up, briefly, the binoculars and the boy behind them didn't disappear. From his high vantage point Dylan could look into many rooms of our house, if he wanted to. Still, I did nothing to change my routine. I wasn't going to embarrass the boy. I didn't want him to feel ashamed. Parker and I had both grown up with enough shame.

For the next several days, around three o'clock, I could count on a pair of eyes watching me. Aside from Dylan, the Shiners kept their blinds closed, so he was free to let his eyes roam. It didn't bother me.

If anything, it was amusing. Parker never offered himself as audience to my process, possibly because he thought I might find it irritating, but more likely because he would. Now, with someone watching, I had no choice but to concentrate.

Absorbed in my work, I'd often forget he was there. One afternoon, after toiling for a few hours on a new piece, I decided to jump in the shower for a much-needed break. I was toweling myself off when I headed to the kitchen to fix myself a coffee. While the pot brewed I took off the towel to wipe under my arms, and that's when I looked out across the way, and there Dylan was, standing by the window of his bedroom. His chest bare, his underwear around his knees. His hands on his crotch. Moving.

We locked eyes. Briefly. It was like telepathy. The look on his face was pleading, heartfelt and tender, but sort of angry, too. His mouth hung open, dumbstruck and hungry. Not half a second, but it still sent shivers through me.

I knew I had to draw the blinds. I could have at least headed to the bedroom to put on some clothes. Every thought, instinct, and reflex unanimously said *go,* and yet I didn't. I had made myself a cup of coffee and I was going to drink it, in my house, on my couch, naked. I'd walked around naked in our apartment before. Parker and I both. It wasn't such a big deal.

A jumble of thoughts entered my brain. Lacrosse captain Steven Bishop in my eighth grade locker room, whispering to me after he caught me staring that I was welcome to suck his dick as long as I asked him nicely in front of his friends. The plush new couch I was sitting on, how Parker and I hadn't even christened it since we'd moved in. I thought about our sex life back in Chelsea, and for a moment, I got carried away with nostalgia. My heart was thundering and I could feel myself getting erect. I don't like little boys, never have. If anything, Parker's the one with the twink fetish. But there I was, getting hard. I didn't move. I didn't touch myself. And I never looked back at him. It's creepy to admit this, but what I kept telling myself was: Just give him enough time to finish. Just this once, let the fantasy be consummated. Wouldn't it be healthier? Even if I never walked around naked again, at least he would have that. I didn't want to scare him several years deeper into the closet, like me and my years of torture in high school and college.

Ten minutes later I went to the bedroom and put on a pair of pants.

Of course I felt weird the next day. For the next few days, I avoided the studio at certain hours, busying myself with errands around town. Parker was convinced he was going to land the promotion any day now, and he wanted us to throw a housewarming barbecue to "cinch the deal." We were going to invite neighbors too: people Parker had met on his train rides into the city, at the Stop and Shop, even the "delightful" older woman who had given him the application to the church bake-off. He wanted me to search the nearby stores and find some hometown specialties that would add that extra dash of authenticity to our shindig. "Nothing too Manhattan," he said. "The boys have had enough of Basque cheeses. Let's go locavore."

He also mentioned installing a pool in the backyard. "Paula and Kevin's kids might like it," he said. "And what's his name, the Shiner boy."

"Dylan," I said.

"Right," Parker said. "Dylan."

These capitulations to domesticity repulsed me, but I said nothing. Because thanks to Dylan, my time in the studio was finally beginning to bear fruit. I had hatched a seed of inspiration from our tacit moments together, nursing them into what I thought might become a breakthrough piece. It was more abstract, darker than usual, not as flippant as a lot of my work. I knew it was just plain strange, and yet, in its refusal to be anything, it was somehow managing to be completely itself.

After switching to morning studio hours, however, I began hitting walls, and I panicked. I couldn't give up, not when I was so close. Maybe I was being irrational, but I went back to the sunroom several days later at three o'clock, only to find Dylan no longer watching. Not that day, or the next, or the day after. Had my absence scared him away? Or had he simply moved on? I was so anxious to finish I began to get superstitious. What if I needed Dylan's stares for motivation? What if without them I would lapse back into the creative void? I closed my eyes and stared at my near-finished canvas. I pictured it in my mind, and then I pictured myself finishing it, and the person finishing it didn't have any clothes on.

So I took mine off and kept working.

Three days later I was in the sunroom when I noticed Dylan walk out into the Shiners' backyard. He held an easel and a small canvas in his hands, and he set them down by the fence, beside Barbra's rhododendrons, facing our house. It was strange seeing him outside, at eye level. He looked more substantial in the daylight.

I was wearing my smock and nothing else. Dylan gave me a smile that told me I needn't be embarrassed. I stood behind my canvas and smiled back. He laughed and began mixing his paints. He set them down, made a frame with his thumbs and index fingers, and held them against his left eye. I pointed at myself. He nodded.

I watched him. Every so often he'd look back toward his house with what I imagined was fear. He made a few broad brushstrokes, and then he paused, holding his thumb against his mouth. He looked right at me, put his hands on his shirt, and mimed pulling it off. I hesitated. Was he serious? I tugged at the strings of my smock and he nodded. I shook my head. He mimed again, his gestures more exaggerated this time. I shook my head again. He laughed. Blood was filling my head. I sneezed out of nervousness.

There was no excuse for taking off my smock, but it's what I did. I stood there for a few seconds, and the whole time I was thinking, *This might help me get somewhere.* I thought back to the first time Parker had convinced me to eat a steak after I'd gone vegetarian for almost two years, how the tender flesh and salty juices awakened something in me I hadn't even realized was dormant, how different my work became after that day. So I found a chair, turned it so it faced Dylan, and sat down. I closed my eyes. I would be the subject now.

I guess I didn't hear the screen door open. When I opened my eyes I saw Stan, eyes bright and wide, tossing a football in his hands. "Heads up," he said, throwing the ball, which landed by Dylan's feet. I heard it bounce and wobble against the ground. Dylan froze. He looked at me one last time and then dashed inside his house. I reached for my smock as quickly as I could but I wasn't fast enough. Stan's eyes had followed his son's over to me, and I knew what he saw. I knew what he was thinking.

When the doorbell rang I almost didn't answer it. Parker was out running errands for the barbecue and I was afraid to handle this alone. Sighing, I threw on a sweatshirt and jeans and headed to the door.

Stan Shiner's breath smelled sour and hot, like pickles peeled off a hamburger. He pushed me against the wall as soon as I let him in. "What were you doing?" he said.

"Nothing," I said. "Painting. Listen, Stan, it's not—"

"You were *naked*." Stan shook his head, like the word stupefied him. "Why were you naked?"

"I'm sorry. I guess it was inappropriate."

"Inappropriate? *Inappropriate?* My son is thirteen years old."

"I'll draw the blinds from now on," I said, curling my head away from his face.

"Have you done something with my son?" Stan's voice was cracking. He picked me up by my armpits and held me off the ground, his eyes centimeters away from mine and seething with the kind of pure disgust I had only thought possible onstage, in an Arthur Miller play. My arms, which should've been pushing him away, instead lay dead at my side, and my mouth, which should've been denying his accusation, instead called out, in vain, for Parker. I was being slammed against my own wall and my first thought was about the vase on the credenza, how Parker's aunt had given it to us as a "future housewarming present" six months ago and how upset Parker would be if it fell.

"What have you done with my son?" Stan growled. He threw me across the room. I landed hard, just a few inches from the glass coffee table. I was too disoriented to get up, let alone to answer him. For a second I imagined having done things with Dylan, if only to justify Stan's blind rage. I wondered why he was home from work so early that day. I wondered if Dylan knew he would be.

Stan pulled my head off the ground by the back of my shirt. "You think this is fun and games, you sick fuck? You move into our neighborhood and this is what you do?"

My eyes stayed shut, anticipating a blow to my face. I could hear noises in the background, beyond Stan's vindictive barks, past the spit that had landed on my left cheek. Parker had come home, and from the way he said "Stan, what's going on?" I could tell he had yet to accept the reality of what was happening.

"Whoa, guys, easy does it now . . ." Parker dropped his bags and circled back toward the fireplace, his palms out in front of him in a gesture of civilized arbitration.

"Easy does it?" Stan spat each syllable. "Your fucking boyfriend is a pedophile!"

"I am not," I said. "Parker?" I looked at him, hoping something would trigger inside him.

"Listen, Stan," Parker said, his hands up in the air, his tone slow and deliberate. "We'll talk this out, okay, buddy? But you're gonna have to let go of Chase first."

"Or what?"

And then I saw a woman's legs, standing by our door. "Stanley. What in God's name!" Barbra's wail was low, very low. If Stan's face spelled outrage, hers spelled it in even bolder letters. She rushed over and grabbed the arm that was still clutching my collar. "Let go of him, Stan. Now!"

"Can't we just talk this out?" Parker's voice had gotten shaky. He had moved closer and I could tell he was afraid, but I wasn't clear of what, exactly. I couldn't believe he was still lingering there, with half of me on the floor.

"Stanley!" Barbra continued to wrestle Stan's hand off of me. But he just gripped my shirt harder, and when I tried to reach around and break free, he grabbed both my hands with his fist and shackled me. I felt small, helpless, humiliated.

"Talk about what? Fuck you both, you and your faggot boy-friend."

"Now wait just one second," Parker said. But it was too late. Because that smack—oh, it was something. Even though I saw it make contact, it was more the sound of it than the sight, this awesome collision producing an echo so hideous, so brutal, so startling and real.

"Stan Shiner, let go." The poison in Barbra's eyes, the fury that possessed her at that moment, like she had been waiting to give that smack for so long. "Get out, and walk home. You will never use that word again. Got it?"

Stan looked confused. His eyebrows did a little dance and the muscles on his neck pulsated. He looked at Barbra like he didn't recognize her. Finally he let go of me. His lips sputtered, and his breath came out staccato. "Barbra, he's our son," he blubbered. "*Our* son," he repeated, his eyes beginning to tear.

"It's okay, Stan." She reached for her husband, and as she took him he collapsed into her arms. "Let's go home."

Barbra held fast to him. The vinegar had gone from her voice. She looked possessed, the way her eyes fixed on Stan, like she wasn't sure where her rage had come from and how she'd managed to switch back to compassion so quickly. Stan turned to face Parker and me one last time, a wounded drunk in a bar fight, eager for more but content enough with the damage done. He banged his hand against our wall. "I don't understand," he said. "I don't."

Stan tore away from his wife and stumbled out our door. I tried to stand up. Parker approached Barbra with his hands cradling his face. "I'm so sorry," he said to her.

"Why are you apologizing to me?" she said, looking at him with pity.

"I'm sure it's just a huge misunderstanding," Parker continued.

"I have to go." Barbra looked at me. She reached out to pat my shoulder, but then pulled back before making contact, her hand retreating to her own forehead. I could sense her embarrassment. She headed out the door.

"Are you all right?" Parker said. He helped me back to my feet and guided me to the sofa.

"No," I said. "I'm not."

"What the hell got into him? Why did he call you a pedophile?"

I didn't want to speak. I searched his expression but apparently my silence irritated him—he sauntered off to the kitchen for some paper towels to clean the mark Stan had left on the wall. I watched him open several cabinets until he found the Windex. He should be helping me, I thought. He should be getting me an ice pack, making tea.

"I was painting in the back. I was . . . I wasn't wearing clothes and Dylan saw me."

"Seriously? That's it?"

"That's it."

"That psycho barged into our house for that?"

I nodded.

"But there's nothing more to this story."

I looked at Parker hard. He was furiously rubbing the wall. Was this his idea of comfort?

"You think I fucked around with our neighbor's son?"

"I never said that," Parker said. "It's just . . . the whole naked thing, Chase."

I walked over, still unsteady, and stared at him with disgust. "I walk around naked, Parker. I did it all the time in Chelsea. So did you."

Parker went over to the kitchen and unhooked the Dirt Devil; apparently Stan had set free some dust mites in his wake. "We didn't have thirteen-year-olds next door in Chelsea."

"Are you serious?"

"Don't get worked up. Of course he was wrong. But I'm going to call Barbra. We'll talk things out. No big deal."

"Right," I said. "I think I'll call the cops instead."

Parker folded his arms. "And tell them what, Chase? Stan will make up some story about how we're fucking recruiting their kids."

I watched as he vacuumed around the edges of the carpet. It crossed my mind that if someone were to look into our house at that moment they would have no idea we were fighting. Maybe that was the point. But I wouldn't have that. Not anymore. "This is fucking ridiculous. Do you hear yourself, Parker? Recruiting? Dylan is gay. He's old enough to know. He was fucking masturbating—"

Parker put down the Dirt Devil. He looked at me like I had just thrown up on him. "You saw him masturbating?"

I closed my eyes. The truth was prickly and suffocating when it should have been liberating. Did Parker even deserve it? Did I even care anymore? "Once. He leaves his shades open."

"You watched him masturbate. A *barely* teenage boy."

"I didn't watch." I hated the fact that I was explaining myself. Why was I the one explaining? "It was a split second. And I've never seen it since. Thirteen-year-olds masturbate, Parker. I certainly did. So did you."

Parker's composure began to crack, the colors of his face continuously distorting, like a mood ring gone haywire. "So, what? Did it make you feel attractive? Do you somehow feel young again?"

Maybe if he had raped me right then and there, I could have forgiven him. Maybe if he had thrown me over the kitchen countertop, my hands searching for purchase on the unfinished surface where adobe tiles would soon be arranged in classic geometric patterns, maybe if he entered me without lubrication or warning or apology, in front of our large windows, I could have discounted his betrayal, traded the pain I felt for a pain I longed to feel. Instead Parker looked at me like I was the only air conditioner on the assembly line that had failed the Energy Star emissions threshold. Where was his new, improved, mature boyfriend, the one who was supposed to come with the house? I half expected a white glove to come out of Parker's pocket, but I knew he wouldn't use it the way I wanted him to. Instead he'd snap it on and run his fingers across the surface of our relationship and find the filthy dust that had been gathering for months now, dust that only now he was willing or able to notice, no doubt surprised to see how careless he had become.

"Did you get hard when Stan hit me, Parker?" There was no going back now. I got up and planted my face inches away from his, whispering in his ear while I rubbed his crotch. "Was that hot for you? Is that why you didn't even raise a fucking finger to stop him?"

Parker broke free and walked away. I watched him as he paced around, stopping to rearrange the azaleas in the vase on the dining table, stalling to come up with the perfect response. "If Dylan wants to masturbate he could go on the fucking Internet. You knew that. But you encouraged him. You did this on purpose. You don't want to be normal. You want us to fail."

"Is the piss-loving part of you normal, Parker? Or the fisting collection on your computer? Or does that part not count, because you hide it?"

"He's a child, Chase. Don't you get that?"

"He's their *gay* child. This is preposterous."

"You're preposterous!" Parker's eyes were swelling. He was finally shouting too. "You think you've made a statement with your behavior? You've accomplished nothing. You'll just be hated. And now they'll have reason to hate us more. How does the cause advance?"

I flinched. So this was what our relationship was reduced to.

"What if I don't want to be part of your cause, Parker? What if I just want to be me?"

"How you lie to yourself." He ripped the azaleas from the vase and threw them on the floor. "You think you don't want acceptance? Your art is all about acceptance! You want it just as much as I do. You just want it on your terms. But *no one* gets those terms, Chase. You could have had a show last year. You didn't because you didn't want to compromise on the fucking wording in a brochure. You're completely out of touch with reality."

I swallowed hard. Finally, some truth, ugly as it may be. "My whole being here is a compromise," I said. "I did it for you."

"Exactly," Parker said, jerking his head in disgust. "Good thing you won't have to compromise anymore."

He looked at me one final time before going up the stairs. I heard a door slam, and the sound of drawers opening and closing furiously. Was he packing his things, or mine? We weren't married—what was to stop him from kicking me out? I had no rights to anything in this house. Other than my canvases and clothing, everything was Parker's. I could be the fall guy, and Parker could keep his fantasy home and new neighbors and make amends, because he wasn't one of those fags, no sir, not good old Parker, he was the *right* kind of homosexual, the safe kind. He'd even believe it himself until one day he'll go to shake Dylan's hand and Stan will cringe ever so slightly, and he'll know just how narrow the margins of tolerance really are.

Dazed, I went downstairs to the sunroom. Removing the burlap covering the easel, I studied the image I had created, the naked figures in the void, their distorted faces and bodies, their oversize genitals, their faces frozen in screams. At first I had imagined these men were representing Dylan. But now I saw that they could be any one of us—Parker, Stan, Barbra, me. Certainly me. There was no point in hiding, and even less of a point in being free. The piece didn't need any more work. It was ready.

And I am ready. Ready to cast *Midnight Picture Show* out of our living room. Or better yet, put the new piece right on our lawn, so everyone can see it. I know it's a pointless gesture. But my rage is defining me, and I'm eager for a pointless gesture.

Outside a mild breeze blows through the elms, a tranquil rustling that stabs at me. The stillness of our neighborhood is supreme, and here I am, with a canvas in my hand, feeling awkward, as if on stage. I sit down in the middle of our lawn and lean the painting against me. The sun is making me squint. I look up to Dylan's bedroom. The blinds are tightly shut, and will likely remain that way for a long time. Is Parker right? Was I just looking for an out? And what about Dylan? Was I really trying to save him, or had I only used him? He's going to feel great shame for what he did, a shame he'll soon associate with sex, and sooner or later, he'll end up like Parker, wallowing in private fetishes, deifying the normal because he can never feel part of it.

The sun doesn't let up. I can feel my face tremble in the heat. In a few minutes I'll have to go back inside. In a few minutes I'll pack my meager belongings and leave my coward of a boyfriend forever. But for now I look up at Barbra's bedroom window and I think maybe it's okay. Maybe Barbra will change things. I imagine her sneaking a peek at me through the blinds, and I picture the look on her face, a yearning look just on the verge of finding peace. She's staring down at me, but she isn't angry or upset. She's even giving me a little wave.

THAT PERFECT POISON

Here's the problem: I don't understand my exterminator.

It's been pestering me for a while now. I've been trying to address a weakness in my novel that is difficult to identify, let alone to explain. I've fitted Boris with great idiosyncrasies, wrapped him in a smooth, elegant plot. I've struggled to make his desires specific yet universal, his flaws deplorable and yet somehow charming. But at a certain point I've stopped knowing him, my increasingly vague descriptions of him like tiny placards announcing my dim authority to the reader.

Last August I tried to address this problem by attending a writers' conference in Olympic Village, California, a picturesque, commercialized oasis nestled in the mountains near Lake Tahoe, complete with Starbucks and Ben & Jerry's. Like the others, I had come to be inspired. The faculty was a lineup of well-respected writers. We were the chosen, selected from a formidable pool, put up in posh seven-bedroom homes with names like Minnie and Bethany that perched on small lanes jutting off the principal road to the main lodge. Basically it was summer camp for adults.

The third night the Hot Tub Party was at Annabelle house. Miranda and I showed up late. On our way over we talked about how strange it was that, partnered people notwithstanding, no one was hooking up yet. We walked in and everyone was there: Sue Ellen our hostess, with the sad eyes and weathered smile; Axel, smoking weed like a nineteen year old should, flaunting his inflated Boston accent and Chia-Pet beard; Chad the Los Angeleno, whose novel had only come out in Bulgaria, his silk shirt two buttons shy of being completely off. And Emma and Richard, joined at the gay man/ straight woman hip since day one.

At twenty-two Emma was an endless fountain of energy and cheer, the kind of overbearing joyfulness that only years of medication could have cultivated. And Richard was my nemesis. Or at least, he was supposed to be. I was having a hard time coming to terms with how I felt about him, given the circumstances.

What were those circumstances? Like I said, I'm writing a novel about exterminators. About a year ago a friend of mine e-mailed me a blurb about some guy who'd just published a novel about exterminators, with a plot somewhat similar to mine. Then this guy ends up in my class at the conference. Richard.

Our first day at workshop he seemed pleasant enough. Friendly, yet guarded, almost bashful. He didn't want to talk about his novel, claimed he was embarrassed by it. I had read the first chapter on Amazon and could understand why. Still, I found him intriguing— he wasn't exactly handsome, but he was boyish and smooth and I liked boyish and smooth and he seemed exceedingly smart and well dressed and I liked those things too.

Miranda—not only my house and classmate but also my instant conference BFF—took an instant dislike to him. "There's something creepy about Richard," she said. "He looks unformed. His skin looks like it hasn't hardened yet, like a pig in formaldehyde."

When she told me this I laughed but didn't comment. I quickly decided that hating Richard would be a cliché; people would simply interpret any negative reaction I had as petty jealousy. Instead I'd try

Eric Sasson

to appreciate him.

At the party I grabbed a Yuengling from the fridge and approached Richard and Emma. The lack of sexual shenanigans at the conference somehow found its way into our conversation.

"Last year I hooked up at Bread Loaf," Richard said, his eyelashes all aflutter.

"Really." I stretched the word, asking for more.

"With two Fellows. Just random hot guys." The way he said "hot," like it was important to him.

As I was congratulating him Jesse came over. Someone we hadn't met yet. Jesse was tall, lanky, pixieish; both his belt and hair were spiky. He looked unwashed and proud of it, and he couldn't have been a day over twenty-five. His eyes were constantly wandering until they fell upon you, and when they did they looked at you deep and hard and flirty, telling you he had something on his mind and it was up to you to find out what. I was instantly smitten.

"So you guys write stories?" Jesse asked no one in particular.

"I'm finishing up my novel," I said, beaming at him.

"Richard's novel came out last year," Emma said, ever the proud fag hag.

Jesse's eyes widened; he seemed impressed.

"My second book comes out in the fall," Richard added.

I thought back to how self-effacing Richard had been in class, his modesty so genuine that you wouldn't even question it. He certainly didn't mind talking now.

When the conversation split off, Jesse stood closest to me.

"So what's your book about?" I asked.

"Bored people," he said. "Promiscuity." He drawled it, rolling his eyes on the last syllable, like a line he'd practiced in front of a mirror.

I admired his lips; they were plush, and I imagined, quite chewy. He seemed aloof, yet he laughed at my jokes; his affectations were thin and his sincerity kept seeping through, despite himself. But I wasn't the only gay man in the room.

Soon after, Louise rushed over to ask me if I wanted to join her skit for the Invitational Follies, a student-run show that would close the last night of the conference. While I was distracted Jesse turned away. He showed me his back, and as soon as he did, the entire evening lay out before me: He and Richard were going to connect. Their witty banter would bubble and spark, they'd break off into a private conversation as the freshly infatuated often do at parties, building a wall which they'd gradually reinforce. Their flirtation would have legs, momentum that would carry them somewhere intimate, exploratory.

Seeking escape, I wandered outside to the hot tub to join the potheads. We made up all sorts of ridiculous phrases in our wasted state. We talked about dead writers we'd like to fuck. I offered a young Hemingway and Axel brought up Anne Sexton but Chad outdid us all, describing how he'd take Sylvia Plath from behind with her head still in the oven. Axel started sounding off about Maryland, where he's from, going on with all sorts of pointless statistics.

"It's getting better but it still has a long way to go. Did you know that in the nineties, twenty-five percent of the population of Baltimore was lost to murder?"

"Wow," I said, in my wasted state. "Why didn't they just move?"

And then everyone laughed, at my absurd yet earnest misinterpretation. I went inside to grab another beer only to find Richard chatting with some other guy while Jesse lingered— lingered!—beside him, his eyes fixed on the ground. I was confused.

Eric Sasson

Had my predictions been wrong? I wondered if Jesse was aware of how he looked, standing there waiting for Richard. I wondered if Richard knew he was waiting.

By midnight everyone had cleared out, the seven of us remaining all stoned or drunk or both. The other guy had long left when Richard bid us good night, casually adding that he and Jesse were leaving together to go to "the mall," his tone a perfect balance between careless and cavalier. I watched Jesse nod along with this declaration, observing the man he'd go to the mall with, observing him with approval.

"Isn't the mall closed already?" Axel asked, too fucked up to recognize the euphemism.

A deep emptiness burrowed into my gut. Richard had trumped me again.

Boris is an industrious exterminator. He masters his trade, understands his poisons, can time and species indicate his prey's droppings. In my novel he's working on a formula for a new kind of pesticide, something he believes will revolutionize the industry. He doggedly hunts for the right mix of chemicals and ends up sharing his passion with George and Natalie Baines, a charming, affluent couple who own one of the homes on Boris's pest control circuit. George, a self-made pharmaceutical man himself, is intrigued with Boris's ideas and offers to help him out with the start-up costs.

As much as this thrills Boris, he's also torn. George is successful, smart, put together—yet he ignores Natalie; it's clear that he doesn't understand her or appreciate her talents. Boris has longed for the gorgeous and ostensibly lonely Natalie Baines ever since she offered him a cappuccino on his first-ever visit. George is usually at work when he comes, and Natalie likes to sit Boris down and talk about his plans, unlike his other customers, who seem to place him on equal footing with the rodents he disposes of. He finds comfort in these stolen moments with the mysterious brunette, whose eyes and words both suggest a deep ambivalence toward her husband.

Then, one day, on one of his regular bimonthly visits, Boris comes across a set of papers in the Baineses' master bedroom, papers filled with formulas and sketches that apparently refer to a giant project that George's firm plans to undertake. The details are hazy; still Boris is shocked by what he reads. Several of the compounds listed are not only illegal, but very dangerous. He'd thought George's company specialized in anti-inflammatories and arthritis medications—yet there he is, with what might as well be blueprints for biological weapons!

Boris is racked with doubt. George's financing could help him greatly; yet he loves Natalie. Does she know about the plans? And if not, doesn't she deserve to? Would it be possible for him to win her over now?

Knowing he must honor Natalie, Boris decides to be forthright. The next time he visits she serves iced caramel lattes. Her sundress is white and her eyes sparkle. Right before he leaves, he tells her everything, explaining the implications. The way her eyes widen confirms her ignorance. She looks wounded and lost. She thanks him for the information and tells him she'll look into it. He cautions her to seek legal counsel. *Your husband might be dangerous,* he says. *I won't say a word, but I thought you had to know.* She takes his hand, looks into his eyes, and thanks him again. *Let's not change our routine,* she tells him. *Next time you visit, I'll have a plan.*

The next day at workshop both my piece and Richard's were up for discussion. I ended up turning in a chapter of my novel I'd already put through six drafts and had several friends critique. I could have turned in one of the less polished chapters, but I felt timid, almost paranoid, at the thought of doing so. I wanted to define how I'd be judged. I couldn't very well let Richard compare my exterminator to his unfavorably.

My classmates' comments were positive, more or less. Richard's excerpt from his new novel, ambitious yet unfocused, elicited a less sympathetic reaction. I couldn't help but smile as the others ripped into him. I offered a few criticisms but made sure to offer a balance of praise as well. When allowed to speak, Richard said nothing. Instead he thanked us for our input.

After class Emma took Richard's hand as they walked outside. I hurried to catch up with them. "So how was the mall?" I asked. Richard feigned bewilderment. "Oh, that," he said, rolling his eyes impishly.

"So?" Emma asked. "Was it flipping?"

"Oh, there was flipping," Richard said. "Quite a bit of flipping."

Again I was amazed at how up front he was. Richard was so reserved about his work. Yet this was something he needed to brag about.

Half an hour later I'd already shared the news with Miranda.

"Apparently our dry season is over," I said.

"I can't imagine why," Miranda said, trying to console me. "He's a troll."

"Perhaps Jesse is turned on by two-book deals," I said.

"Ha! Who isn't," she said. "But seriously, Talon, your piece kicked his piece's ass."

The rest of the day when I saw them together, which was rare, I couldn't make sense of them. They seemed to be *too* platonic, distant to a fault. I wondered whose choice this was. Did this aloofness add to the excitement, or was it just a by-product of someone's ambivalence? I wasn't sure whose, but I could venture a guess.

Two weeks pass. When Boris returns to the Baineses' mansion, he's surprised to find George in the library with Natalie. George sits cross-legged, imperturbable. Natalie is gazing out the window. Boris can see only half of her face, her expression lacking the emotional contours he's grown accustomed to.

George gets up, hands Boris an envelope. "Here's a check, " he says. "This is your last day. Thanks for your work."

Boris puts on a perplexed smile. "Is the compound not working?" he asks.

"It's not about your damn compound," George says. Natalie is still staring out the window. *Biding her time,* Boris thinks. "Listen, Boris, I know your job requires you to speculate. But this is our *life, man.*"

"I know my chemicals, George. Indolizidine is illegal. It's a poison-frog alkaloid."

George shakes his head and sighs. "You got the chirality wrong, genius. It's not indolizidine. Indolizidine is the left-handed molecule. The one you saw was right-handed, and totally harmless. You could have asked me. Or even told Natalie to ask me. Instead you filled her head with crazy ideas. Although it's not hard to figure out why."

Boris looks up to Natalie. For a fraction of a second her eyes fall on him. They do not seem to be judging him, or pitying him. Instead she's taken on a cold, expressionless stare, which destroys him.

"You don't even love her," Boris says.

George takes out a cigar from a box. He looks at it, considering it, along with Boris's words. "Oh, and you do? Or is it that you just don't like me?"

Boris's lips tremble, but he says nothing. He wonders if he should run to Natalie, shake her out of the coma of her indifference. She wouldn't have to stare out windows silently, not with him. He too will be a success one day, didn't she know? He was on the verge of a major breakthrough with Differol, a nontoxic, environmentally friendly compound that seemed to drastically diminish the procreative drive of several species of ant and termite. And now this.

George lights the cigar, slaps a hand on Boris's shoulder. "Listen, Boris, a lot of people are brilliant and still don't know a thing. They let pettiness get in the way of good judgment. Think about it, my friend. Good luck to you. Natalie, say good-bye to Boris."

Natalie steps away from the window and approaches Boris with her left hand extended. As stiff as her handshake is, as rehearsed and ungenerous her smile, Boris is still smitten. He still loves her.

That night Minnie house, our house, threw a party/reading. Our conference-mates arrived in droves, because there were snacks, and free booze, but most important, there was a chance to share your work with an appreciative audience.

The reading went off spectacularly. I read a juicy excerpt from my first chapter. Both Richard and Jesse were there, at different ends of the room. Richard chose not to read; presumably his book tour had satisfied those cravings. Jesse, meanwhile, solicited Louise to read on his behalf. The pages were caustic and witty but also rather sad and knowing. Jesse sheltered his face with his hands while Louise read his words. His timidity was precious.

Later on, I noticed Axel and some others out on the patio smoking yet another joint, with Jesse sitting beside them, looking hopeless. I joined the table and partook. Jesse refrained.

"How old are you?" I asked him.

"Thirty-four," he said, tossing my own age back at me.

"You're a bad liar," I said. I wondered if he was trying to seduce me. But he kept looking through the window at Richard, who was now enmeshed in conversation with Greg. Greg was older, in that distinctively elegant way that urban gay men grow older. His muscles were thick, his chest broad, his face a symphony of clean, rugged lines. Greg also had a novel out, from which he'd read. I wondered if Greg was to Richard what Richard was to Jesse.

Jesse and I soldiered on, discussing favorite authors, other conferences we'd attended, how our workshops were going. The conversation was too deep for the other stoners at the table, who shortly left us alone. Jesse seemed happier with them gone. He began flinging witticisms at me, his smile opening slowly, deliberately, like a flower that knows where the bee will land.

"I like your dimples," I said.

He nodded, placing this too in his arsenal.

Still the problem was the hurt; it registered in his eyes too clearly. The more animated he became the more I thought: He wants Richard to see. He wants Richard to think that he too has moved on. But if *I* knew he was doing this, then surely Richard wouldn't be convinced. Surely the cause was lost.

Later, I was chatting with Emma when I heard Richard say "Can we meet up tomorrow?" to Jesse, and it was the question mark that said everything, the way his voice rose to it, that told me a pact had been broken. Richard lingered in painful small talk after Jesse left. Then I saw him leave with Greg. I didn't know if this was meaningful. I didn't think Greg was attracted to Richard, or even if Richard wanted Greg. Greg was older, I told myself. I don't know why that reassured me.

The next day, Miranda and I dissected the party over morning coffee. I unleashed my play-by-play analysis while she tried to give me some needed perspective.

"All these interpretations! It's positively Talmudic," she said.

"You think I'm overreaching?"

"We Fictionists." Miranda sighed, blowing her bangs away from her eyes. "Eternal slaves to subtext."

"But what do you think is going on?"

"You know I don't like Richard," she said. "I'm sure he's the villain. Although sometimes it's not that easy. Depends on the genre."

"Did you know that he was an exterminator before he wrote the book? Apparently made a lot of money at it too."

"And this makes him a good person?"

"No," I said. "But it doesn't make him a bad person either."

It's all downhill for Boris after his falling-out with the Baineses. He's lost without Natalie's attentions and hates himself for being so reckless. He feels disconnected from his work. The figures in his formula, which used to fall so elegantly into place, are no longer lining up as they need to. His drive has disappeared. So the world won't have his special pesticide, so what? Would it make any difference?

And here is where I lose touch with him, as we enter the final act. I know he can't win back Natalie's love—if he ever had it at all. And I certainly can't imagine just *handing* him the magic recipe, allowing him that creative and financial breakthrough so his business can take off and he can get rich and famous and meet that special someone and live happily ever after. What would be the point in such a transparent contrivance?

No. He must reveal himself to me otherwise. He must discover himself. But how?

Friday night was our last night of the conference. Dinner was an alfresco buffet set in the courtyard behind the funicular station. Most of us were already there when Richard walked in with Greg. They sat down at a table for two, in perfect view of Jesse, Chad, Miranda and me, sitting at a communal table. Miranda and I shared a glance.

"So what are you taking away from the conference, Jesse?" Chad asked.

"Well," Jesse said, in what I imagined he thought was his cryptic voice. "It's certainly taught me to be pure." Then he turned to face me. "When are you flying home?"

"I'm not," I said. "I'm going to San Francisco for a few days."

"Oh. Do you have a ride?"

I already knew Jesse had driven from San Francisco. "Yeah," I said.

"What a shame." His eyes narrowed. He looked up to the gloaming sky, then back at me, with his left eyebrow arched. "Well, I'm sure you'll have a lot of fun there."

A few minutes later I hauled Miranda to the dessert table.

"Did you hear him? He's pissed at Richard, and I'm the rebound."

"Jesus, Talon," Miranda said. "Do you really want to get involved?" Our friendship was barely a week old and already she was mothering me.

"He's flirting. He's hot. Why say no?"

"Subtext," she said, wagging her finger in front of my face. "Don't let him suck you down a rabbit hole."

After dinner we all headed to the Follies. Louise's skit was sophomoric; I was glad not to have participated. Richard and Emma played characters in a spoof on *The Wizard of Oz* written by a participant who wore the same t-shirt advertising his novel every day of the conference. It was even more dreadful than Louise's piece.

I expected to spend the night with my housemates, those I had grown closest to over the week. But Jesse bee-lined for me as soon as it was over.

"So what's up for the evening?" He was hugging himself and massaging his triceps.

"I don't know," I said, feigning nonchalance.

"You guys throwing another party?"

"No. Something more intimate. Last night and all."

He sighed. "Intimate. I see."

I smirked. "You're fucking with me, aren't you," I said.

His eyes dilated. "About what?"

"Your age, for starters," I said.

Jesse laughed. "That's not the only thing I'm fucking with you about."

I can't say I was shocked by his forwardness. Building on his invitation, I grabbed his neck and whispered in his ear: "Why don't we find out more about that then."

My heart was thumping. Someone offered me a ride back to Minnie, which I refused. More people came to ask me what I was doing. *I'm getting laid,* I thought. I didn't care about the context. In fact I appreciated it, supposing that with this I might catch up with Richard somehow. Besides, I was turned on, acutely and viscerally—

my lust weighed me down and sent me soaring at the same time. We were leaving together. We were going to find a spot and have hot monkey sex.

We headed over to Jesse's car underneath a canopy of stars that a New York sky hasn't produced in over a hundred years. The lot was deserted, and I could almost breathe the disappointment in the air. Tomorrow we'd all be returning to our normal lives, where we had responsibilities and families and jobs and the crushing monotony of the ordinary to deal with. We could no longer wake up to a day of nothing but the sweet fantasy of craft lectures and editors' panels, sermons of loving reinforcement that reminded us that what we were doing was valid and meaningful.

Jesse didn't look at me much. When he did he seemed sorrowful, as if he was performing some sort of duty. I didn't like this look. I couldn't suffer the mystery behind it. I had to address the pain on his face.

"There's a backstory here," I said, just as we were about to reach his car.

"Backstory?" he repeated, his voice wavering. But his expression said otherwise, a quiet shame percolating into his eyes.

"Yeah," I said, opening the car door. "But maybe you don't want to talk about it."

"No." He nodded without looking at me. "Let's talk."

The seats were cluttered with library books, empty coffee cups, different-size Tupperware with all manner of knickknack within. He reached over into the glove compartment and pulled out a Book of Love CD. I was impressed—eighties New Wave at its most tragic and obscure.

"It's sort of obvious what's been going on," I said.

Jesse grimaced as he took this in. "Obvious, huh? You're on

Wayne, right?" he said, about to turn left on my street. Strange, I thought. Did he just want to drop me off?

But I knew that couldn't be it. "How about we go for a spin?" I said.

"Okay."

The night was cold and exquisite. The drive, on a serpentine two-lane road unacquainted with streetlamps, Lynchian. We were heading up into the mountains and the towns, when they came, were so small they passed by in a flash. One minute shops and restaurants and the next, open road, houses camouflaged into the shrouded hills. The lake was to our right, the water too dark to be seen. We knew it because we could smell it. We knew it by the lights that flickered in unpredictable patterns at great distances, the lights of anchored boats.

"It's not fair," I said. "How he's acted with you. It's unkind."

Jesse tapped his fingers against the steering wheel. I don't know why I danced around the specifics; I suppose I was enjoying the Whartonesque avoidance. And Jesse responded in kind, when he bothered responding at all. Eventually we realized we didn't know where we were driving, so we turned back to the first town and parked.

We found a lighted trail and followed it down to a sculpted path that hugged the lake. We walked along until we saw a bench, the silence broken only sporadically by a light breeze that brought with it the tangy scent of juniper. The whole episode reeked of romance, pulsed with the throb of opportunity. Still, I wouldn't say we were flirting, exactly. Or if we were, it was with a hint of elegy, of something lost. *We're sitting by a lake,* I told myself. *There has to be a kiss. There has to be; the story forces it to rise.*

"So," I said, edging a bit closer to him. "Tell me what happened."

And he did. He was reluctant at first, but gradually, he grew more confident, his words like tiny picks chiseling away at my misconceptions. "We just made out. We went for a walk down by the ski lift, and I told him I often went there for walks by myself. I told him I wanted to climb one of the poles to the top and take in the view. He suggested we do that the next night. He told me he just wanted to get to know me better. He sounded so sincere."

I sat there, shaken, my jaw tight and my fingertips numb. It never occurred to me that they hadn't slept together. I was going to be a revenge fuck, but only because Richard had jilted Jesse *after* they had sex. I nodded my head, offered a simple but unconvincing "okay."

"Try to understand," he continued. "I never dreamed of making any real connections here. I'm not used to letting my guard down emotionally. But we went back to my place and I felt so comfortable with him I asked him to read the first chapter of my novel. He said he'd love to and he did. When he put it down he looked at me like I had scared him, and he said: it's brilliant. *Brilliant.* Then he promised me he'd put me in touch with his agent as soon as possible. He didn't have to say any of that. He could have said thanks, it's good, or any other bullshit, and moved on. But instead he said that.

"What I don't get is how easily it was aborted. It went from that to nothing so quickly. He didn't even talk to me at the party. I still don't know why. Does he think I'm that untalented? At least if we'd had sex I could have brushed it off as a lie to get into my pants. But now it's like he couldn't even *sleep* with me after he read my stuff."

His eyes were tearing up. He was trying to hold back, I could tell, but he wouldn't succeed. And my heart broke open for him. It sounds metaphorical, but I felt it: a crack in a valve and a cold liquid pouring into my insides. Quickly I had to adjust, become the wise older man. I wanted to make him see that everything would be fine. Men are assholes, I said, and Richard no different. You deserve better. You just have to believe in yourself, I said, trotting that nugget out with all the other lessons I'd learned along the years. But had I really learned any lessons?

I kept reaching for him. Even when his arms had formed a fortress around his knees, I kept forcing my hands up his pants legs, telling him I was cold and needed to warm myself up. I was cold, but it was hardly that. I was struggling with simultaneous feelings of lust and empathy. Wasn't I, in my own way, just as fearful of Richard's rejection? Wasn't I just as afraid my novel would never get any notice?

"We should go. You're cold," he said, laughing.

"A few more minutes," I said. I tried to look him in the eyes. I realized we'd never hook up now, not under these circumstances. And that angered me. It shamed me.

"Richard told me that you guys had sex," I said, my hands still on his legs.

I watched him shake his head. He let out a thick laugh and then stared out into the water. I wanted him to hate Richard. But what if it had the opposite effect and made him feel worse? Neither of us spoke for the next few minutes. The silence was poisonous; it forced me to retrace the lines I had mistakenly drawn. Only now I could see they all led back to the same source: my own needy, bruised ego.

"Let's head back," he said, finally. I studied his expression. He was smiling, and I wanted to believe he was feeling better, that at least one of us was.

We didn't talk much on the way to Minnie house. That is, we did, but about other things, as if we both knew better than to rummage further. When he dropped me off he reached over and offered me a hug.

"This was good," he said, patting my back. "I can leave the conference with a positive memory now."

In that second, I hated him. I didn't want to be a positive memory. I wanted him to want me just like he wanted Richard to want him. It was as if he had transferred his frustration to me. There was the initial thrill of lust, but now I'd have to get over something far stickier: his vulnerability, and how it had exposed my own.

Inside, Miranda and my other housemates were gathered around the kitchen island, high on leftover wine and tarot card readings. I took up a cup and attempted to smooth into the festivities, but Miranda knew better and pulled me aside, so I could share with her what happened. When I was done she cupped my face with her hands.

"What can I say? You're better off." She mussed my hair. "We sort of knew, didn't we, that something like this would happen? I told you Richard was evil."

I nodded. It was so easy to peg Richard as the villain. But was it true? Maybe I was the villain. When Jesse approached me, I knew he was on the rebound, flirting with me only to validate himself. And when I asked him for a ride, was I not thinking: *I'm going to have sex with him.* Wasn't that my overriding motive?

It only occurred to me later that Richard could have picked up on Jesse's other inclinations, his need to turn this conference fling into something it could never be, and, quietly but without malice, decided to cut it off before things got thorny. Perhaps he was letting Jesse down easy, in the only way Richard knew how, which was to not speak about it unless pushed, much as he did with his novel. And even if that wasn't true, it *could have been* true, just as when sitting with Jesse out at the lake, I could have taken advantage of the situation, or Jesse could have just fucked around with me. We could've never had our talk and instead reconfirmed, passionately, our cynicism about the pettiness of people in general.

Richard's second novel came out last week. Advance word of mouth has been strong; he's already been reviewed by a few name critics. Word on the street is it's far more personal, this novel he'd set aside to work on the more commercial exterminator thriller. I imagine him standing in front of a podium at a Barnes & Noble in downtown St. Louis. He's wearing a Diesel shirt and jeans with crisp lines, about to field questions from a group of perky midwesterners eagerly testing new selections for their book club. He'll charm these Emmas-in-waiting with seemingly off-the-cuff anecdotes about a gauzy childhood; he hasn't given a passing thought to Jesse or me in months.

I called Jesse with the news a few days ago, a perfect excuse to disguise my need to check up on him. I'd prepared an exquisitely derisive comment about Richard to cheer him up, and he in turn rewarded me with a solid laugh, a moist vibrancy in his voice that others, who weren't as well tuned to his affectations, might have mistaken for resilience or sanguinity. He talked about making progress on his novel and a possible life-changing move to Atlanta, already sounding nostalgic about the sobering dampness he'd leave behind in San Francisco. And I talked about the agent who had sent me an encouraging rejection letter, the contests I'd be entering, an upcoming seminar in Saratoga Springs. We rode along with each other's words and neither of us delved or asked difficult questions about the lives we had returned to because we understood; we were trying not to let each other down.

Here in New York, I'm still trying to understand my exterminator. I want to be fair to him in the end, allow him a chance to regain some of the dignity he's lost by acting prematurely on his tenuously held assumptions. I want him to go to work knowing that he must, not only because the world needs its pests controlled, but because he needs to accept, for himself, that the work he's doing is valid, without trusting to the support of bored, lonely housewives to affirm him as a man. He needs to disregard the whims of the masses, sit down at his lab table, and keep fiddling with his chemicals, so that one day the mix will be right, and he will discover that perfect poison, the one that will shake the very foundations of this exterminating world.

ACKNOWLEDGMENTS

Some of these stories have appeared, in slightly different form, in the following publications:

"Floating" in *The Ledge* and *The 2010 Robert Olen Butler Prize Stories*.
"Getting There" in *The Puritan*.
"Body and Mind" in *BLOOM*.
"Cruising" in *THE2NDHAND*.
"Remains of a Once Great Civilization" in *The Crucible*.
"The Coming Revolution" in *Limp Wrist*.
"The Margins of Tolerance" in *Nashville Review*.

So many people to thank. If this were an Oscar telecast, I'd certainly be cut short:

Thanks to Amy Hempel, for teaching my first-ever creative writing workshop, and to the NYU Graduate Creative Writing Program, and my professors there: Edwidge Danticat, Deborah Eisenberg, Ted Solotaroff, Paule Marshall and E. L. Doctorow.

Thanks to all the conferences I've attended for their support, including the New York State Summer Writers Institute, the Key West Literary Seminar, the Squaw Valley Community of Writers, the Summer Literary Seminar in St. Petersburg, the Southampton Writers' Conference, the Sewanee Writers' Conference and Aspen Summer words, and to my instructors, particularly Rick Moody, Kathryn Harrison, Catherine Texier, and Elizabeth McCracken. All my conference friends: I hope you know how much you mean to me.

Many thanks to those who helped these stories improve: Alex Yates, Anna

North, John Reimringer, Andrea Dupree, Jennifer Itell, Jeff Voccola, Viet Dinh, Ben Nolan, Lilli Leggio, and especially Aharon Levy. And the many members of my workshops over the years—too many to list here but I must mention: Christina Phelps, Doug Silver, and Lee Kaplan.

Shout-outs to my other writer and nonwriter friends, for their advice, ears, shoulders and laughs: Liz, TJ, Michael, Zachary, Will, Francesco, Brian, Ruth Anne, Sally Jane, Nadia, Elana, Jenny, Claire, Patrick, Nick, Adam, Heather, Roxanne, Maria.

Thanks to the Sackett Street Writers' Workshop and especially Julia Fierro, for her confidence in me. Robert Hedin and the Anderson Center of Minnesota: thanks for a peaceful, productive month of work.

Jeff Bucari and Jason Covert: your patience is why the cover is so awesome. Steven Sergiovanni at Mixed Greens Gallery, thanks for the use of your lovely space. Jane Elias, thanks for your exceptional editing skills and friendship.

Loreena (White) Lewis: thanks for Beaufort, Sheppy and your unwavering faith. Marcos Namit: Larf.

Joe Taylor and Livingston Press, you made this possible. I didn't dare believe it was.

A final thanks to my brother, for becoming the lawyer in our family, and to my parents, for not pushing me to become one too, and willing me to pursue my passion. All my love.

ERIC SASSON received his M.A. in Creative Writing from New York University. His story "Floating" was named a finalist for the Robert Olen Butler prize. Other stories have appeared in *Nashville Review, BLOOM, The Puritan, Liquid Imagination, Alligator Juniper, Trans, The Ledge, MARY magazine and THE2NDHAND*, among other places. In 2010, he was awarded a residency fellowship to the Anderson Center in Minnesota, where he completed an edit of his first novel. He lives in Brooklyn, N.Y. www.ericsassonnow.com